ABOUT *That* DATE

THIA FINN

About That Date
Thia Finn

ISBN: 979-8-9913692-1-3

Edited by Swish Design & Editing
Proofreading by Swish Design & Editing
Book Design by Swish Design & Editing
Cover design by Designs by Dana
Cover Model by Wanderbook Club, Alejandro
Cover photography by Wander Aguiar
Cover image Copyright 2024

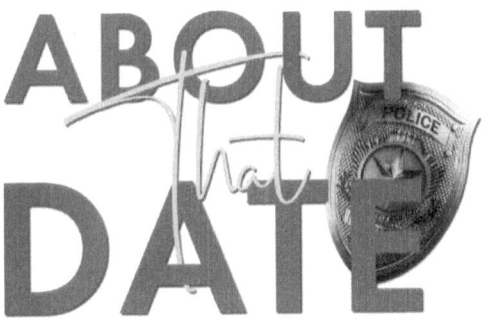

1

Allison

Floating.
Turning.
Suspending.
Hits, shattering glass, bumps, side mirror flying.

I watch wadded-up tissues, the dog's leash, papers, and the new Starbucks cup I purchased to match Junie's, filled with coffee, rise into the air. The scalding liquid touches my face—no pain registers.

Metal crunches as I float midair in the passenger compartment. *Is this how astronauts feel when they move in the shuttle?*

My head bangs against the headrest, but it doesn't hurt.

Stop. The seat belt holds me against the seat, but my head hangs straight down. All the blood rushes to it, adding to the strange feelings I'm having.

I try opening my eyes to focus, but the world spins, making me instantly shut them.

A loud tat, tat, tat. My heart races to escape my chest, but the incessant thump tells me I'm alive.

I work to open my eyes again. It's hard. It hurts. Pain shoots through my leg.

My head lolls to the left on its own. Kellen hangs unmoving beside me. I see him, but I can't say his name.

Muscle memory allows my arm to move across the console to him. I always touch him when he drives. Kell likes us connected.

With all the effort I can muster, I nudge his arm lying twisted between us. It's not supposed to bend in that direction. He needs to fix it.

Kell fixes everything. He's good at it. Be a good husband, Kellen, and straighten this out for me. My head spins too rapidly to say words. He can only stare at me, his head lolling slightly to the side as it hangs. His body is held back by the seat belt. He doesn't speak either.

Another voice registers. A fist bangs on the window beside me. Huh, it didn't crack like the windshield did.

A silent laugh leaves me. The noise only happens in my head.

Stop banging. My head throbs with each hit. The

window cracks before pieces of glass fall from it a few at a time as the man hitting them bangs away. That's weird—the pieces are landing above my head.

My window broke—Kellen will be mad about that. But when I turn to him again, he hasn't moved from the same position as before.

Hmm. That's odd. He can't be comfortable.

"Ma'am. We need to get you out," a uniformed man says.

I glance at my husband. He doesn't try to stop the stranger from reaching over me to undo the seat belt.

No, no, no. I can't go with a stranger. I want to scream, but nothing works. No voice, no sound, no fight. I'm too tired to fight. How can I be exhausted? I need to rest for a minute while I wait for Kellen to get me.

Arms slide around my middle, holding me in place as the seat belt falls away. The man slowly spins me so my head comes out through the window first. Then he starts to roll me over.

Oh my God, that hurts. Stop! You're hurting me.

The pain pierces. It's too much.

My mind drifts away.

Ian

WTF! I find myself lying in the weeds ten feet from where I started. Only a moment ago, I was standing by the passenger window of a small SUV, writing a warning ticket. Now, I'm in three-foot-tall weeds on my ass.

Glancing to where I feel a stabbing pain, I see a stub from a broken tree limb jamming into my forearm. Beside me stands a huge wild pecan tree. Two feet to the left, and I'd be hurt a lot worse than I am.

I shake my head, trying to regain my senses, before I pull the offending branch out. It's only then I realize there's a vehicle on its roof not far down the highway. Since no one stands around it, the occupants are trapped inside or too injured to crawl out.

My body revolts and sways as I get to my feet, but I know time is short for getting whoever is in there out. Fuel might already be leaking which means fire—the last thing I want. The people need to get out, but I can't see anyone moving.

I check on the occupants of the SUV where I stood before, and they both give me a thumbs up. I don't have to worry about them right now. Hitting the radio on my shoulder, I call for an ambulance to get to the scene as soon as possible.

My concern now narrows to the people in the other car. It crosses my mind that I got out of one dangerous police job only to be thrown into another—literally.

Chapter 2

Allison

People talk around me like I'm not right here.

I can't open my eyes. Trying as hard as I might, I will my eyes to open, but they refuse.

An annoying sound blares close to my head. It beeps constantly. *Please turn that damn thing off.* No one listens.

Someone stirs on the other side of my bed. I feel them staring at me. But it hurts to think, so I drift off to the silence inside my mind.

It's the screaming that wakes me—my own. My eyes fly open wide, watching as strangers race through the wide industrial door.

"Mrs. Waller, try to calm down. You're okay. Lay back, please." Someone—a nurse, I think—pleads with me to relax.

Realizing I'm sitting straight up and how much it costs me to do so, I lay back but refuse to close my eyes. When was the last time they were open?

"What's going on?" My voice is barely a whisper. "Where am I?"

"You're in the hospital in Houston," another stranger in scrubs tells me.

"W-w-why?" The word finally pushes past my lips, but I fear the answer. Do I want to know? Is it going to be something I truly want to hear?

"You were involved in an automobile accident. Let me get your family." The nurse and others silently step from the room. I hear them talking outside the door, but their words don't register.

The door flies open again, this time hitting the doorstop, and both of my kids bound through before stopping abruptly. Jackson silently moves to the opposite side of the wide bed from Junie. Their warm hands envelope mine, offering the comfort I was missing.

"Oh, Mom. It's so good to see your eyes open," Junie murmurs as she leans down and kisses my cheek.

"Yeah, Mom. You gave us a real scare when you didn't open them after the first few days," my son adds, leaning down for a makeshift hug. His six-foot-two frame continues to be awkward for him at twenty. We always laugh about him trying to maneuver his long legs in small spaces.

"Sorry, guys. I hate I worried you. What do you mean a few days?" My eyes scan the sterile room. "How long have I been here?"

The two cut their eyes across me, meeting each other's, before my son speaks, "Well, you've been out for six days now. Today is day seven."

His face tells me there's more to this story. Jackson was never good at hiding things. Kellen and I always told the boy to steer clear of Vegas. He'd never master a poker face.

"What's going on, you two? Tell me the worst first and get it over with." It took me a minute to realize Kellen still hadn't entered the room. "Where's your dad?"

I'm sure he's taking care of something important while the three waited for me to wake.

"You suffered a pretty bad concussion in the wreck, Mom. The doctors said it would just take time before your brain decided to wake up," Junie adds, still not looking at me.

"Oh, wow. That must have been scary for y'all waiting for me to wake up." I glance between the two. "But what's your dad taking care of? Must be something important because I thought he would be here waiting too."

Tears well and roll down Junie's face. I look to Jackson.

"What's the matter? Tell me now." I try to keep the fear from my voice, but the longer they remain speechless, the more panic takes over.

"Jackson, answer me."

The terror seeps in. Deep down, I know what's coming.

No. No. No. This can't be happening. It's not the right time.

We just became empty nesters. As we'd made our way home after moving Junie, our youngest, into her dorm room, we'd laughed at all the things we were going to do with the house childless for the first time in twenty years.

The university seemed enormous then, unlike when we moved Jackson in two summers before. Something about leaving our daughter made me teary-eyed as I watched our little girl standing and waving on the sidewalk in front of the twelve-story building filled with excited freshmen. I remember feeling the same way when we left her with the kindergarten teacher on the school walkway.

"Well, Mom..." Jackson leans both elbows on the railing of my bed, "... what do you remember about the wreck?"

"Just tell me, son."

"The doctor said it would be better to let you recall the events first. So, what happened? Do you know?"

My hand covers my eyes while my brain searches for the last thing I remember.

"We were laughing about something and then... and then... your dad... he... uh..." Where is that memory? It's right on the tip of my tongue.

"He... ugh. Kellen stopped laughing for a second, and I saw a police car on the side of the road ahead with a car pulled over. I thought we were both looking at it, but your dad never said anything."

Tears from shock spring from my eyes.

"He veered too close," my voice raises. "I screamed at your dad to watch out, but he sped up more, and he hit that car! Not the police car, but... but the one stopped!" My words stutter out, and my breathing becomes erratic. There isn't enough oxygen reaching my lungs. I grasp my chest.

"I can't breathe. I can't breathe," my scream sticks to my tongue. Alarms and bells ring around me. Blue-clad workers run in. I can't breathe. I'm going to die! I'm going to die!

People talk, but I can't understand the words. With my mind spinning, everything comes undone inside me. Words keep tumbling out.

"No, no, no. We hit the people. We hit them from behind, going down the side. Then we start spinning and flying through the air. But then the car started to roll over and over in slow motion. My body was suspended with each tumble. Stuff in the car floated with me. I watched my coffee mug and my ChapStick moving in front of my face."

I suck in a breath, the moment in my head playing on a continuous loop. *I'm going to die. I'm going to die. No, God, please not now. Please.* I close my eyes and pray. The memory finally ends, and so does my mind. It shuts down. No thoughts. No words. Nothing left.

I open my eyes and stare at people now standing in the room. They let me get it all out until I couldn't'.

A young nurse steps forward and mercifully turns off one of the horrid, blaring medical devices.

"I think that's enough for now, Mrs. Waller." She turns to the kids, who look traumatized by my rush of words, and motions for them to leave before smiling at me comfortingly.

"You've remembered a lot at once, ma'am. Let's see if we can get you to rest a bit. This is causing you undue stress from the looks of your blood pressure."

The pretty redhead pulls a syringe without a needle from her scrub's large pocket. She screws it into my IV and pushes the plunger, injecting the line.

"This will help you for now," she informs me. "Your doctor doesn't want you to get too excited."

My body floats. Not like in the car but like I'm high on drugs. Did I take drugs?

"Are those drugs?" My speech slurs. My tongue refuses to articulate words.

"Just a tiny bit to help you remain calm for a while longer."

"I don't want drugs. I want to stay awake. My kids need me. Where's my husband?"

I'm not sure they heard me. I'm not sure I'm talking.

No more words come. My mouth fails to cooperate,

and neither does my mind.

"Mom, we need to talk." Jackson walks through the door. "It's been two days now, Mom. Putting off the inevitable isn't going to change things."

My son sounds like an adult. He is an adult and has been since he left home at eighteen, but until now, I have never taken that idea too seriously. Today, his voice is strong and demanding instead of timid and questioning.

Jackson always deferred to Kellen and me for the hard stuff, and even then, mostly Kellen. Now, I'm the only one he can do that with.

The last two days played havoc with my mind. Coming to the realization that my kind, attentive husband didn't survive seems ludicrous.

I meet Jackson's eyes and see a man standing here, watching me. He won't shirk responsibilities. He never does when he has work to do. Now, the work involves making life decisions. I know he's ready for it. We raised him and Junie to be that way.

"You're right, Jacks." I hold my hand out, wanting to touch him. To hold on to him. To allow him to be the man he can be.

"Okay, so do you have questions for us?" Jackson asks me.

As if on cue, Junie opens the door like a wind blowing through a mountain pass. "Oops, sorry. I'm running a little late."

She produces a bouquet of fresh flowers, placing them on the wheeled table at the foot of my bed.

Jackson turns and grins at her. God, these two. I'm so happy they like each other.

"Yeah, yeah, I was just asking Mom if she had any questions."

"Oh, right. The doctor said we should try to answer them or maybe fill in the blanks you have." Junie's face doesn't show the happy-go-lucky girl we took to college that day. Worry lines form on her forehead as she looks at me.

"I do. There's a lot I've missed while I was out."

"Right. But most of that doesn't matter. What matters is moving forward. Getting a grip on what needs to be done."

I feel my forehead scrunch. What needs to be done?

"Then tell me, oh, list maker. What's on this list? Where's my trusty spreadsheet you always send?"

"We told you. First, let's answer questions, then we'll move on," he replies.

"Jump to the elephant in the room then. Tell me what happened."

They volunteered, and I want to know.

Jackson drags a chair to one side of the bed, and Junie follows suit. "Well, let's see. An officer writing a ticket on the passenger side of the car he stopped. Dad sideswiped it, causing the policeman to be knocked several feet away from the car."

He stops and studies my face for a reaction. I don't give him one.

"He's okay, though," Junie quickly fills in. "Just a cut on his arm from something he fell on."

"That's good." The response isn't much, but it's all I've got.

"The impact caused your car to start rolling over and over. They think Dad was doing about seventy-five when it started, which caused the car to roll several times before stopping on the roof."

"I think I remember the rolling." That small tube of ChapStick drifts in my mind again.

"Yeah, you mentioned watching stuff fly around in the car when you woke up once," Jackson responds.

"Go on, please," I push. If I'm going to hear this, I want it all at one time. Maybe I can deal with the pain all at once.

"So, anyway, the policeman said he got up and checked on those two people who were okay. No real injuries and that's a good thing." His innocent smile comes and goes quickly.

"Yeah, that cop was something else because after he checked on them, he came and crawled down to see about you and Dad," Junie adds to her brother's recounting. "Can you believe he did that after flying through the air and cutting his leg open?"

Jackson gives his sister a dirty look as if she said

something wrong.

"It is miraculous he was able to check on us," I say. "I guess his training kicked in over the pain."

"That's right. Adrenaline does weird things to people," she continues. "So, he saw you hanging there, but he had to use his stick to knock in the window. That's pretty amazing too."

"Yes, amazing, honey." I try to smile but can't muster the feeling. I know what's coming with this story, and I know the ending. It's not good.

Jackson picks up the story. "He kicked out the window, and you were screaming. He can't recall if it was at him or Dad." My son keeps his gaze on the hand holding mine. "Doesn't matter. Anyway, he can't get you out because the airbag deployed at some point, and your seat belt had you locked against the seat."

I release both their hands and reach for the back of my head. The memory of being locked in that seat belt and bumping my head on the headrest rushes forward. All in all, that was a minor injury compared to the rest of the damage.

"Pretty sure that left a bump on the back of my head, and the bruising from the seat belt is finally fading some." My hand rubs the traces of black and blue visible across my chest and down to my left hip. Touching it still creates pain and stirs the unwanted memories inside me.

Junie pipes in, "Yeah, the doctor said seat belts

sometimes do damage, but what would happen without one is definitely the greater evil."

"Junie, please. Trying to be positive here," Jackson scolds. "So, the policeman reached across and undid your seat belt, which made you drop down on his arm because he tried to stop you from falling. He didn't want to do any more damage to you since he didn't know the extent of your injuries."

I nod. Some of this is familiar to me. He wrapped one arm around my middle after I landed on the other outstretched one, slowly pulling me out and away from the car. I remember thinking how relieved I felt to have someone wrapped around me. He wasn't there to offer comfort, but his body warmth did that anyway until he left me on the dirt with tall grass blades sticking into me.

When I close my eyes, thoughts drift in, and I remember watching him move quickly back to our car, where he got down on his hands and knees on the driver's side. It was impossible for me to see what the officer was doing, but when he popped back up, he made his way to the car we hit, where the passengers stood off to the side of it.

It hurt to think about those moments, so I turn back to my son who is studying me with sympathetic eyes.

"Go on. I'm ready," I assure him.

"He moved you farther away from the car while he waited on the ambulance."

"Oh, right. The louder the siren got, the more it hurt to hear."

"Yeah, the cop said you hated the sound, but there was nothing he could do until they stopped and turned it off," Junie adds to the tale. "They took over from there, and the policeman had to stay and work the scene."

"But wasn't he injured too?" I ask.

"Yeah, but it was just some scratches the EMS bandaged for him. He's fine now," she offers.

"How do you know he's okay? We should check on him, at the very least."

"It's all right, Mom. We've seen him a few times since he's come by to check on you. He kinda wants to ask you a few questions."

"About the wreck? What could I possibly say that he doesn't already know?"

My son wraps his warm hand around mine again. I think it's as much for his comfort as it is for mine. "Mom, he wants to know what was going on before the wreck."

"What? Nothing was going on." Jackson makes it sound like we were drinking or something. He knows better. "We were talking and laughing one minute and flying through the air the next."

I close my eyes as that image comes back—floating, suspended, coffee burning me.

"He wasn't implying anything like that, Mother. He just wanted to know if something happened that could explain the wreck."

I can't turn away from them with one on each side, so I shut my eyes. I'm exhausted from talking about it, but they haven't mentioned their dad yet. Knowing what happened to Kellen will hurt, but I need to understand.

"Tell me about your dad, please?" I ask quietly, not wanting to hear. But if I have to learn the news, I'd rather it be from my children.

The two stare at each other, and that look crosses between them. Finally, Jackson opens up. "When the officer got to Dad, he was gone. There was nothing that could be done, Mom. The paramedics assured him at the scene he had made the right call to get you out and leave Dad until they arrived."

Tears stream down both the kids' faces, and I join them for a brief cry.

I feel guilty that they've had to shoulder all this without me. We have relatives who live hours away, so these two have had to step up and be the people we raised them to be.

"What's going to happen now?"

"Your doctor talked to us about waiting to hold the funeral until you could attend. He thought it would be better for you to get closure on all this."

"Besides, since Covid, funerals take place several weeks after the death. At least that's what he said." Junie hiccups, tears still streaming.

"I'm sure that's for the best. We can plan it

together. Your dad and I never talked about funerals. We both thought we had a long time before facing anything like that. I guess you never know."

Junie leans over and hugs me. I know she's hurting. Dealing with all these events is a lot for anyone, much less an eighteen-year-old.

"Listen, both of you. They are going to let me out tomorrow if everything is going okay. I want you to consider going back to school and trying to see your professors."

"No way we're leaving you, Mom," they both say at once.

"We've discussed it already," Junie informs me. "I can stay home and defer to the spring semester for a start date. I talked with my advisor about it, and she thought that was the best plan."

"No, that will not happen. Your aunt Elizabeth can stay for a week, and by then, I'll be okay on my own. Then we can start dealing with the funeral. She'll stay longer if I need her to."

Again, that look passes between them. When did our kids get to be so in touch with each other that one glance relayed everything they didn't want to say?

"I'm not backing down on this, kids. You're allowed two more days, one to get me home and one to drive back to school. I expect you to get caught up as soon as you can and make decent grades this semester. It will be difficult for you both, but that's what I want. Your dad would want that, too, so it's settled."

My son rubs his hand down his face and lets out a huff. "We figured you'd be an iron-ass about this, but Mom, we can take the semester off. One semester isn't going to change things that much."

"Yes, it will. You'll both have an extra semester before graduation and all the expenses that go along with—"

Junie jumps in before I can finish my sentence. "So, we also talked about the cost. Maybe it would be better if I stayed home with you and went to community college for the first two years. That would save a lot of money."

"Stop!" My voice raises more than necessary. "Both of your college funds were set up from the day you arrived on this earth. College is covered. Y'all know this. We both paid in all these years to make sure getting a college education would never be in question. You're going off to school, Junie, for however long it takes. And you, Jackson..." I stretch my hand out to hold his, "... you will graduate on time if at all possible. There will be no more talk of this nonsense from either of you. Is that understood?"

I can be the tough parent when I need to be. Kellen and I shared this position throughout our kids' lives. That wouldn't change just because he wasn't here to help, not until they didn't need me anymore.

God, I don't want that time to come, but it won't be long based on how they've handled everything up until now.

Allison

After dinner via a delivery service, I tell the kids they need to leave. I'm sure they're exhausted from all the days here with me, all the decisions they've made, and all the worries I've put them through.

I turn on mindless television to break the silence in my room. I'm not sure how that will work when I go home. Wandering around our home, knowing I'll be here alone forever, will lead to many sleepless nights ahead of me.

Kellen rarely took meetings that kept him away overnight, but even when he did, the kids were there to create some havoc. The only havoc I have to look forward to now is the occasional barking dog.

Maybe I'll get a dog now. It's been years since we

lost our sweet mixed rescue, Busy. The kids jumped on the name when Kellen suggested it because she was always busy getting into something. His other option was Nosy, but that was a no-go. Not that she wasn't, but it sounded too strange. So, Busy it was. Busy, Buzmeister, Busy Bee, Buzz Girl. We used all forms of her name at some point. Losing her hurt all of us for months, and we decided not to replace her for a while. Maybe 'a while' has passed.

A soft knock sounds on my door. I call to come in, and the door opens with a stranger on the other side. The uniform immediately gives it away.

"Mrs. Waller, I'm Officer Windsor, Ian Windsor." He steps forward and offers his hand.

I immediately stand. "Hello."

As hard as I try, I can't remember his face. I shake his hand briefly, but he holds onto it for a few seconds. His warmth helps calm me.

"I'm sorry to bother you, but I figured if I came during visiting hours, I could talk to you," the fair-haired man says softly.

"I was told you wanted to question me about the wreck. I'm not really sure how I can be of any help with my memory like it is." Those last few minutes stay buried deep inside. I want to forget forever.

"Oh, I was told you remembered some of the event. May I ask a few questions? And if it's too much, please just say so." He smiles at me. Not a big, wide grin, but a kind upturn of his lips as though he knows how hard this is for me.

"I'll try is all I can say."

He nods while looking straight at me. "Great, that's all I can ask for. So, was anything unusual going on with your husband before the accident?"

My eyes cut to his. Is he accusing Kellen of something with this question?

"I mean, was he angry or agitated?"

"No, he was fine. We were laughing about being empty nesters so early in our lives."

"Yes, laughing, that's good. So, the two of you were both doing okay?"

My eyebrows raise. I'm trying to follow his line of questioning but am put off by every question.

"Yes, we were doing great," I finally answer. It hurts to think where he might go with this. Should I be angry or indifferent?

"That's awesome, Mrs. Waller. Do you know if your husband had any health issues prior to the weekend? Was he feeling good about moving your daughter off to college?"

He looks down at his phone as if he were reading notes from it. I wonder what else he has stored in those notes.

"Yes, we were excited about Junie leaving for school. She's looked forward to going since the moment our son left. Not that she didn't milk being an 'only child' for the two years. She bragged constantly to her brother that he got screwed being an only child for his first two years." Thinking about her ribbing Jackson makes me smile and snicker. She loved giving him hell about it.

"That's great. I'm sure it was wonderful for the two of you to have that bonding time with her. I wish I'd had it with mine."

His brow furls as he says it as if it's not something he wants to discuss. None of my business anyway.

"And health issues? Any that you're aware of?" He looks at me through soft lashes as I lay propped up in the hospital bed.

"No, he was as healthy as a horse, Officer. I mean, it's been a while, probably a couple of years since he had a full checkup, but you know how that goes. We put off things we don't like doing and going to the doctor for Kellen was more on an as-needed basis." I let my mind drift back, trying to remember how long it had been. Oh well, it doesn't really matter now. "Why do you ask?"

"Just like to cover all the basis, Mrs. Waller." The reply sounds like a rote memory thing for him.

"Please call me Allison. I mean, after saving my life and all, I think we can move to first names."

His midnight-blue eyes bore into me. "Mrs. Waller... Allison... I didn't save your life. I only removed you from the car in case it was to catch on fire. You were talking but in pain. I hated moving you in case of doing more damage, but I smelled gasoline and feared it might ignite. That's why I went back for

23

your husband immediately, leaving you on the grass."

"Thank you for that. Thank you for everything, Officer. I know I probably didn't tell you that the day of the wreck, but under the circumstances..." I let my words fade off.

"No need to thank me, Allison. And please, call me Ian."

"I'm sure you always say that because you're doing your job, but honestly, one of the things I do remember was your arm wrapped around me, holding me when I came loose from the belt and moving me to the grass. It was a connection I needed at the time."

Tears well in my eyes. The memory floods my mind—a strong arm is holding me against the seat back, and then the belt is letting go. I only dropped a little and straight into a muscled arm that quickly pulled me out.

"I've wondered if, somehow, I knew Kellen was gone. I've woken up a few times remembering his eyes looking at me."

I haven't cried much since the kids told me the truth. As long as I'm in this hospital, I don't have to face the reality that Kellen is not going to be there when I get home. I know this will all be hitting me square in the face in the empty house.

Seeing tears roll down my face, Ian steps back and pulls a chair to the bedside. Does he pity me? I don't want to be pitied. I want to be strong. I'm a survivor.

"I'm really sorry, Allison. I knew it would be hard for you to answer questions, and I wanted to get this over with as soon as possible so you can move on."

"Thank you. I'm good. It just hit me all at once. The aftermath of the wreck doesn't seem real while I'm stuck in this sterile, white room with a view of a roof." I try to lighten the situation.

"Yeah, your view leaves a little to be desired." He follows with a brief laugh.

"Speaking of view, where exactly did the wreck occur? I never asked that before."

"It was on Highway 71, just outside of La Grange."

"That's a long way from here." His answer surprises me.

"The EMTs thought life-flighting you was the best idea since they didn't know the extent of your head injury. They couldn't keep you awake on the scene, and with your eyes showing signs of a concussion, they didn't want to chance it."

While listening to Ian talk about the details, it strikes me how different his details are from the ones kids shared. But they weren't there. Ian witnessed every single minute of that horrible time. I hate this for him, but then I remember he sees terrible events often.

Obviously, the scene takes up space in his mind even after a few weeks. That disturbs me. It wasn't his doing—though the car stopped on the roadside probably took a tremendous blow. I don't quite remember, but I recall a white blur somewhere in my mind as our car sideswiped them.

The thing I didn't see was what happened to Ian. I would never have known if the kids hadn't told me about him flying and landing on the dirt.

"Ian, is there anything else you can tell me about my husband that my kids didn't know? They only have your account of the events, and I'm not sure what you shared with them."

If enough people tell me the story, allowing me to relive it enough times, maybe I'll understand it. I don't know if I need all of this at once, but I may never see Ian again, and he holds one side of the secrets of that day. If only Kellen had lived. But that's something I'll have to deal with later, privately.

"Honestly, Allison, I've told you all I know." The tall policeman stands and walks to the window, his back to me. "You know they did an autopsy on your husband, right?"

"What?" My voice strains. "Why would they do that?"

"A fatality occurred. He died outside the hospital. They do this to determine if his injuries caused his death or if something else happened."

My eyebrows scrunch together as I try to understand what he's saying. Surely, the injuries from the wreck caused his death.

"No, I didn't know they did an autopsy. Thank you for telling me."

"They'll also inspect the car to see if something went wrong with it to cause the wreck. Could have had a flat. At that speed, it can cause a car to roll. Or maybe something mechanically broke under the car, making your husband lose control, ending with the rollover."

He glances over his shoulder at me before turning back to look up at the sky. "You never know until all the investigative work's done."

I stare at this kind man's back, trying to remember if anything snapped or if Kellen said something to me about the car. Nothing about the car comes to mind as my eyes take in Ian.

For the first time, I realize he's about my age or a little older. His arms are muscled but not like a bodybuilder or anything drastic. Moving me from the car probably required a lot of strength, especially since he had sustained his own injuries.

Being a policeman must require him to stay physically fit. The job is grueling enough, I'm sure. I wonder if working out is a requirement to keep his job or if it is a coping mechanism for him with all the bad things he encounters. Police maintaining good physical condition never occurred to me before now.

Ian turns from the window, where the early September skies are already turning dark. "I guess I've bothered you enough for now, Allison."

"No, you showing up has been eye-opening for me. I'm glad we had a chance to chat, not that the information we shared was pleasant." I know I should smile, but it's just not in me. What's there to smile about?

"It never is. Wrecks can be the worst part of my job if I let it affect me. I try not to get too deep into the information. Makes living a little easier when I go home."

I nod, realizing the situations he encounters must be horrible for him. I doubt I could do his job. Nothing about being a policeman sounds appealing to me.

When he turns around, he catches me staring at him. Not that there is anything salacious about my gaze, but Ian gives me an intense look.

"The nurse says you're leaving tomorrow, so I'm glad I had the opportunity to talk to you now. You and your family have a lot in front of you. I wish you luck and hope you can find peace in your heart when this is all settled."

"You're very kind, Ian. I appreciate all you did for us. For me."

He stops at the door and looks back. Deep blue eyes meet mine, and an easy smile crosses his lips. "Take care of yourself, Allison."

"Thanks, Ian. You too."

The door slides closed with a definitive click. The sound marks the end of a chapter in my life.

Allison

One of my kind nurses pushes my wheelchair while Beth walks beside me to the car where the kids are waiting. My sweet sister carries flowers and the supplies the hospital insists I take. Junie and Jackson stand beside Jackson's Bronco. They both look too young to be college kids, but today, I can't help but notice that Jackson looks just like his father.

Jackson and Kellen share so many traits. When I gave birth to him, there was no doubt he was his father's son. Now, it's as though I'm looking at the version of the man I married—Jackson is even around the right age now.

Kellen and I met in college. We already had two full years to enjoy being irresponsible coeds, living off our parents' dimes. We were on schedule to graduate with stars in our eyes and were both ready for marriage.

I knew I'd met my soulmate the day we met in the cafeteria. He'd banged into me with a tray full of food. He dropped it to keep me from dropping my own. We shared my lunch that day and every day after.

By the end of our junior year, we were in love and wanted to spend the rest of our lives with each other. Our senior year, we moved into an apartment together, much to my parents' displeasure. But they understood being in love. My mom assured my dad it was best to let it happen. She wasn't wrong.

We tried to be responsible, but circumstances changed a bit when the first fall leaves started collecting on the ground. My morning sickness soon took over.

The two of us were ecstatic over the pregnancy. And I still walked across the graduation stage, almost eight months pregnant with our son.

Our parents took some time to come around to the idea. Like it was going to change, right? But seeing that sweet baby cuddled between us in the hospital bed melted all four hearts as soon as the now grandparents walked through the door. Love at first sight took on a whole new meaning for each of them.

Our parents still insisted we have the wedding we'd talked about before the discovery of a little one on the way. Jackson made the cutest ring bearer the following summer as his dad pulled him down the aisle in a red wagon.

In his tiny suspenders and navy bow tie, he'd climbed out of the wagon and held Kellen's hand, walking up to the preacher and waiting for my dad and me to make our way to them. As soon as Jackson saw his grandpa, he'd squealed some unintelligible one-year-old words at the top of his lungs. Kellen held onto him to keep him from toddling to meet the two of us. Everyone laughed, and it set the tone for the rest of the wedding. One that had turned out to be all we'd hoped for and more.

Now, here I am, twenty years later, being pushed by a nurse down the walkway to my little boy's car. My beautiful children are waiting at the end of this aisle but no Kellen. While I'm not walking alone, it feels like my right arm is missing.

Where's the man I married for better or worse? He vowed to love me until the end of time. Twenty years is not the end of time. It's barely any time at all.

A wave of anger followed by tears washes over me.

He left me…

He promised me forever…

He told me I'd never be without him…

Beth hears me suck in a breath and stops the nurse.

"Allison." My sister bends to look me straight on and blocks my view of the kids. "I know you're not okay no matter what kind of brave front you put on.

31

And it's okay to be sad. It's natural. There are lots of steps for you to go through to get over this. You'll get there, but today... today, girl, you need to show your kids you're going to make it so they'll realize it's all right to move on, too, to live the lives they were meant to lead."

Her words puncture my pity party long enough to let me pull myself together. "We'll talk later, right?" I whisper.

"Yes, we'll talk all night if you want, but right now, suck it up and be their mom."

Beth's harsh words help get me past this hump. At this moment, I know they hold the determination I need to get me through. My children need to see I will be all right when they leave. Witnessing me fall apart won't cut it.

I raise my hand, wave at my kids, and motion for us to proceed to Jackson's SUV.

Junie opens the door, watching my every move. "Is everything okay? Why'd y'all stop back there?"

"Your mom thought she'd left something in the room. I assured her I gave it all a second look," Beth tells her as the nurse clips the locks on the chair.

"Do you need help, Mom?" Jackson asks. He stands at the ready between the SUV and me, the back-seat door open. This is a good decision on his part as riding up front might set off my anxiety.

I stand and step toward the opening, but the memory of my last car ride flashes before my eyes. I close them, take a deep breath, and release it slowly. If I climb in this car, I'll face the ride home. I'm not sure I can do it.

I open my eyes and see the four people—even the nurse—waiting for me with looks of pain, fear, concern, and love.

I can do this. I can be strong. We will make it from here. The words turn over in my head as I reach for the seat. I take another step forward, raise my foot, and place it on the floorboard.

I will move on. I will make it. I will be strong for myself and my kids.

Even though my entire body hurts climbing into the car, I do it. Stiff from days in the hospital bed, I readjust myself in the seat. The doctor assured me I needed to move around as much as possible to work out the soreness. He is right. Jackson grabs the seat belt, buckling it around me.

"I could have done that, son."

"I know, but why stretch if you don't have to? Let us help you, Mom. We need to feel useful."

A slow smile slides across my face. My boy came here trying to be helpful to me. I guess it's ingrained in him.

Once I settle and give the word, Jackson pulls out of the parking lot. I'm not going to lie. Being in the car scares me, but I don't want to make everyone else worry. The last few weeks caused enough of that for all of them.

Jackson's hand reaches back to me, and I fold my hand in his. He gives my hand a squeeze. "You doing okay?"

I nod and take a deep breath.

"You're not fooling any of us, Mom. The further we go, the whiter your face gets. It's going to be all right. You need to sit back and try to relax. We'll be out of the city in about thirty minutes, and the rest of it should be easier for you."

"I know, but seeing cars zip around us causes me some anxiety I've never had before."

"The doctor said as much," Beth pipes up. "But you have to get used to it if you're going to face driving again sometime soon."

My head knows she's right, but my heart says otherwise. Even though Kellen drove that day, I could have been behind the wheel. Would we have had the accident then? I did most of the driving when we were in my car. Why didn't I drive us home?

Watching me from the corner of his eye, Jackson asks, "So what did the policeman have to say? Or did he only ask questions?"

I applaud him for trying to get my mind off the situation. Taking a deep breath, I finally speak. "Finding out if there was more to the story than what he got from the scene seemed important to him. He wants to do a thorough job of recreating everything to know exactly why it happened."

"What difference does it make now? Dad's gone,"

my sweet daughter's voice cracks as she speaks. Junie's words break our hearts, but she needs to grieve in her own way.

"I'm not sure exactly why it matters. Obviously, it does, or he wouldn't drive all the way to the hospital to find out."

My sister leans forward, putting her hand on my good shoulder. "Did he offer any other information we didn't already know?"

"No, not really. He said our car was inspected to make sure something mechanical hadn't happened like a flat or something breaking underneath. If it did, Kellen will be cleared of any wrongdoing."

"What the fuck, Mom?"

I whip around to stare at my son. "Jackson?"

He never talks like that to me.

"Sorry, but are they trying to say Dad did something to cause the wreck? Like he was intoxicated?"

"No, the officer didn't imply anything like that. They simply need all the answers to make a complete report." However, I had wondered the same thing about Officer Ian's line of questioning.

"I call BS on that, Mom," Junie adds. I guess they think because they are technically adults, they get a pass on language. I'm not sure how I feel about it, except F-bombs are not high on my list. Not that I don't use it when the situation calls for it, but to hear it come out of an angry Jackson—yeah, I'll need some time with that.

"Why, Junie?" I ask. "He's only doing his job."

"It sounds like there's more to it than just the police needing to make a report. I mean, could they issue Dad a ticket now? What good would it do?"

My sister squeezes my good shoulder once more before letting me go. Jackson makes a face at Beth in his rearview mirror. I turn and look at Beth and I realize her law radar is going off.

"What's going on, Beth? Do you know something I don't?"

"Honestly, Ali, I haven't had time to sit down and look at the situation well enough to advise you. I'm not a personal injury lawyer, but there is a law in Texas about medical emergencies that cause accidents. If Kellen was having a medical emergency, then the people he hit, or the officer in this case, can't sue you for negligence."

"What I'm hearing is the officer writing the report has the say on who's at fault. Is that right?"

"Yes, so I'm sure he wanted to be thorough about his report. And if it comes back that Kellen was at fault, then you'll more than likely be looking at a lawsuit. If there were a mechanical reason for the wreck, your insurance company would probably take over and sue the auto company for damages. You'll never have to be involved with that."

"Oh, wow. This could turn into a huge mess for me to deal with."

"Don't worry, Ali. I'll be with you every step of the way. Let's wait for the report to see what's going on." Beth appears calm with all of this, but she has a poker face when it comes to lawyer stuff.

I watch the cityscape turn into rural areas. The traffic wanes, making me realize we won't be on the road much longer. Returning to the house, knowing Kellen will not be there waiting for us—the family we built together—causes my heart to ache.

Chills travel through my arms and spine. I shiver. As much as I tried to prepare myself in the hospital, I know nothing will give me the confidence I need to face the house—our home—without my husband.

It's the home we built together just before Junie was born. Our first two-bedroom house had quickly grown too small the year we pulled Jackson's old baby stuff from storage. Kellen and I poured over the floor plan he'd designed each night after our son went to bed. It was going to be a forever home for our growing family, so we worked to make it the most livable space. By the time Junie was three months old, we'd moved the four of us in.

Everything good about our family happened in this house. Junie took her first steps. Jackson lost his first tooth while standing in the kitchen. They both took their prom night photos by the fireplace. There, Kellen and I toasted all but one of our twenty anniversaries.

No more birthdays together.

No more toasts to celebrate.

No.

More.

Kellen.

I try to tuck the morbid thoughts away. The sound of Jackson's blinker catches my attention as he turns into our driveway. I watch as he pulls around and into the garage beside where my now totaled car normally sat—his dad's spot.

A fierce pain rips through me. I can't breathe. My hand reaches for my chest in a useless effort to rub the pain away.

"I think I'm having a heart attack," I eke out with the little oxygen left in me. My sister's hand is on the back of my neck, pushing me forward so my head is between my knees. "She's having a panic attack." Beth's voice barely registers before her hand leaves me.

My door flies open, and her face appears beside mine. "Come on, Ali, breathe with me. In, two, three, four. Out, two, three, four."

She counts it over and over while I attempt to keep up. Slowly, air returns to my lungs, finally inflating for use.

I hesitate to sit up. What if I start hyperventilating again when I see the house?

Realizing I have to face the inevitable, I push myself up but keep my eyes straight ahead, trying to avoid even one more in-my-face reminder of my new world. As I slowly turn to see the empty spot, warm tears slide down my cheeks.

"Sorry, Mom," Jackson says gently. "I guess I should have parked in the driveway until you got used to the empty space."

"It's okay." I lay my hand on my son's strong arm. "I didn't realize it would have such an effect on me seeing his car not there."

I look back at Junie and move my hand to her knee. "He's really gone, isn't he? You two have had to face it all alone. I'm so sorry I wasn't here to help you."

"Mom, you have nothing to be sorry about. We're just happy you're home now. We can all be together."

I nod at my daughter, who is resilient in every way. Even through tears like mine, Junie's holding her emotions in check enough to speak. Her words comfort me more than she'll ever know. God, what would I do without these two right now?

Allison

Between the exhaustion, lingering pain, and medication, the next two days crawl by, though I'm sure the kids' opinions differ from mine. They begin putting their lives back together, prepping to head back to school.

I promise them both this will work out, especially with their aunt here to oversee my recovery. Knowing she can be an iron-ass when needed, the kids eventually give up on convincing me to let them stay.

It's not that I don't want them here. If I could, I'd lock them in the house and keep them safe for the rest of their lives. Unrealistic, I know, but what mom doesn't feel that way at some point? But while it's a time of crisis for me, my precious children need to move forward like I'll eventually have to do.

I wake early the day they leave, wanting to be as helpful as possible. My contributions lead to an argument. They prefer me to sit idly by while they load their cars.

Watching them, I try to understand how life will be with them gone. There is so much to do, and there are decisions that their input would be helpful on. But this is my new reality, and I need to handle the day-to-day chores.

No one ever said life would be easy—not that my time with Kellen was always a bed of roses. This is different, though. I must face the world with a brave face and a new outlook. Just thinking about it overwhelms me.

Kellen and I shared responsibilities for the past twenty years, and now, they're all mine. I'm not sure I was cut out to do life alone. But if I have to, I plan to jump in with both feet and face it head-on like I do everything else.

Their cars are almost packed. I open the front door and step into the hot sun. Texas in early September can be brutal, and today is one of those days. I know I can't do this heat for long, so I move to the shade of the large oak.

Our parents gave Kellen and me the tree the year we moved in. We both babied the young tree and got excited when we watched the new leaves return each spring. Our children played under it when they were little. Jackson broke his arm while climbing it when he was eight. I remember him lying on the ground crying after Junie ran in to get me.

I'm pretty sure Junie had her first kiss under the oak when Chase, the cute boy from across the street, came over five days in a row to *hang out* with her on the swing Kellen had hung years before. I thought it was cute. Her dad, not so much. I had to keep him from storming out there.

Fortunately for the boy, Junie didn't find the kiss to be all she'd hoped for. Chase still came over, but it was only to visit. They ended up best friends all during junior high and high school. Chase decided to go to college out of state last year, so who knows if they ever talk anymore.

I sit in the swing while they finish the last few loads. The number of things they both brought home surprises me until I remember Junie's hasty decision to move home and attend community college.

"Did you empty your dorm room, Junie?" I call as she walks past with another armload.

She arranges the items in her trunk before joining me in the shade.

"I thought I was moving home, Mom. I figured if I could get enough in the first load, there wouldn't be too much left."

Taking her hand in mine, I squeeze while I pull it onto my leg. The connection calms me, her warm hand a huge contrast to my cold one. When were my hands last warm? I believe the cold settled in the minute I woke in the hospital. Nothing keeps them warm for long now.

"I'm proud of you and Jackson. You know that, right?" The last thing I want to do is upset her before her two-hour drive, but my time for words will abruptly stop when they pull out.

"You'd think differently if you could watch a video of the two of us the first few days at the hospital," she says softly. "We were a big mess. I'm sure we worried everyone who came to visit."

I turn, surprised. "A lot of people came to see me?"

I'm not sure how I felt about that. Friends, relatives, and gossips watching me sleep as I lay unaware kind of freaks me out. How did I look to them? Why would anyone want to drive over an hour to stare at me?

Junie stares at me. "I can read your mind, Mom. You looked fine like you were sleeping. We only allowed a few people inside other than family. Grandma called constantly, wanting to know if she should come stay and take care of Jackson and me like we were children again."

"Oh honey, you'll always be children to your grandma." I laugh.

"She wanted to come and made us FaceTime at the hospital and at home with her a few times so she could see for herself. After that, she decided to wait and come when you got home. Aunt Beth stopped that. She volunteered to spend some vacation that was going to waste. Seems she understood how Grandma being here would probably send you screaming back to the hospital. To the psych ward specifically." It was Junie's turn to laugh.

I love my mother, I really do, but she can be a bit much after a few days. She and Dad came often when the kids were young, and we enjoyed it. Dad's restlessness after a few days saved many a visit from turning into a disaster. He would announce they were leaving, and Kellen and I would breathe a sigh of relief.

I never worried about them coming when Dad tagged along with her, but when she came alone, a weekend was enough. She expressed her opinion about everything Kellen and I did with Jackson because, according to her, we were such young parents.

The two of us read enough books and visited with our Lamaze group of parents often to have great backups for everything that went wrong. Of course, nothing we chose to do for cholic or diaper rash was the right way to handle it. It made for some strained days. My dad recognized it and gave me a knowing look before he told Mom they would be leaving the next day. Kellen and I secretly hugged him tightly when they started for the car. The two of us whispered more thank yous than we cared to admit.

Like I said, though, I do love my mom and know she

means well, but two hens in the hen house create issues. I did not need more issues, so thank God for Beth.

"If you'll get that small box by the door, Aunt Beth, I think I'm ready," Jackson calls as he walks out the front door with an armload of clothes on hangers.

"I swear the two of you own way too many damn clothes and shit," Beth walks out with the last box.

"Beth, we try to encourage them not to use bad language," I warn.

"For the love of God... gosh... they're adults, Allison. We don't have to be so prim and proper anymore. They need to know the real me like they've been seeing since I've been here."

"Yes, but you and a sailor have too many similarities when it comes to language. I guarantee they learned new words this week."

"Always happy to help expand their vocabulary," she adds while my two kids have a field day laughing.

"Please, Mom." Junie giggles. "I live in a coed dorm with too much testosterone and your son. Don't get me started on his potty mouth. You'd be looking for the soap."

Jackson turns from the back door and side-eyes his sister. "You're one to talk. If she only knew."

I can see this escalating into an argument between the two. They do love each other, at least from what I've seen during this time.

Anxiety is high with the circumstances, so I decide

shock therapy will be a big hit. In a loud but stern voice, I stand from the swing and yell, "Shut the fuck up, both of you. We'll have none of that damn bickering you're both famous for."

Drop-dead silence.

The looks on their faces are priceless.

Until Beth starts pointing at my kids and laughing. Full-on belly laughing. Tension immediately dissolves when they both join her. I join in, and the mood lightens even more.

"Hmm. I guess I'll throw away the swear jar." I gasp between laughs.

"Nope," Jackson jumps in. "I'll take it to school and blow that fucker up in the science lab."

I can't retaliate over his word choice, so I agree to let him take it.

Beth and I stand in the driveway and wave at them. I find it comforting they are leaving on a lighter note. I woke up dreading the moment they'd go. It stood a good chance of being an all-out cry fest, and I didn't want any of that happening.

We watch as Jackson drives down the street, trying to keep up with our speed demon, Junie. The girl only knows one speed—fast. Beth's arm rests on my shoulders, and the thought of moving into the house makes me cringe.

"Well, damn. Guess they are really gone, right?" I ask.

"Yeah, Mom, they are off to live their lives like you

both would want them to," Beth assures me.

Turning to her, I try to smile but fail. "I know you're right, but that doesn't make me like it anymore."

"Nope. Sucks, doesn't it?" She pushes me toward the house.

The time for crying would come later when I was alone and missed them terribly. Right now, I have a list to make for the upcoming chores Beth and I need to complete before she leaves.

Walking at my new slow speed, I make it to the kitchen table and pull out my to-do pad. I thought about writing on it all morning but wanted to get the kids off. They cared too much to see it. Guilt over leaving me already hurt them. The last thing I want to do is add to it by writing chores out.

"I know you've been dying to make a list," Beth comments as she shuts the back door behind her. "The wheels in your head have been on full spin cycle since you got out of bed."

She knows me too well. I've always been a list maker—it's how I kept my sanity having two little ones so close together. With today's scene, I'm glad we had them when we did.

"Sorry, there's just so much to get done, and my thoughts are fleeting at best right now. If I don't capture them when I think of them, I'll never get it all done."

"What's on that list that won't keep another twenty-four hours? You've only been home one full day, Ali. A day off won't hurt you. The doctor told you to rest."

I turn to her. My sister used to be so judgmental, but the last few years mellowed her. Losing her long-term boyfriend to a much younger woman made her take a good look at her life.

She went from staunch and unwavering to happy-go-lucky and spontaneous. She laughs more, takes more time off, and spends more time with friends and family.

We love her any way we can have her, and this new version is a breath of fresh air we all enjoy. Before, we dreaded having her in our home. Now, we love her being around.

"Hey, I wanted to tell you how happy I am that you're staying with me for a bit. I don't think I can make it without you. And the kids, they would have never agreed to go back without you being here. So, thank you." I stand and draw her in for a tight hug.

"I wouldn't be anywhere else right now, little sister. You and the kids mean everything to me. Seeing you hurting kills me inside."

Leaning back, I stare hard at my big sister. She's five years older than me, never married, and lacks prospects now. With how things turned out from the dick she lived with for all those wasted years, she's missed out on having a family of her own. He'd refused to have more children since he had two from his first marriage, and she'd agreed to it.

Kellen and I wondered if she didn't want them or wanted him enough to agree. The time she spent alone with our kids said the latter was correct. Beth would never admit it, and I refuse to bring it up. It doesn't matter now because she's been perimenopausal for a couple of years now.

When I feel tears stinging my eyes and threatening to spill over, I pull back. "There's time enough for tears later. Do you have some items to add to the list? I mean, you've had far more time than me to think about all that must be done."

"Has to be or needs to be? Two very different things, Ali."

"Yes, but I want them all on here, and then I'll prioritize them."

"What, no spreadsheet to cover two full legal sheets?" Her smile tells me she's secretly laughing at me. If the kids were around, they'd be agreeing with her.

What can I say? I love a spreadsheet.

Allison

"How about we go look at what's in the freezer? Your neighbors loaded it up with food for you. There *might* have been cakes and pies in the beginning." She side-eyes me.

"Oh, I don't recall seeing any in the kitchen when we got home."

"Someone had to eat them to keep them from going stale. The three of us took it on as a mission." Her smile might be contagious if I cared about food, but right now, eating repulsed me.

"You each volunteered to take one for the team then, huh?" I smirk.

"Absolutely. Glad you see it our way," she says over her shoulder, reaching into the refrigerator for a half-filled bottle of wine. "We thought it would be better than tasking you with making important choices later on."

She holds up the bottle, offering me a glass, but quickly pulls it back. "Damn, sorry, you can't have any with the meds. Maybe in a few days." Tipping the bottle of white, she fills her glass before pulling out a bottle of water for me.

"This hardly seems fair. You get cake and wine, and I get water with cheese and crackers?"

Beth sets the already nibbled cheese board on the island. The cheese smell makes me turn up my nose, so I scoop a few crackers to munch on instead. They seem the least offensive.

"What can I say? We did think about you while we mindlessly ate it at night watching TV."

I turn to stare out the window facing the backyard. "I'm sure you did. The grass needs mowing."

That was Kellen's job. He loved his John Deere lawnmower and treated it like a treasure.

Beth stands beside me. "Yeah, Jackson wanted to do it before he left, but you shoved them out the door faster than they planned to go."

"I had to do it, Beth." I tip the water bottle for a small sip. "They would have stayed the entire freaking semester if I let them. Their lives can't come to a screeching halt because of the accident."

"We talked about what your feelings would be on the matter when I first arrived. As much as they didn't want to go, they knew what you would say."

"Then why did they even argue with me over it?"

I feel her eyes boring into me. "They hoped you'd change your mind, especially after you got home. Just like they predicted, you didn't."

Beth's glass lifts, and she takes a healthy drink of the gods' juice.

"If you hadn't been here, it might have been different." I put my arm around her waist and pull her to me. "What the hell am I going to do, Beth? You can't stay forever."

She pulls me to her by the shoulder. "You're going to take it one fucking day at a time."

"One fucking day is the truth."

By day three, I swear the two of us answered a gazillion messages.

The kindness of our friends and neighbors had poured in while I slept the days away in the hospital. We decide to tackle my list next. My sweet sister took pity on me and typed it into a spreadsheet for us to divide and conquer. It's the little things.

Number one on the sheet stands out because it's the worst part.

The funeral.

It's not something I want to deal with, *ever*, but I

want Kellen to be honored in a way that's a testament to the kind of man he was, especially to those who had left the gazillion messages—Kellen's golf buddies, fishing buddies, church friends, work friends, and more. They all left voicemails or stopped by the house.

How did my kids handle all these people? I look at the list in wonder. Many are people they barely know or haven't ever met.

Kellen and I never talked about our deaths. Would he want to be cremated instead? I think I remember, at some point, he'd made a comment about the ridiculous cost of funerals when his grandparents passed.

We were young, and the shock of losing them made us feel adrift for months, with only the two of us against the world. Will I feel that way again after this numbness wears off?

"Beth, this wears me down," I tell her through tears. Crying taxes the little bit of brainpower I still have.

"How about some lunch and a snooze? It'll make you feel better, and maybe you'll feel more like tackling the funeral thing then."

"Let's call the funeral home and make an appointment before that." I know if we don't set a time to start this, it'll be put off another day.

"Good idea. I'll make lunch, you call." She hands me my phone from the counter and turns to the refrigerator.

Our town has one funeral home, so the choice is easy. A calm but upbeat voice answers and leads me through a series of questions to consider before we arrive tomorrow. What's the day? Clothes? Time? On and on. Nothing I want to think about.

How do you choose the last clothes you'll ever see your husband in? He looks so hot in his black suit, but black? Do I want to always remember seeing him that way? Kellen wasn't a suit kind of guy anyway. He liked a golf shirt or a plain tee.

What will everyone think if I put him in one of those two shirts? I huff over the plate of salad Beth sets in front of me.

"Sorry, we have so many salads that will ruin if we don't eat some of them," she says with a grimace.

"No, it's not the food. Should I be worried about what people think when they see him buried in a golf shirt?"

"Allison, really? You shouldn't give one fuck about what other people think."

"Yeah, yeah, I know, but I don't want them walking away thinking I was too cheap to put him in a nice suit."

There was a time when he didn't own a suit. That money had to go elsewhere with two kids running around. Between doctor bills, insurance, and daycare, we had no extra money for foolish things like suits. Keeping the kids in clothes and food was far more important.

"Who cares what they think?" Beth stabs her salad with a fork. "Girl, you need to be real here. Would Kellen rest easy knowing you'd put his suit on him for the last time? Hell, if it were me, I'd put him in his favorite cargo shorts and a T-shirt."

Beth speaks the truth. If any of his friends stopped by, ninety-five percent of the time, they'd find him dressed exactly like that.

My forehead lands on the back of my hand on the island top. I don't want to talk about this. This is wrong. I can't be burying Kellen.

We were both ready to find each other again. With the kids finally out of the house, we could rediscover each other like we did when living in that little apartment and finishing school.

Kids took so much energy, but in the last six months—with Junie graduating and doing her own thing—we found more time on our hands. Time for each other. We decided to spend time together doing the thing we loved again, reconnecting as a couple, as lovers.

Like most couples, our love life suffered because of kids. There was never enough time. Rendezvous for the two of us were few and far between with ball games, band practice, and taking kids here and there.

We made a pact that a few times a week, we were going out to do something we wanted to do—plan it and do it, with nothing to get in the way. Concerts were not going to wait. Dining at specific restaurants around the city was going to happen. Meeting friends for drinks or a show was on.

And sex. Sex was on whenever the mood struck us. No being quiet because the kids would hear. No stopping and moving upstairs when we kissed in the kitchen. The counter would do. The rug in front of the fireplace would work.

I sit straight to face my sister, a blush crawling up my neck as I think about it.

"Are you okay?" she asks.

"Yeah, I'm fine. Just thinking."

The look I give her must be revealing because her smirk tells me she knows where my mind went.

"Okay," she drags the word out. "I can't do anything to help you with that."

"What?" I try to pull off an innocent look but fail.

"The look says it all, girl." Her finger wags in a circle around my face.

"It's so hard, Beth."

"That's what they tell me. Been so long, I wouldn't know." One eyebrow goes up in question. "But then, do you ever really forget?"

"We had so many plans with the kids leaving."

"Must have involved a lot of sexy times."

"You'd know with kids in your house for the last twenty years of your life."

"Yeah, that ship sailed a long time ago." I hear the disappointment in her voice.

I take her hand in mine. "That wasn't meant to hurt

you, but we've always had kids around. Good thing we were together for a few years before."

"Right, I get it. You were both looking forward to being a couple again instead of a mom and dad."

Warm tears roll down my cheeks again. God, will this ever stop? I can't spend the rest of my life crying over what will never be.

"Oh, Ali, I'm sorry. Don't cry. You're going to make it. You're the strongest person I know. Look how great the two of you made it work when you got pregnant. And let's not even talk about what great parents you are."

"Were," I add. "We were. Now I get to be a single parent."

"True, but they're grown, so now you'll get to be a single person again when the time comes for it."

"No, I can't do that." My eyes open wide. "There'll never be someone out there as good as Kellen."

"That's probably true, Ali, but you're young. You can't honestly think Kellen wouldn't want you to find someone at some point. Not now, maybe not in a year, but when the time is right. You've got forty or more good years to live. Doing it alone isn't advisable. Take my word for it."

My head cannot wrap around something like this right now. "Let's work on you first, then. I'm not on the market, now or maybe ever."

This conversation wears me out even more. I rise and put my dish in the sink. Eating doesn't sound so great now.

"I'm going up to take a nap." I snatch my phone from the island. "Call if you need me."

The throw at the foot of the bed is soft and velvety, feeling scrumptious when I pull it over me. Junie gave it to me for Christmas since I'm always cold. The throw caresses my skin with each movement of my legs. As I drift off to sleep, I love cocooning in it.

Kellen comes in from the backyard, where he's been tinkering with his lawnmower. I hear him wash his hands at the utility sink while he hums a tune probably stuck in his head from listening to the radio over his earbuds.

I'm lying on the couch, midday, a rare occasion. He walks in and sees me watching a movie on the television. He joins me on the couch, lying behind me, as I watch 365 Days. This movie can only be described as soft porn by some viewers, and I'm some viewers.

I look up and see the people in the movie have moved to the other side of our den, where a bed sits. We don't move from our position, but Kellen and I continue to watch, never saying a word. The two actors notice us watching and motion for us to join them, but we decline.

Instead, we create our own scene but on the floor, still in the same positions. Kellen's hand slides under my tank top, where I'm braless. He takes his time to caress my breast, pinching and pulling on my nipples. Kellen's hardness begins to slide up and down in the crease of my ass as we watch the questionable scene unravel before us.

He moves my hand to my breast. "Keep doing this for me, babe."

He walks his fingers over my skin, touching and drawing circles with calloused fingers, creating delicious friction. He reaches my jogging shorts and slides his hand inside—straight to the slick folds that wait for him. He knows exactly what the nipple play does for me.

His fingers tantalize my clit, circling the nub of swollen nerve endings. When I begin squirming and moaning loudly, he knows I need more. Sliding his middle finger inside me, his thumb continues to assault my clit in delicious ways.

"You're ready for me, aren't you, babe?"

I can only nod as I begin to writhe and use his finger to fuck myself. He adds another finger, stretching me a little more. My back bows with the surge of need he creates in me.

The people on the bed are now hanging over the end, watching us, as the hot-as-hell guy continues to fuck her from behind. We've never had sex with others watching. It's not something we are into, but we go with it. Kellen moves between my legs, sits up, and begins to remove my shorts. I whip my top off, freeing my swollen breasts in the cool air.

"Look how responsive she is to him," the man says. "It's the way it should be when it's your true lover."

The woman rolls over and kisses her partner. She's now lying under him, but he doesn't take his eyes off us. He seems fueled by our coupling and spreads the woman's legs, entering her again.

A sheen of sweat from being outside glistens on Kellen's skin, but it feels so good as I run my hands down his body, ending at his shorts. I put my hand around his length, straining to be released from the material that separates us.

"Take it out, babe," Kellen instructs me, so I open his shorts and pull down the front of his strained boxer briefs allowing his swollen cock to break free. It's smooth and hard under the hands I wrap around him.

"Let me taste you," I tell him. He sits up and pulls me to him.

"Swallow it up for me," the man on the bed utters in a deep voice. "Let him know how much you love the hard cock that's about to give you unlimited pleasure."

I sit up and lean over, licking around the head and causing Kellen to growl. Taking him in, I suck as I continue to slide further down the smooth, solid length.

"Push her past her limits," the female above tells Kellen. "She can take it."

"I don't want to hurt her." My husband speaks

softly, but I feel his hand wrapping in my long hair and pushing me down further than I've ever taken him before. The forceful way he pushes me makes me want to please him more.

Bobbing up and down his length until I swallow him all, I run my hands down his bare thighs, cupping his balls with soft fingers, rubbing, squeezing, and pulling easily.

"I'm gonna blow, Allison." Kellen's strained voice tells me.

His rigid cock pops free from my lips. "No, I need you to fill me first."

Rising, I watch the two on the bed as the man enters her from behind again with her ass in the air. The hulk of a man roughly pulls her onto his dick.

"We can do that, Kellen." We've explored many positions, but nothing like what the couple does.

Kellen sits back on his calves and lifts me to my knees. He uses his hard length to tease me by running it from my clit to my small rear opening. Up and down, up and down. He has me writhing on the sheet below me.

"Kellen, now. I need you now."

Instead of entering me, he slides down on his stomach and assaults all of me with his tongue. Circling my clit over and over, he knows exactly what to do to make me come. He enters a finger and bends it forward, rubbing that special spot, building an intense orgasm.

But before I can reach that pinnacle, he pulls back, looking at me with smoldering eyes that tell me he's ready to push this exquisite torture to the next level. I'm so ready for him to take me hard and fast. My need is more intense than ever.

"Are you okay in here? You've been making all kinds of weird sounds and moaning. I was afraid you were having a bad dream."

Allison

My eyes pop open with my sister standing over me. I'm rolled up in my soft throw, but I feel the evidence of arousal trickling between my legs.

Good thing my subconscious didn't have me acting on the erogenous dream. How embarrassing it would be for my sister to find me in the throes of passion while dreaming.

"Yeah," I eke out, unable to find my voice. "I'm fine. Bad dream. Thank you for waking me."

All the memories of the great sex we were finally enjoying, with Junie gone all the time and Jackson away at school, had rushed into one hot but strange dream.

The realization they were going to be gone fulltime

hit us both one day as we lay side by side on the den floor, just like in my dream. We laughed while talking about all the great sex we would have when she truly left. Yes, we would miss them both, but we had each other.

The watchers in my fantasy baffle me since I've never considered what it would be like to have someone watching us. Voyeurism isn't something Kellen and I ever talked about. I'm not into sharing my husband with another woman, so I guess I'll tuck that mystery away for another day.

At least we did have each other. Now, I'll simply be alone in this big house. No one's body warmth in the middle of the night when something wakes me. No one to cuddle with on cold nights. No one to hold me when I've had a bad day.

As I unwind from the small blanket, I realize Beth is waiting for me to share the dream. If she thinks I'm divulging what the dream was about, that would be a big no.

"There's too much I'm going to miss with him gone, Beth. So many memories to push aside for now to deal with life."

Perching on the side of the bed, I look at her. She suddenly gained the role of becoming my rock. I hope she's prepared because this will be a long haul. With my eyes wide open, I look at her hard. "You're planning to stay for the week, right?"

Please say yes, please say yes.

She pulls my hair over my shoulder. "I'm planning to stay as long as you need me. Maybe I'll move here. Who knows?"

"I couldn't ask that of you. You have a life back in Dallas. Friends. A job."

"You know I can work from anywhere since Covid. My company leased out the office space to someone else already. As for friends, most of my friends are 'our' friends," she air quotes, meaning her now ex. "Wonder which ones will he take with him?"

"Regardless, you have a life you've built there, Beth. Don't move for me."

She breathes in deep and releases out slowly. Is she trying to make up her mind? I don't intend to influence her one way or the other.

"Honestly, I'd be moving for me. I've missed you, and now that the kids are gone, this seems like a good time to make the move. You know, a fresh start and all that."

I lay my head on her shoulder, and she takes my hand. "Aren't we a pair of sad old ladies?"

"Hey, speak for yourself. I'm a sad young lady, and you're a rock star for getting through all of this like you have."

I make the rock star sign with my hands and bob my head to imaginary rock and roll music. "Okay, all you rockers. Let's get this party started. And by party, I mean let's go find another frozen casserole and eat dinner."

The two of us ride to the funeral home, but each mile hikes my anxiety by leaps and bounds. We barely make the appointment on time, and by the time we leave, I feel drained of everything I'm made of. The whirlwind of emotions makes me want to run out screaming like an apparition appeared in each casket we viewed. How do people even do that job?

"What now?" Beth asks as we exit the parking lot. "Care to go drink brunch?"

"You must be reading my mind because the first thing I thought of when we walked out was where we could go and get drunk. Stinking drunk. Sit at the bar and tell them to keep them coming till I am blacked-out drunk."

Beth looks at me like I've lost my mind, and honestly, I feel like I have. My mind, my body, my life. All in one fell swoop.

"You know you can't do that, right? Your spreadsheet takes precedence over day drinking."

"Who says? I'm the boss now. Like the Missio song says, 'I do what I want.' Now and forever." I turn and stare at her. "Sounds badass, huh? If only I felt that way."

"Let's go have a couple of mimosas with some lunch. You'll feel better or at least be tipsy enough you won't really care," Beth snickers. "The rest of the entries we can handle from home."

After three Sunrise Mimosas, my well-meaning sister cuts me off. She nurses one the entire time we sit at the high-top table overlooking the lake. We order a light lunch which I only nibble on. The idea of eating food today makes me want to throw up all the alcohol.

My sobbing starts after I've downed the first half of the third, overly potent, drink. Beth fights with me to leave, so I gulp the rest before she takes me home. I crawl on my couch to cry myself into a fitful sleep.

The escaping slumber doesn't last long because my phone starts the ridiculous chime Junie programmed for her number.

"-lo," I mumble.

"Mom?" A bright voice questions.

"Yeah."

"What's wrong? Are you sick? I knew you'd get sick with all of this. You always do when you get super stressed out. I'm coming home right now."

Beth takes my phone away, turning on the speaker. "She's not sick, Junie. She's a little drunk."

"A little drunk?" I hear my sweet baby repeat with a snicker. "Is that like a little pregnant?"

"No!" I shout. "I just had a teeny bit too much sunny drink."

"Sunny drink, huh?" I hear laughter in Junie's words. "I don't think I've ever had one of those, but good for you. You deserve a break, Mom."

Moving to a sitting position, I look around me. Nothing's changed, I see.

"Yes, I do deserve a break, honey. The gods aren't being cooperative with that, though."

"I can come home for a few days if you want."

"No, I don't want. Go to class, learn a bunch, and be a kickass graphic designer. That's what I want." I know that my slurred speech sounds ridiculous, but it's true. She needs to live her life. If I've learned nothing else with all of this shit, life is too short to not live life to the fullest. Isn't that what the posters for old age say?

The thing is, I'm not old. Kellen wasn't old. We're barely in our forties. He never got the chance to start a bucket list, much less tick off the best items.

"Mom?" Junie draws my attention back to her.

"Yes, I'm here."

"Did you decide on a day?"

She doesn't have to say the word 'funeral,' I just know. "Yes, it's going to be a week from Saturday. That way, you two can come home after your last class on Friday, make visitation that night, and do the service on Saturday morning."

"That's fast, isn't it?" Her words sound hesitant.

I wish I could see her face, but I don't want her to see mine since I know I look a total wreck after the morning I had. Is she crying?

"Oh, honey, I think it's been long enough with me

being in the hospital for so long. We need to find closure. We need to move forward. It'll be hard, but we'll be together. We'll muster up the courage to pull through."

Please let my words mean something to her. If only there were a way for me to believe in them too.

Time passes quickly, and I soon find my little family standing at the front of the chapel, greeting people. People look at us with sympathy while offering warm words of condolence. The surreal situation taxes me heavily. I try hard not to cry, but it's impossible. My kids look as miserable as I feel.

Before I can blink a few times, the casket lowers into the ground, leaving the three of us surrounded by family and dear friends. I feel the sweat rolling down my spine under the Texas September sun.

Why did I choose this stupid dress? I swear it's going into the trash when I walk in the door at home. Who decided black was the right choice for funerals anyway? The only time Kellen liked black was for lingerie and sexy cocktail dresses showing lots of cleavage. Yet here I stand in a plain black-sleeved sheath he would have hated.

Does this day have to go on forever? Can't they all go home and leave me, no us, alone? I know my kids are hardly looking forward to entertaining and listening to stories they've heard dozens of times from people they barely recognize.

Beth and the three of us enjoy listening to soft

music and having drinks on the patio, so why do we have to do something else?

I let out a breath I didn't realize I was holding and turn to her and the kids. "Guess we'll see all of them at the house."

Jackson looks around as people make their way to their cars. "You think they'll all come?"

"God, I hope not," Junie adds.

"No, but a lot will," Beth answers them. "You know, the ones who expect to be fed for just coming out."

This gets a smile out of the three of us. She's right. I was thinking the same but was too worried my words would come across as crass at this point.

"Let's get it over with then," I tell them as I start toward the car.

A man stands close to a tree off to one side of the grassy area where we are standing. I didn't notice him during the service. Dressed in a button-down and slacks, he looks like he belongs here, but I don't recognize him. Kellen knew a lot of people and worked with many I didn't know.

He angles toward us as we walk across the grass toward the street close to the burial plot. Oh my God. Does a stranger expect to talk to us right now? I can't handle one more kind word at this point. If I run fast enough, can I make it inside the car before he gets here?

"Yeah, yeah..." Jackson says, "... that's the policeman who pulled you from the car, Mom."

I remembered that he came to the hospital. Jackson told me he talked to him a few times before I woke up.

"Do you not remember talking to him, Mom?"

"Yes, I think I do." I stare at the man as he gets closer. "He came to ask questions about your dad and the wreck. Like what happened before the crash."

I feel tension rise inside me. If he's here to ask more questions, I'm not having it. This is not the day.

"Hello. I'm Officer Ian Windsor. We spoke at the hospital," he says the words as a reminder to us. As if we need one.

Please go away.

"Why are you here?" Junie asks. Blame it on her youth, but I'm glad she asked. At least she is honest enough to say what we're all thinking.

"I came to pay my respects to your family," he responds with a brief smile. "I see a lot of accidents. Most turn out okay, but then this kind of wreck happens, and people's lives are forever changed. Mine included."

His face morphs into one of sadness.

I never considered how accidents affect the people working the scene. In his case, he was part of the scene. He watched it all unfold—the rolling, the landing, the screeching.

My screams.

Kellen's first moments of death.

How could he not be traumatized by the scene? Flying through the air also involved him. I feel like a horrible person when I look at him now.

Stepping forward, I offer my hand. "Thank you for coming, Officer Windsor. We appreciate all you did for us that day. I don't know if I told you that in the hospital. Please feel free to come to our home and enjoy the meal set out. We would love to have you there."

"No, no. I can't do that. This is your family time. I don't want to intrude on your private moments." He glances over my shoulder to where the dirt covered in fake grass waits to be shoveled over the casket.

That explains why he stood back from the group during the graveside service. Respect is a rare quality these days.

I drop his hand and watch him glance over the kids before focusing on me. A flash of memory hit. When those dark blue eyes land on me, I see them looking on as he pulls me from the passenger seat. He holds me up with one strong arm, extracting me from the crunched frame surrounding me.

A flash of the horrid scene invades my memories, causing tears to well. As a fat drip spills over and down my cheek, I feel compelled to hug him, so I step forward and wrap my arms around him. He hesitates to respond to my awkward, tight embrace, but eventually, a warm hand lightly pats my back.

"Thank you so much for all you did that day. I don't remember everything, but brief moments of the scene pop into my head at the most difficult moments. It happened just now and reminded me of you getting me out of the car."

"You're welcome. I'm just glad I was there to get to you that quickly."

I pull back and step away from the closeness we share. "I insist you stop by the house. You can follow us there now."

A tentative look crosses his face, and I realize he must be debating the thought.

With a small smile, I almost beg, "Please come. It would mean the world to me, to us."

"Maybe just for a minute, then."

"Well," I nod and turn toward the car. The others follow without saying a word.

Chapter 8

Allison

Drifting through the house, I speak to people, but I'm not truly aware of what I say. They repeat their kind words over and over each time they address me. I see some are uncomfortable expressing condolences, so I avoid more eye contact with them and move on to the next.

To call the situation strange is an understatement. Do we ever know the right words when someone dies? I'm on the receiving end and can't find the right words to say back. I'm sure I repeat graceless words dozens of times in the span of a few hours.

When I pass the windows to our backyard, I notice Jackson speaking to the officer. Ian is the name he asked to be called. The two seem to be having a lively discussion. I hope Jackson finds some comfort in talking to the man about Kellen's age. Maybe the two can find things in common like the ones he shared with his dad.

Junie walks up behind me, wrapping her arms around my waist, and spots the two men standing under the trees just off the patio.

"What do you think they're talking about? He doesn't even know that guy," she comments. The negative tone in her voice says she doesn't understand the scene the same way I do.

"Oh, I don't know, Junie. Man things."

"Mother, really? Man things?" She doesn't laugh, but I know she found it funny.

"Sorry, you caught me off guard. I was thinking they might have some common interests like sports or cars or, I don't know. Like Jacks used to do with your dad when it was the two of them."

"Don't say that, at least not today. You can't compare a total stranger to Dad."

Without even trying, I've made her angry. I know it's the grief talking, so I ignore her curt words.

I turn and urge her toward the foyer. "Come help me say goodbye to the people. The sooner they're gone, the sooner we can relax."

Jackson appears next to me as I close the door behind several guests.

"Sorry, I didn't know it was time for people to leave." The look he gives me says he's more than ready for them all to be gone. I understand it because I feel the same way.

I pull him in for a side hug. "That's okay, honey. Your sister was with me until a minute ago. She disappeared with a friend from school."

"Ian and I were talking about growing up here."

"Really? He grew up here too?" Kellen and I moved to this town after our son was born. It was close enough to our parents but not in the same small city.

"Yes, he grew up on the other side of Calvary but left for college. He did the police academy in Houston but got a job in Columbus after he graduated. Said he hated living in the big city, so he only applied at the small towns out this way."

"Sounds like you got his life history."

"Yeah, he's pretty easy to talk to. I guess when you're a cop, you figure out how to talk to everyone you meet... sorta like Dad could." He looks down at me with a shy smile.

At least he wasn't worried about comparing the two like his sister.

"That's true. Your dad could talk to a fence post." We both laugh.

These memories are the kind I want to keep close for the kids—Kellen's quirks that made him the type of man he was. That man was far from perfect, but he was one of the good ones.

I catch myself already referring to my husband in the past tense. Did my mind automatically know to do it? He's only been gone such a short time. I drop my head as my eyes water.

Please, God, let this be over. I suck in a deep breath to keep from breaking.

We close the door to Kellen's parents, who are as devastated as the rest of us. His older brother, Kerry, hugs the three of us last.

"You know where I am, Allison, kids." He looks over Junie and Jackson, who stand attached to his sides. They've always had a close relationship with their uncle, who could be a twin to their dad.

"Will do, Uncle Kerry." Junie hugs him once more.

Tears spring up in Jackson's eyes, and his uncle hugs him close like he did when Jackson was a child. Kerry whispers for only my son to hear, and finally, Jackson pulls back, nodding. I pray they always share this tight bond. Kerry is not Kellen, but it's the closest to his dad Jackson will ever have now.

My dad walks in from the patio with Ian following him, sharing a smile that immediately disappears when they see my in-laws leaving. Dad knows the tight bond between Kerry and the kids, so he turns to the den—hopefully to find my mother.

Ian waits until Kerry clears the doorway before he approaches. "Thank you for having me today. I never meant to stay so long."

"No, I'm happy you came." I smile. "Sorry if you got trapped outside with talkers always looking for a new ear to bend with old stories."

Ian looks over his shoulder into the den. "Oh, we were sharing war stories from the deer lease. Your dad has a lot of them."

I see my dad helping Mother up to go. "That he does. We've heard them too many times to count."

"Listen, I want to talk to you or you and your kids about some things, but now is not the time."

My head turns up a little. "Oh? You have some information we haven't been given?"

"Yes, I believe so, but I can call or stop by to talk later in the week if that's okay with you."

"Sure. The kids are leaving tomorrow, but my sister will be here with me."

Ian offers his hand, and I shake it as Junie and Jackson join us. They all say goodbye before Ian makes his way out the door. I'm happy my kids didn't hear Ian ask me about coming by. They both need to return to school tomorrow to get on with life. Having to return to their routine will be good for them.

As Beth, Jackson, Junie, and I shut the door behind the last guest, we look at each other. What do we do now?

"I don't know about the rest of you..." Beth pipes up, "... but I'm having a tall glass of the expensive wine. We damn well deserve it."

Moving into the kitchen, we pour wine for each of us. Junie might not be old enough to drink legally, but wine is a staple in our home, so she's already had some for several years. I laugh at myself. Who am I kidding? She's a college kid. If all she has is an occasional glass of wine at school, I should count myself lucky.

The comfy chairs in the den call to us, so we spread out and prop our feet. No one says a word as we each enjoy the quiet.

Jackson places his empty glass on the coffee table. "I guess that went well. I've never been to a dinner after a funeral before."

"Count that as a good thing, dude." Beth pats him on the back. "I hope you don't have to go to another for a long time. You're too young to be dealing with shit like this."

My breath comes out in a huff. "True, but our parents are getting older."

"Mom, please." Junie whines. "Can we not talk about death anymore today? I'm sick of it."

"Sorry, I know you are. Let's talk about what you two have coming up at school. Football season?"

As the remainder of the day passes, we keep the conversations rolling with nothing important. We clean up the mess, snack, and watch mindless television to keep from thinking.

My mind replays snippets of today's conversations with Kellen's friends and coworkers. I know some stories I need to file away to share with the kids later.

When they're ready. When I'm ready. Today is not the day.

Ian's request pops up, making me wonder what he

could possibly know that we don't. As the investigating officer, I suppose he wants to close the case. Will that be the last of it? Kellen's life will end with a probated will and a police report?

I find the kids sprawled out, drinking beer and watching a comedy they've seen often but laugh every time. A few empty bottles rest on the coffee table, where I am sure I'll find more when I get up. I'm okay with that. Downtime is good for them.

The silence in our bedroom hits me when I walk in. Standing at the foot of our king-size bed, it doesn't call to me, but there are no other empty rooms for the night. Maybe I'll switch this one out for a queen size later. It won't feel so big and empty.

"Damn, this is depressing," I say to no one.

After a shower, I follow my usual routine to prepare for bed—one ingrained into me. The white ceiling stares back at me, but I lay thinking about last night's dream. Kellen's essence is still on the sheets when I roll toward his pillow, wrapping my arms around it.

"Yeah, definitely changing the bed out soon." I take a few deep breaths and fall into a wine-induced sleep.

Beth and I watch the kids head out to school. I insisted they get an early start, which didn't go over well. They wanted to linger as long as possible, hoping I would change my mind. But no. They need to get back to their regular routine and get on with life.

It won't be easy for them. Beth and I discuss the signs to look for if they become overwhelmed with grief or depression. Hopefully, the rigorous schedules they opted for keep them too busy to get bogged down in either.

When the phone rings, I dread the idea of talking to anyone else today. Can I please have one day to wallow in my misery? I guess not as the incessant ringing continues.

"Hello," my tone might be a tad sarcastic.

"Mrs. Waller, Allison?" the deep voice rumbles through the phone. "This is Officer Windsor, Ian Windsor."

"Oh, yes. Sorry if I sounded rude. The kids just left."

"I hate that I caught you at a bad time, but I'm coming to your town today and thought it might be a good time for us to talk."

Looking around the house, I realize putting off the visit isn't going to change things, so I might as well. "Sure, we're not going anywhere today."

"Thanks. I'll be there in the next thirty minutes if that suits you."

"That's fine. We'll see you then." I end the call, hating that I even answered it. But Ian carries information I probably need, so I don't know why I procrastinate.

"Who was on the phone?" Beth asks as she comes downstairs dressed for the day. There's a mess everywhere in the house to straighten up from the reception. While it's not terrible, a good cleaning would do it and me good. Hell, diving into a monotonous chore to keep me busy sounds like a plan.

"It was Officer Windsor. He wants to stop by to review the information since he has to come over here today."

"Great. We can put off this mess for a while longer."

"Quit being a neat freak. It'll get done when it gets done," I bark at her.

"I'm not that bad. It's better for our brains to have an orderly living space."

"Might be better for yours, but mine says, fuck it. It'll be here tomorrow."

"No can do, sis. If you don't want to help, that's okay. I understand, but I can't look at it for one more day. Part of me wanted to do it last night. Falling asleep with a mess drives me insane."

Seriously? All my fucks were gone by the time I went to bed, and sleeping didn't replenish the stock. I guess we'll have to rely on hers for a few days.

After putting on nicer clothes, I brush my hair for the first time since before the funeral. Was looking presentable even necessary at this point? Ian saw me at my worst, hanging from my seat belt.

The doorbell chimes in less than thirty minutes.

Well, at least he's prompt. Not that I care either way.

Beth answers the door, a breezy note in her voice. Is she flirting with the cop? Now? The accident didn't change her life, so she has every right to be happy. Why not flirt with a hot guy? Her freedom from the douchebag gives her permission to do what she wants. Her words make me happy briefly as I walk down the hallway to the front door.

"Hello, Officer Windsor, uh, Ian. Come in, please," I offer.

He steps in and looks hard at me like he's trying to judge my level of crazy for today. On a scale of one to ten, I teeter on a six or seven.

"Ian, please, Allison. I promise not to take too long today. You two probably have a lot to take care of."

I glance around at the hasty job Beth did in the den area. She made it more presentable for company. The leftover mess in the dining area still waits.

I offer him a seat, happy at his words of brevity. Get in, speak, get out. It works for me. Hopefully, it's one last step in the nightmare I want out of.

Allison

As Ian spreads paperwork on our wooden coffee table, I realize scratches cover it, overlooked for years. Having survived both kids growing up, it served us well.

I glance around. Maybe our whole house appears full of nicks and dings. Right now, my life consists of damage and loss. Remodeling the house will wait.

Is this a sign of how complacent we'd become? Comfortable in our lifestyle to the point we let things go? Kellen's death has shaken me up in unimaginable ways.

Will I look at the world with fresh eyes any day soon? Part of me likes to think we tried to be up to date, and then I see ignored items and pause. If only he'd lived so we could move forward together.

Kellen dying too soon makes me wonder how I want to exist from here. Living in the moment scares me, but I realize I need to, except I'm not sure I'm ready to jump off this crazy train around me and try life yet. I need more time.

Ian squeaks his shoe on the floor, jarring me back to reality. "I don't know if you've been notified, but the autopsy results were released. I went by to get the report and finish up the paperwork. The evidence found bears looking over... some possibly for your insurance company to see."

Hmm. I never thought I needed to do more than I've done. Surely, they'll pay for everything. Isn't that why we paid dearly for twenty-plus years?

"You make it seem like something they found has a major impact on the accident."

Ian turns to look me straight in the eye. Sitting side by side on the couch, I watch his blue eyes darken even further around the edges to form a ring of black. This enhances the indigo, a beautiful contrast. Thick, feathery, black lashes frame the perfect irises—something women go through torture for.

"I must be honest, Allison. The findings surprised me."

"How so? I mean, it was an accident. He veered too near the car, right?"

Watching me closely, he reveals, "He did, but more than that came into play."

He takes a deep breath, slowly releasing the air. What he is about to say is going to be important.

"The bottom line is Kellen died from a heart attack. The report says almost immediately. The doctor labeled it a widow maker." He looks at the paperwork in front of us.

In a dumbfounded attempt to understand what Ian is saying, I stare at the side of his face. A heart attack can't possibly be true. A soft laugh escapes me. "That's impossible. Kellen was in great health."

"He appeared that way on the outside, but inside, he was a ticking timebomb. Were you aware he had heart issues?" he asks, finally looking at me instead of the papers. Was he afraid to watch me break when he told me? He has no reason to fear that because this is all BS.

My eyes widen. "No way. I would have known. I'll call his doctor right now to prove it."

Kellen's general practitioner checked him out every year. We didn't keep secrets from each other, especially about health.

The doctor ran routine tests just like he did with me. Have I looked at his test results lately? I'm not as dependable about going for checkups, but Kellen is... was.

While calling the doctor's number, I think about doctor visits and realize Kellen had gone more this past year. He'd played it off as nothing to worry about—sore throats, allergies, pulled muscles—

normal things for someone his age. Was Kellen being honest with me?

The ring starts on the other end, connecting me to our doctor.

"Dr. Heinz's office," his receptionist answers.

"Yes, this is Allison Waller, Kellen's wife."

"Oh, Allison, we are all so sorry about the sad news. He was a great guy."

Dr. Heinz treated the whole family for as long as we've been here. Once the kids got older, we left the pediatrician for Dr. Heinz. I wanted the family all at one practice.

"Yes, I need to ask about some medical issues Kellen had. Is it possible for me to speak to the doctor?"

"Uh, well. Let me ask him. Are you listed as having the right to see his record? You know, the laws and all. We adhere to the HIPAA laws."

She questions me, knowing Kellen is dead. What difference does HIPAA make now?

"I want to know what all Dr. Heinz was treating him for, please." I try not to sound pissed off with her comment. It takes everything in me not to yell into the phone.

"Right. Let me see if the doctor is available to speak to you, Mrs. Waller," she replies with a snit. I guess I struck a nerve by demanding information I have every right to.

"Now we will get some answers," I assure Ian.

Kellen did not have a heart attack. Plain and simple. The coroner got this wrong. I would know if he had heart issues. Kellen never kept secrets from me.

"Hello, Allison. This is Dr. Heinz. My receptionist pulled me from an exam room, so this must be an emergency."

"Yes, it might be, Doctor. I've just been informed that the wreck that took Kellen's life was caused by him having a heart attack while driving. Tell me this isn't true, Doctor. He would have told me if he was having heart problems."

I hear papers being shuffled around, then the sound of tapping on computer keys. My heart feels like it's in danger of exploding with the waiting, the unknown.

"You are listed as able to see his medical records per the paperwork on file." A squeak of his chair blares through the phone. I picture the doctor leaning back before speaking to me.

"Allison, did Kellen share with you what's been going on medically for the past year?"

I swallow past the lump forming in my throat before I barely get a 'no' out loud enough for the doctor to hear me. Please, God, please tell me he never kept it all from me.

"I treated Kellen for blood pressure problems and high cholesterol for over a year."

"What? I never knew this. I've never seen him take anything other than vitamins."

How could I not know this? Why keep it from me? What the hell, Kellen!

I don't know whether to be furious, disappointed, or hurt. All these years, we'd talked about how we were stronger together with no secrets—secrets like the ones we'd watched our friends' marriages crumble from. The lies started when secrets ate away at their marriages. Weren't secrets lies in this case too?

"He asked that I not share this with you, but with his passing, I see no reason not to. Your children need to be told because this seems to be a hereditary issue."

"You're saying he should have told them to be checked for cholesterol and blood pressure. Doctor, they're young. Why scare them if it's not necessary?"

"Yes, that's exactly what Kellen said about telling them and you. He felt like they had years before dealing with it. He knew if he told you, they would know too soon."

How selfish to keep this to himself. Kellen loved his children more than anything. When did he plan to tell them? After a heart attack? After we buried him?

Anger rushes through me until I can't sit still. I pace around the den, feeling Ian watch my every move. I really don't give a single fuck about that right now. He can leave. He said what he came to say.

"But they need to be tested now," the doctor adds. "They need to know what they can do now to prevent anything from happening."

My head spins.

"Oh, wow, Dr. Heinz, is there something that can be done to make sure they don't develop either of those?"

My heartbeat races, and my nervousness shoots through the roof. How could Kellen be so irresponsible with his kids' lives? Damn, damn, damn. He knew better.

After giving me a minute to digest, Dr. Heinz continues, "There are several things that can help them, but they'll need to see a doctor to get started on the right path. Diet and exercise, possibly medication. Are they still home, Allison?"

"No, but they can see a doctor in Austin or come home and see you. As long as they start preventive measures now."

I continue pacing, my hand on my hip, eyeing Ian as he follows my moves. *Just leave, dude. I don't need you judging Kellen or me.*

Dr. Heinz must hear the frustration in my voice.

"I'm sure you'll do everything that needs to be done, Allison," he reassures. "Feel free to have them call the office if they want to ask anything about the testing they both need. I'll make sure my staff is aware."

"Thank you, Dr. Heinz. I appreciate everything you've told me. If only Kellen had listened."

"Well..." he pauses, "... I'm sure you'll find a lot of 'if

onlys' over the next year or so. They will not change anything. It's best to put this behind you and remember the good things about your husband. My condolences to you and the kids."

The phone call ends, but information whirls in my head.

He used kind words to help me feel better, but right now, I don't want to feel better. I want to be angry. I am angry. I'm beyond furious. I feel my feet hit the floor and realize I'm stomping in my treks across the room.

Glancing over to Ian, I stop myself from the temper tantrum. His witnessing my fit makes me feel childish. But dammit, I am livid with my dead husband. What a selfish piece of shit he was for keeping this from me. From us.

"I take it the news from the doctor confirmed the findings are correct?" He keeps a straight face.

"If you say, 'I told you so,' policeman or not, I will smack you in the nose. I pack a powerful punch."

I see his face and realize my words only sound harsh and probably ridiculous.

"Why, Mrs. Waller, are you threatening an officer of the law with bodily harm?" He ends his question with a smirk.

A smirk? How dare he make light of this when he doesn't even know how serious this could be. My actions, crazy or not, say exactly what I feel inside. He can just deal with it.

Ian's solemn countenance tells me he understands, but I didn't appreciate his look.

"I feel like some part of this tells you more than you knew before. Information you can deal with."

"What?" I ask, still fuming inside.

"Think about it, Allison. This means your husband didn't make a mistake. He had a medical issue causing the wreck. Kellen only sideswiped the car, so he kept it from rear-ending the other vehicle, which would have resulted in much more damage. Someone could have damn well been killed, or me." He speaks each sentence faster than the one before. His volume climbs.

My mind accepts all his quick speech. I know it's the truth, but thinking about it brings all the scene back in a rush.

He veered too close to the stopped car. I yelled it at him. The impact with the sideswipe happened under my nose. Flying through the air made my heart rapid-fire. Landing upside down with Kellen staring at me. Fighting to get out.

My hands come up beside my ears, holding my head as my mind wrenches through the scene repeatedly. It's too much. Too much for me to understand or deal with.

Loud screams pierce the air until I feel strong arms wrap around me. They hold me in place to stop my body from rocking. A tremble takes over, shaking me from head to toe. And still, the arms keep me tight against another human as Ian offers solace for my crazy.

Soft words of comfort eventually penetrate my thoughts. The calming effect finally reaches every part of me.

When was the last time I felt this way? Like I can breathe without it hurting. Like I can let go and just be.

Ian holds me as we stand in the middle of my den. With my arms trapped under his, I bend my elbows to reach around his narrow waist, basking in the comfort of another human.

God, I need this. Warmth only another person can offer. My head turns so I lay on his chest. My nose captures his manly smell. Relief washes through me. For the first time in days, maybe weeks, I feel safe. Even if it's only temporary, I'll take it.

I'm not sure how much time passes, but I realize Ian has let me go. With his hands clutching my upper arms, he takes a step back. The look on his face says he understands my need for the hug, the human contact.

How often is he forced to embrace people crying for anyone to offer support? Does he always come forward? This must wreak havoc on him to relate devastating news to families.

"Hey, you okay now?" His quiet words bring me back to the moment.

Stepping away, I take my place on the couch where

I started from.

"Yes, there's just a lot to think about. To take in and make sense of. You know?"

"Yeah, I'm sure there is. Does it feel as though every day something new presents itself? You know, like make decisions or tell strangers what you need to proceed?"

"You don't know the half of it. With the funeral out of the way, there's all the will stuff to deal with. Lots of decisions to make."

"Oh, right. I think you need to take a minute before making any big decisions until you're sure and ready. At least that's what I've always heard after a major life change."

"Yes, I plan to take my time and do everything step by step. Could be a long haul for me."

"I'm sure you'll get it all done in your own time." He looks around the house, and I realize he sees Kellen's touch everywhere—as it should be.

"Guess I've done all I came to do. Sorry to be the one to break all of that to you, but I felt like I needed to come tell you." He moves toward the entryway, and I follow.

"I'm sorry if I said anything that..."

"No, you don't owe me any kind of apology. Your life has been turned upside down. I'm happy I provided you with one step to closure."

I open the door, leaning my head against the end. "Yes, thanks for that."

"And look, if you need anything, please let me know. I'll do all I can to help you."

My head bobs. "Will do, Officer."

A beautiful smile flickers across his face.

"That's Ian to you," he says, turning toward his car.

I can't help but grin back at him. Someone needs to scoop that guy up. He's too cute to be alone.

Allison
Two Years Later...

"No, Junie, you're not taking a gap year in the middle of college," I hear the exasperation in my voice, and she hears it too.

"Look, Mom. I know this isn't an ideal time, but school is pressing me to declare a major, and I'm not ready to. Honestly, I have no idea what I want to do with my life at this point."

"All the reason to stay where you are and surround yourself with all the options available."

"No, you're not listening. That's the reason I need to get out and see what's going on in the world. Make informed decisions from experience instead of reading some dumbass brochures put together by a graphic designer from a foreign country."

Folding clothes, I put them away in my newfound drawer space, finally empty after clearing out and donating Kellen's items. After two years, I realized it was time to get started.

Once I began, I couldn't stop until everything personal had been mulled over and either donated or stored away for the kids. The few pictures of the family placed strategically remind me of the best times of our lives.

With Beth living down the street now, we tackled the task together. We laughed, cried, and drank a lot of wine.

She reminds me daily that the time to start dating is now. Two years is long enough to mourn. I'm not sure I believe her because she's never been married, but breaking up with her boyfriend and moving to our town gave her a new perspective.

I'm quickly discovering that dating at forty-two is just damn weird. People don't date. They mingle, choose a partner for the night, and slip away later to lick their wounds or bask in the afterglow of sex.

Honestly, I'm not sure I'm cut out for it. Kellen was the only one I've ever been with. The idea of meeting someone and jumping into bed that night, or even a few meet-ups later, scares the hell out of me.

And the way they talk to each other. I'm not a prude, but the words they offhandedly use make me cringe. Kellen and I tried our best to control our language once the kids came along.

The last thing I wanted was for Junie to stand up on the pew at church between the two of us and yell out, "Oh shit," or "What the fuck." And what about her brother calling her a cunt?

If that had happened, they could have held my funeral at that exact moment. My headstone would read, "Here lies Allison. She died of mortification."

"Look, Junie, I know choosing a career is difficult. In reality, you'll get a degree you might never use, but you're too far in to drop out." I shut the bottom drawer and stand.

A slight pain in my lower back makes me wince, and I remember the doctor telling me that at my age, I need to stop leaning over and squat instead. Squat? He must be joking, but that reminds me that I need to go to the gym.

The house of pain calls to me every time I drive by. If nothing else, I should try a yoga class to stretch the tight muscles out. Do men around my age hang out at the gym now? I never paid attention before—maybe because Kellen was with me when I went.

Junie's aggravated voice pulls me back to the conversation.

"I'm not dropping out, Mom. Just postponing graduation to travel with several of my friends. A guy is even going with us, so it won't be just girls."

"Is that supposed to make me feel better knowing some strange man is traveling with three females?"

"Yes, it should." A loud exhale comes over the phone. "He's just a friend, and none of us like-like him. He wants to travel, and we're going, so why not have him go with?"

"Did y'all discuss possibly only taking off one semester instead of the entire school year?" A semester should give them enough time to discover what they want from life, right?

"No, we all decided the whole year would be a great time to backpack across Europe. Look at the world with fresh eyes. See what's going on around us."

"Living in Europe is not going to show you what's going on in the US, Junie. I'm assuming you plan to get a job in the US after college."

"See there. I really don't know yet. Maybe I'll want to work in London or Paris. I can see you are not okay with this." Her voice sharpens. "We'll talk later after you've had time to consider the idea."

I keep my words even and try to keep the judgment out. Getting Junie worked up over not getting her way makes life difficult for both of us.

"Maybe. Probably not going to change my mind about leaving the US. A lot of Europe is in turmoil right now. There's war in the eastern part, and no one knows how long that will last." I sound like a mean mother, but her safety comes before anything else.

"Right, we'll talk later. Bye." The call goes dead.

Junie is almost twenty-one. The money in the trust for college will be turned over to her that day. I will not have any say in what she does. What were Kellen and I thinking, making it twenty-one instead of twenty-two? With any luck, maybe the other parents will feel like I do and nix the idea.

Guess I better start thinking of better reasons for her to stay in the US. I doubt she'll listen to me, though. Jackson and Beth have far more pull than I do.

My phone rings again before I can turn off the lights to go to bed. Maybe Junie thought about it and changed her mind. Except it's not her—it's Beth.

"What's going on?" I asked.

"You'll never guess who I ran into tonight."

"Nope, you're right. I don't even know where you've been."

"If you'd listen to me once in a while, you'd know I started a class at the gym. You know, the one I've been trying to get you to go to forever."

She's right, but ugh. Is this a sign from the big guy upstairs telling me something? First the doctor, and now Him?

"You're right. I'll get myself together for next week. Promise." She may have to drag me kicking and screaming, but she doesn't have to know that yet. "Anyway, you went and ran into a man, I'm assuming."

"Damn right, I did, but not *some* man. I ran into a hot, luscious, sweaty man. Wow, he did look good too."

"Yeah, I got that from your description, Beth."

"Good, only this is someone you know." She teases.

"If it was someone I went to high school with, the answer is no. Don't even bother asking." The absolute last thing I want to do is date some asshole from high school who knew Kellen. Too much past there for me to deal with.

"Nope. He didn't know you in high school, but he knows you well enough now to ask how you're doing."

"Great. Just tell me, Beth." I have about as much patience as Junie.

"The policeman who worked your case was there, and *oh my God*, he is one hottie to look at while he works out. Muscles just right for squeezing. Gets me wet just thinking about it."

"*Beth*!" I yell into the phone.

"What? It's true. He made my shriveled-up lady bits straighten out and take notice."

Laughter bubbles as I think about her running on the treadmill with all that going on down below.

"I'm surprised you didn't fall if he was that good."

"I'm not you, little sister. I know how to multitask when slyly checking out men at the gym. It's the best place I know of to find quickies."

"Eww. Gross. In the gym with musky men?"

"Hell yeah, woman." She breathes heavily through the phone. "That's like cologne to me. Give me a hot guy with his muscles pumped up from working out and a mat on the floor any day."

"Jeez, Beth. You make sex sound like the WWE."

"Don't get me started on cage fighting. Those guys, uh."

"Okay, stop. Just stop. You're making my brain hurt thinking about this."

"Your brain is the last thing that needs to get excited. The cobwebs you're growing will need excavating by the time you jump some bones."

"Please stop, Beth. I don't want to think about that yet. I haven't even thought too hard about an actual date."

"High time you do, sis. You're still young and getting into your prime. Have some fun. Do the nasty with a few, and you'll see what you've been missing."

"And you're gross. Besides, when's the last time you've been out with a man?"

"Like as a date? Years. Doesn't mean I haven't been bumping uglies with my share since moving here."

"What? You don't even know that many people here anymore."

"And your point? I don't have to know them to fuck 'em." She laughs.

My sister working her way through the eligible men in town scares me. What if I meet someone, and he has had sex with Beth? Nope. Not happening. That's one item at the top of the checklist of men not to date.

Needing to change the subject, I ask, "So you saw Ian, huh?"

"Yeah, and he didn't give me a second look. He did

ask about how you were doing, though."

The last time I saw him, he held me while I cried my eyes out. I promised to call him if I needed anything else, but the closest I came was staring at his card on the front of the refrigerator.

I'm not sure why I kept it since I had no desire to use it. The kindness he showed during the whole ordeal expressed what a great man he was, but at that time, I didn't want anyone but Kellen.

I'm still not sure I want anyone other than my husband, but my heart knows being alone for the rest of my life will be lonely. I wasn't made to live alone for forty or more years. The thought of growing old and alone causes tears that threaten to spill over my eyelids.

"I'm going to go, Beth. We'll talk tomorrow." My voice breaks, leaking my feelings. I never want to cry on someone's shoulder again from losing Kellen. It's over and done.

"Hey, I didn't mean to upset you, Ali. We've talked about this forever. You know Kellen would never want you to be alone. The kids mentioned to me the last time I saw them that they hoped you would find someone who treated you great and made you happy."

"Jacks and Junie told you that?" My tears dry up quickly.

"Yes, they did. We all see you're lonely. You had a mate for a long time. But I doubt you'll always be that way. At least consider dating and meeting men. See what's out there. Who's out there."

"I know you're right, but it freaking scares me to even think about dating."

"It scares everyone these days, girl. You have to bite the bullet and do it. After a few, you'll get used to it."

"Do I want to get used to it?" I feel my heart speed up thinking about meeting men.

"Well, for now, think about it. Doesn't mean you have to act on it tomorrow."

"You're right. I will. Promise." I'm not sure if I'm saying these words for Beth or myself.

"We'll talk tomorrow."

"Yeah, goodnight. Love you."

"Love you, too, sister."

11

Allison

When I lie in bed considering going out to meet men, my thoughts head in one direction first—my body. What will a man think of my curves? Hell, will they even think they are curves and not fat rolls? Call it like it is, Allison.

I haven't thought about my size in a long time. I went to the gym off and on since Kellen and I were married, but with his passing, that's been the furthest thing from my mind. With so many other worries, I know I've gained a few pounds. Stress eating is real. Can I blame the wine consumption on that too?

Our babies weighed over eight pounds. They took a toll on my hips and stomach. Instead of looking like a Barbie, I'm more like a Bridget from *Bridget Jones's*

Diary—pretty face, great personality, rounded hips, and a few extra pounds I tried like crazy to get rid of after Junie came along. The weight loss was slow, and I never reached my goal. But Kellen loved me at any weight, so I stopped obsessing over the added love handles. I avoided the scales. Still do, if I'm honest.

Let's face it. I like to eat good food and don't even question drinking a bottle of wine here and there. Since the funeral, I've consumed more than I ever have, even in my college days. I'd give it up, but I'm not a quitter.

Rolling over, I slide my palms down my sides. The waistline doesn't go in like it used to, but it's not too bad. My hips feel like they are the right proportion to my waist.

And then there's my thighs. Damn those things. I push in the extra, only making the insides touch even more. They do have some extra I hadn't noticed. Maybe I've had more wine than I thought. So much for the thigh gap.

Did I ever have a thigh gap? Even as a teen, I don't remember having that, so I won't even consider it. Who thought thighs need to be skinny anyway? Can't be anyone I know. It's genetic, I guess.

My hands cover my breasts. At my age, perky isn't the right description. With a gentle squeeze, I imagine what a man feels when he caresses them.

I plump them up and slightly pull on my nipples, sending a charge directly to my clit. They still work, thank God.

But what about when a man, a stranger to my body, touches them? Will my body respond? Will I think of Kellen every time?

Warm tears roll down my temples as I tuck my hands under my hips.

"I can't do this." The soft words swirl around the room. "Do I even want this yet? Or ever?"

My eyes shut, pushing more tears down to my pillow. It has caught so many over the past two years.

Two years. How can this much time have passed?

Rolling over to my left side, I stare at the photo on my nightstand. It's one I'd forgotten about but recently found. We went camping when the kids were young, and little Jackson took the off-centered picture.

The idea of removing the rest of the photos of Kellen in the house breaks my heart. I don't think I can do it, but what will a date think about when he sees them?

I would never want to go to a date's home to see pictures of his dead wife. That is a no-go for me. The palpable guilt I'd feel for taking her place hurts me to think about, even now, lying alone in my bed.

So, before the first date, I will remove some of the pictures of us, a little at a time. Our family photos will stay up. I don't want the kids to think I've put Kellen and them in a drawer to forget about the family.

Thinking about family reminds me of what Beth told me tonight. Ian Windsor. I have thought about him a few times when the subject of the wreck comes up in conversation.

Nosy people want to know the gory details—like the ones I'm acquainted with online through social media. Their audacity after Kellen's death amazed me, so I shut down all my accounts. But they still stalked me when I opened them back up.

These people had the gall to ask me for details point blank. Hallelujah for the delete button. I removed most of them the moment I read their questions.

Ian never tried to contact me again after the night I cried in his arms. Thinking about that night, his kindness blows me away. He never questioned me, and I am so grateful for that.

My phone rests on my nightstand. I know he has an online page, but do I want to be that person who stalks a stranger? Hell yes, I do. Grabbing it, I pull up his account. We friended each other shortly after he was here, but neither of us tried to do any more than that.

The page opens to a banner of several police officers posing with plaques in their hands. I'm not surprised he won an award. He thrives in the line of duty.

The small circle has a close-up of Ian's upper body and a face. His hair looks longer than I remember. He looks as handsome as ever in the photo, which, according to my sister, is still true. But considering the source, most men look hot.

A snicker at the thought escapes into the quiet. Because Beth running into him in the gym all hot and sweaty from the workout gave her all the feels, she'll not forget him anytime soon—or let me.

Scrolling down, I read the captions and a few posts with friends. Fishing, hunting, and shooting photos take up the feed. There's no woman.

My eyes drift to the dark ceiling. I wonder if reaching out to him is a good idea. Maybe he doesn't post about his significant other or the women he casually dates.

Maybe he dates men instead. His looks are enough to attract either sex, even if they aren't interested.

Dammit, this is too hard. I will worry about this tomorrow. My phone hits the nightstand harder than I meant, but thinking about Ian—or any man—makes my insides curl up.

As I lie in the dark, another night alone, I see Kellen's face. We never had time to talk about something like moving on. I've cussed and screamed at God for taking my husband and at Kellen for leaving me.

Now, here I am considering dating a new man. Kellen would want me to, right? Living a life alone is not something I would wish for him. He would want me to be happy. I nod at the thought.

I grab my phone before I can rethink this and write a message to Ian.

Me: *Hey, this is Allison Waller. I hope you remember me.*

Backspace, backspace, backspace.

Me: *Hello, Allison Waller here. I just wanted to see how you were doing.*

"Stupid, Allison." Again, I backspace until it's gone.

Me: *Allison Waller here. How ya doing?*

"Yeah, right, Allison. You sound like Joey from *Friends.*"

Me: *Hi, Ian. This is Allison Waller. Hope this finds you doing great. Maybe we could meet sometime for coffee? Just to check in.*

I delete the last sentence and hit send. I don't need an excuse to meet up. If he wants to see me, he'll reply. If not, oh well, I tried.

The phone slips quietly onto its resting spot. I roll over, cuddle the extra pillow that stopped smelling like Kellen long ago and sleep.

A noise rouses me slightly, but I don't move.

The alarm goes off abruptly, ending my peaceful sleep. Then I remember I have a dentist appointment first thing, so I jump out of bed and run to make coffee.

Taking the cup to the bathroom, I gulp it down, only burning my tongue once. I shower, dress, and head out to make it in the nick of time.

"Damn," I whisper to myself, and the hygienist, Wendy, stops picking away.

"What's wrong?" Wendy asks. "Did I hurt you?"

"No, I realized I left my phone on my nightstand."

"I hate it when I do that."

"Yes, and my kids go ballistic when they can't reach me first thing."

"Ain't that the truth," the slightly older woman says.

We've known each other for years, with the whole family coming here

"I feel like my three should implant a tracker on me, which is exactly how I felt when they were kids."

She keeps working on my mouth, leaving me unable to answer. Her words are not wrong, though. A tracker on them as teens would have made our lives easier.

"Yeah..." she continues, "... they want to know where I am, who I'm with, and when I'll be home. I swear they think at forty-eight, I'm helpless."

I nod. Mine don't consider me helpless, but they do worry too much.

"I'm a grown-ass woman. If I want to stay out all

night or, God forbid, entertain a man all night, I don't feel obligated to clear it with them. To hear them talk, though, I'm too old to do any of those things." She pulls the tools out of my mouth.

"I understand. Since Kellen passed, they've both been mother-henning me to death."

"I bet so. My kids' dad is alive. We divorced when they were little, so dating seemed impossible then. But now that they're all out of the house, one's even married, they think they need to keep their nose in my life."

I think about her words. My kids want me to date, but how will they feel when I do? I will not report to them after every date.

"Do you date often?" I pull the napkin from the clips around my neck while she cleans the area. "If you don't mind me asking."

"No, not at all. I date off and on. Had a few relationships. Some short, some long, but I haven't found one I'm willing to give up my independence over. I've been without a man until the kids were out of the house. I think I'm too set in my ways."

I nod, not knowing what to say. Two years isn't enough time to be set in any way, especially since the first year I lived in turmoil.

"I know, Allison, losing Kellen was heartbreaking but not the end of the world. You have to go on with your life when you're ready."

All I can do is nod again. She probably thinks I'm

one strange person with no words.

"We should go out sometime. Having a wing woman along makes it easier, a second set of eyes on the hotties at the clubs."

I swing around and look at her. "You go to clubs to meet men?"

"Sure, why not? They don't all cater to the young and beautiful, you know. There're lots of places in the city where people over forty hang out. Not all men want to be a sugar daddy to some bimbo looking for a ring."

The laughter escapes before I can stop it. "You are too funny."

"I try." She winks and turns to her computer. "We'll see you back here in six months, but let's get together soon." Her card extends from the end of her fingers. "My number's on there. I have yours here. I'll call soon and set up a night for us if that's okay."

"Sounds great. I'm sure my sister would also love to come. She's never been married and is always looking for Mr. Right."

"Good luck to her with that." She laughs. "I'm not sure they exist anymore."

I back out of the parking lot to head home for my phone. The kids or Beth have probably tried to call more than once by now. When a loud growl comes from my stomach, I remember I forgot breakfast.

"I should start at the gym again today. These thighs aren't going away on their own." With no one to respond, the sound dies away before being replaced by the alternative rock on the radio. I love the Missio and Vampire Weekend songs this station plays. Those bands got me through the last two years.

A vibrating noise alerts me when I walk through the door. Someone's message is coming through before I can even get inside.

When I retrieve the phone before heading to the kitchen, I see eight missed messages—three from each kid, one from my sister, and the last from the number I messaged last night.

After the wreck happened, Ian made sure I had his number in my phone in case I needed anything. Never having removed it made reaching out now even easier.

The edge of the kitchen counter pushes into some of that extra weight on my hip as I lean against it to look over my messages. Naturally, I go straight to the kids in case something happened during the brief time I was without this electronic leash.

Reading the usual messages and comments from the two, I move on to Beth's.

Beth: *listen to your voice mails bitch. I refuse to type that much.*

"What a lovely way to greet your sister." I tap to my voicemails.

"Hey, calling to check in because that's what awesome sisters do for each other. Guess you're sleeping in, or you called that hot piece of man from the gym, and he's still heating up those rusty parts for you. Anywho, check in when you get this. Love you."

"So typical for her love messages, except the part about the hot man." My voice bounces off the walls. I want to open Ian's text, but fear causes me to set the phone on the counter and move to the refrigerator.

With the supplies pulled out, I concoct my smoothie before moving to the island to sit and drink it. My eyes bore into the phone the entire time I'm drinking.

"What's the worst he can say, Allison?" I try hyping myself up. "He's married? He has a girlfriend? He forgot I existed?"

But all of those thoughts scare me, so instead of looking, I clean up the mess and go into my bedroom to change. I need to run errands, but I'm not ready to go anywhere yet.

While walking back into the den, I scan around at the photos that haunted me last night. There are more than I realized, but taking an inventory of photos never made my extensive to-do list.

Until now. Now, there is a reason for it. My hand slips down my face. This is harder than I thought. Which ones stay? What do I do with the rest?

The last thing I want is to make hasty decisions because the kids will notice the moment they walk through the door. How will they take it?

I should have asked this question at the dentist today. Maybe if we go out, I can ask her then.

With Kellen here, I never considered taking down pictures. Just another instance I took for granted. It was our home. We could do what we wanted.

But it's *my* home now. Neither of the kids stay here. They live their own lives without my help. Hell, if Junie has her way, she'll be homeless for a year. I know I shouldn't let them dictate what I do in my house.

My hands latch onto my phone. What's keeping me from reading Ian's text? Disappointment in his answer, maybe? Reading it has the possibility of making me happy... or sad.

He's only one guy in a sea of thousands. There must be someone I find interesting between here and Houston or Austin.

It's not like I'm looking to marry the first man who comes along. Remarrying is so far off my radar that there's not a blip to register.

"Okay, Allison. Pull up those granny panties and look at the damn thing."

The fact I chastise myself over something so minor says a lot about my frame of mind.

12

Allison

> **Ian:** *Great to hear from you. It's been a while. Meeting up sounds perfect. Where and when?*
> **Me:** *What's best for your schedule?*
> **Ian:** *You choose, and I'll make it happen.*

Ian's willingness to work around my schedule makes me feel better about asking him. It makes me think he doesn't feel obligated to go.

Now, what do I choose? Dinner seems too intimate to meet up just to talk, and lunch is too fast.

I should have thought this over beforehand. Isn't that all I want to do, talk? Meet a friend who already knows the situation?

Not having to go into all my recent past sounds

much better than starting fresh with baggage to spill.

> **Me:** *How about coffee at Steep/Brew? Do you know where that is?*
> **Ian:** *I'm a cop, remember?;)*
> **Me:** *Oh right! Beth, my sister, said she ran into you at the gym. Why not come on the day you come over for that, so you don't have to make two trips?*
> **Ian:** *Yes, we talked a few days ago. It's not that far so any day is good. Like I said, I'll make it happen.*

Great, he's putting it back on me. If I say tomorrow, I'll seem too eager. Damn, I hate this. Just choose a day.

> **Me:** *How about day after tomorrow? 10ish.*
> **Ian:** *10ish it is. Looking forward to it.*
> **Me:** *Me too.*

I hit send before I can rethink it. "Me too." Wow. Does that sound needy? Oh well, I can't unsend it now. He read it immediately.

With my heart in my throat already, I pull up Beth's contact.

> **Me:** *You got your way.*
> **Beth:** *Oh yeah? Some hottie is going to scoop*

me up and have wild monkey sex with me for forty-eight full hours?

Me: *No, nothing that crazy but crazy for me. I'm meeting Ian for coffee.*

Beth: *What? You followed through? That is crazy for you.*

Me: *Yes, and now I've got two days to worry.*

Beth: *What's to worry about? One hot guy + one needy widow = sure-fire sex.*

Me: *NO, NO, NO. No one said anything about sex. It's just coffee and conversation.*

Beth: *Boringgg! Why do you stall all the sexy thoughts brewing in my head?*

Me: *Because you're like a fourteen-year-old boy when it comes to talking about... everything!*

Beth: *Don't blame me for my dry spell. I'm willing but no takers.*

Me: *Let's get back to me, please. What to wear, how to do my hair and makeup?*

Beth: *I don't know why you're fretting over it, he saw you at your worst.*

Me: *Thanks for that reminder, dear sister. So he'll be expecting a bizarre lunatic talking nonsense, dressed in dirty clothes from moving, and my hair in a ragged ponytail?*

Beth: *Yeah, uh no. When you put it that way, we have work to do before the meet and greet. I'll be by later after I solve work problems.*

Me: *Thank you, love you too!*

Five changes later, I stare at my latest outfit in the mirror. Jeans and a flowy shirt. Not flirty but not frumpy.

"Is this something a mother would wear for coffee with a friend?" I ask no one as I turn both ways in the mirror. "Nope."

The last thing I want to do is come off looking motherly for a first-time meeting with any man. Yes, even though he's seen me looking horrid in the wreck and the hospital.

And I don't even know what I had on when he stopped by to tell me about Kellen's heart attack—that had to be the worst.

Beth approved, so it must be okay. With no time left to change again, I grab my purse, phone, and sunglasses and head out.

As I pull in, I notice the lack of cars in the lot. That's good. We won't have to take just any table. Sitting up front near the windows will make it seem less confined.

Hesitating in the car, a part of me says, "You can run out the door!" Another part cheers me on, saying, "You got this girl. It's just coffee." My roiling insides rebel, saying, "What the hell, Ali? Have you lost your mind seeing another man?" But the real question here is, what does my heart say?

I'll have to revisit that later since I can see him

sitting by the corner window.

Damn, I'd forgotten how handsome he is. Thick lashes surrounding deep blue eyes. Whoa, lady bits. Slow down for a second. Adjust to the 'it's just coffee' right now!

A feeling of desperation hits me with full force. Just because I'm a widow doesn't mean I don't feel the need for intimacy.

I miss so much about a man. The smell on the sheets. The sweet words whispered when you made love or the dirty words when the sex is intense and rough. I long for a night with some of both kinds of sex.

I've woken to an ache inside me like nothing I've ever felt. I want to be treated like I'm desired more than any other person. As though he yearns to be inside me—to watch me while he manipulates my body, wringing out an orgasm powerful enough to make me scream his name.

"Stop, Allison. Stop right now," I say to my car's interior. I feel his gaze as he watches me through the window. If I were close enough to see, I'd bet the blue in his eyes deepens like it did once before.

"Here goes nothing." I step out and walk as calmly as my legs will allow. After that burst of lust, it's a hard task.

Ian stands when I walk through the door.

"Hello," his deep voice greets me.

"Hi, yourself." I'm going for light and airy, but it

comes out grittier than I intend. My hand automatically reaches for his, hoping he doesn't read anything into my words.

"Coffee?" he asks. Seeing he hasn't ordered yet, I let his hand go and turn toward the counter.

"Let me get it since I invited you."

"What kind of man would I be if I let a pretty woman pay for coffee?" His response makes me want to laugh, considering my first words.

Here I am, world. Julia Roberts is ready to take this dating scene by storm. Maybe my clothing choice should have been red.

I glance at my feet, not knowing what to say out loud.

"Please, Allison."

His soft words sound sincere, and all I can do is nod. I'm making it awkward already. I wonder how I'm going to get through the visit. Maybe I should make an excuse to leave. Beth and I should have crafted a plan like girls do for bad dates. A quick call from her ten minutes in would offer the perfect out.

But we didn't, so I'm stuck. Or maybe he's stuck unless he set up an out for himself. Oh God. Why did I do this?

"How do you take it?" Ian asks. "Or do you want a special drink?"

"No. Cream and sugar in plain coffee, please."

He steps away, which allows me a minute to calm down. With my head lowered, I try to calm down. This is normal—two people meeting for coffee, two friends enjoying a moment together. No big deal, right?

A large hand places my drink in front of me, bringing me back to the moment. My mind wavers between being ready for this and being petrified of making a stupid mistake. I take a deep breath and slowly expel it before he returns with my requested trimmings.

"You like yours black, I see." Dumb Ali.

"Yeah, product of police department late nights. Sludge is a better word for what the department calls coffee. Thick enough to stand a spoon in. On stakeouts, we drink coffee from wherever we can get it. Another good reason to leave that life behind."

"I must be a coffee snob then because I'm careful where I choose my coffee." I look at his cup's contents. "Yuck, how can you drink it without cream and sugar? I'd have to pour it like half and half."

He laughs, and it seems to ease the start of our meetup.

We breeze through the pleasantries before he asks, "How have you been making it, Allison? Not the pat answer but the real one this time."

The look he gives me suggests he didn't buy what I offered the first time around. I wanted today to be more lighthearted, but I guess he had other plans.

"Oh, you know, good and bad." I fiddle with the coaster around the hot cup without looking up. "Some days are better than others. Thankfully, the better days seem to be happening more often now."

"Sounds good. I know you took a chance reaching out to me. Reaching out to a stranger must be hard. At least we're slightly past that stage."

"Yes, I wanted to meet with you." My words are hesitant since I don't want this to sound like a date. "When Beth told me she ran into you, it surprised me. Honestly, I haven't started getting out until recently."

"I'm happy you did," he says as he reaches over and places his hand on mine. With surprise, I glance at him, and he's looking directly into my eyes.

My first response is to jerk my hand away, but I take a breath and leave it there. I never expected him to be forward in any way. However, it's not like holding hands. He simply laid his on top of mine. Is he offering me comfort?

Ian must sense my indecision. "Is this okay, Allison?"

The question tells me this is a deliberate move, not a comforting one. All I can do is nod. I need to examine my feelings about it later when my brain isn't freaking out.

The warmth of his hand seems to cause it to misfire. Why does a single touch make those synapses leap into hyperdrive?

He's just a man like everyone I might date out there. There are so many questions waiting for an answer. Do I want to find 'the new one?' Am I ready to have sex with another man? How will the kids take me finding a new significant other?

They seem okay with the idea of me dating, but choosing one single person to introduce into our lives—well, that's another story.

Why am I worrying over something that is five years down the road? There are a lot of frogs in this huge pond, and kissing them all sounds scary but necessary right now.

Ian brings me back, "Allison?"

As my eyes jump back up from our hands, I look at this kind, gentle man watching me.

"Are you sure about this? Because if you're not ready for a connection, I get it."

"You know, I question everything these days. I want to know I'm doing the right thing."

"That's understandable." He squeezes my hand, offering reassurance. "You were forced to move past life as you knew it for twenty-plus years. Anyone would question or weigh the pros and cons of anything new."

"I know you're right, but thinking and doing it are different. While my heart says jump in and enjoy the experience, my brain says stop and consider all sides of your decisions. I never used to be this way." I sigh. "Choices usually boiled down to cost and need. Now I have the kids to consider and what will other important people think."

"Yes, I can see that, but at some point, you have to decide what's best for Allison. Your kids probably want you to be happy. I guess I moved on from what others think about what I do."

"True, and I have, too, or I was that way before. His family might not be, though." I refuse to use Kellen's name while on a date. Beth warned me it would be a definite deal killer.

"Do you feel like they want you to be alone for the next fifty years?" Ian moves forward in his chair but never takes his hand from mine. "I'd say that's pretty narrow-minded of them."

I know Ian's right. My in-laws would never want me to be alone that long. Over the last two years, they have been extra supportive of my decisions. The unconditional help they've given the kids and me has been invaluable.

In the beginning, they were at my every beck and call. They pitched in every semester to make sure the kids had everything they needed, even driving to the university to deliver last-minute items.

After the first year, they backed off and let me live my life. They checked on us but not as much, assuring me they were around if needed.

That doesn't mean I'm beyond caring how they'd feel, though. They lost a son that day and were devastated all over again when I explained he'd had a heart attack.

But looking at this man across from me, I decide fuck it. I want to pursue this, whatever it is. I want to be happy. I want to do something for myself.

A sizzle moves through me as I flip my hand over and join our palms. Ian makes me feel more than I've felt in forever. And I like it.

My lips turn into a big smile, and I know this will be all right.

Ian

As far as first dates go, I'd give this one a ten out of ten. Taking her hand seemed aggressive when I did it, but after Allison had time to adjust, she went with it.

Knowing the situation, I thought about how to let her know I wanted this to be a date and not a friend thing. Being her friend is a no-go for me.

Allison is a knockout. Guys will be flocking to her door once she decides to put herself out there. The idea of her being with anyone else but me makes me see red.

The night I came with the information, I knew I wanted to pursue something more with her when the time was right. Her taking all the time necessary to grieve trumped anything else, though, so I backed away.

Meeting Beth at the gym proved to be a sign that the time to reconnect with Allison was now. Beth shared enough information to let me know she thought her sister was ready. Without coming right out and saying it, Beth dropped perfect hints.

Now it's time for date two. She took the initiative for coffee, but I plan to make this more to my liking without pulling out all the stops. Allison's not ready for wining and dining.

I pull up to her house a few minutes before I'm due to arrive, check myself in the mirror, and head for her door right on time. In my book, being punctual says a lot about a person.

Allison opens the door, and her beauty takes my breath away. She still possesses that girl-next-door look that I know she rocked as a teen. Dressed for doing something outdoors, as I told her we would be, she looks perfect in white and aqua blue.

Her hair is pulled back and clasped at her neck— maybe I'll have an opportunity to take the thick masses in my hands as the day goes on. Those thoughts will stay with me all afternoon.

"You look beautiful," I say as I take her hand and pull her in for a brief hug. I want to touch this beauty as often as possible without scaring her off so she'll get used to the idea. Nothing too close, but enough to keep her aware of me.

The light perfume treats my nose to a floral scent I noticed the last time. It's not overbearing but smells feminine enough. I won't forget it for a long time.

"Thank you. You're not so bad yourself," she replies. "I'm ready to go if you are."

I hoped she might invite me in, but not today. Having me in her space this time will be completely different from the last time when I delivered harsh news about her husband. I wonder if she remembers that night.

Remembering holding her in my arms as she fell apart feels bittersweet. She needed me in a completely different way than I want to give her now. Hopefully, the events we shared back then have faded away.

I want our beginning to be full of lighthearted, fun moments. We can make new memories for her to remember when I'm not around.

"Sure, let's go." I let her hand drop to lock the door, which she fails to do.

"Aren't you forgetting something?" I stare at the door handle.

"Oh, right." She blushes. "I'm bad about not locking this door. Living in a small town, I don't think of it all the time."

"Allison, your safety rates high on my list and not because I'm a cop. I want you to feel at ease in your own home, and all it takes is one time to take it away. One dumbass to destroy that peace of mind."

"I know you're right," she says, giving me a strange look. "But sometimes, I have so much on my mind that I forget I'm alone now."

"Don't worry, Ali. I'll never let you forget when I'm around."

"Yes, sir, Mr. Police Officer." She salutes, which makes me smile. "What? Did I do it wrong?"

"No, you just look so... so... funny doing it."

I wanted to say sexy, but she's not ready to hear it. I wonder how long it will take me to get her comfortable with whatever I say. Carefully choosing my words rubs me the wrong way, but I'll do it for her for now.

We drive to a picnic spot on the lake where local couples and families go for the afternoon. I wanted the date to be in public, and I know many will not linger too much longer. The families will be gone before the sun sets, and the couples usually drift away shortly after.

Since I spend time patrolling the area and know when people come and go, my timing is spot on—one of the perks of being on the force.

Small-town city limits west of Houston practically touch the urban sprawl that eats away at the open spaces. People escape the city to enjoy country life they know little of. This will eventually, if not already, ruin the peace of mind we've enjoyed forever.

I park by a tree that overlooks a nice section of the lake. Boats split the smooth water to tow a skier looking to do a trick or spray a rooster tail at a friend in another boat. It's a great way to enjoy a Saturday in the Texas heat.

This date spot is exactly as I pictured it with Allison. Relaxing, nothing too intimate, but still alone on our small patch of claimed land. We're among the masses without a need to share conversation with others.

"So, what do you think?" I ask as the cork pops from the bottle of wine—the same kind I noticed at her house the first time I was there. Even after a couple of years, I remember the brand.

Allison's chestnut hair, with streaks of honey, contrasts her creamy fair skin, stirring something in me each time I look at her. As she turns her head to look out across the dark blue water, I watch her shoulders visibly relax.

The action makes me think she hasn't relaxed in a while. I intend to correct this at every opportunity. She needs to equate our time together with a different life than she's led since the accident.

"This place is wonderful. I haven't been here in years. I don't think we ever brought the kids out to the lake." As soon as the words leave her mouth, she jerks her head to look at me. "Sorry. I promised myself I wouldn't talk about the time before the wreck."

Her pink lips curl inward as though she's practicing locking her words away.

I reach for her hand and pull it to me. "You have

nothing to be sorry for, and please don't apologize for talking about your life before. It's only natural for you to think about what you all did as a family. It's the majority of your life."

I pull her hand up and kiss the soft palm. Her breath sucks in as my lips brush her skin. This woman responds to my every touch. How will she react when we finally find ourselves alone if she reacts this way when touching is all we're doing? A quiver runs through me as I think about it.

Instead of pulling away, she leans against my shoulder, leaving her hand in mine. This small step gives me hope the day will go my way.

"You brought my favorite wine, I see. How did you guess?"

"It wasn't a guess. I saw it in your refrigerator when I was at your house."

"Let's see, you've been there a total of two times." Her forehead scrunches. "Your observation skills are amazing."

"They pay me to collect information, remember? I find it a useful skill when I want bits of information for later."

"I see." She takes the plastic wine glass I pour her and turns back to the water.

Good job, Ian. You sound like a first-class stalker, especially considering it was the day of her husband's funeral.

"It's very peaceful here. The breeze, the blue skies,

children's laughter. Perfect afternoon." She ends her list by tipping the glass and draining it.

"Happy you're enjoying it. I hoped it would put you at ease."

Her eyes find mine. "What? Do I seem nervous? Too uptight?"

"Yeah, maybe a little." I squeeze her hand. "It's okay, I understand. You're venturing out in a new world."

She pulls up her knees, rests her elbows on them, and lets go of my hand, leaving me with a hollowness I hadn't felt before.

"My entire family started pushing me after the first year to get out, see people, go to new places. I never realized how hard it would be."

"I get it. Dating's not what it used to be." I lean over on my side and watch her.

Dating these days with the twenty-somethings has a new meaning. We aren't that old, but I feel like we have some leftover rules from our parents that they don't adhere to. With Allison, I want our time to be perfect. Showing her I will be the kind of man she deserves takes precedence over everything I do until she realizes I'm worthy of her.

Our first few times together gave us both the opportunity to learn what's important in each other's lives. Her number one priority will always be her kids, and I get that. They should be. Hopefully, at some point, she will figure out she deserves to put herself first for a change.

I know I'm not close to perfect, but I want to be, and not simply when we're together. I intend to work hard to be that person always so she sees me as a man she would choose to be with.

I pick up a few strands of her soft hair that have freed themselves from the clip and curl them around my finger. As I reach up and remove the metal keeping the hair, I hope she won't mind.

"You know, Allison, you are such a beautiful woman."

Her eyes cut to me, and the look on her face makes me wonder if she questions what I'm saying.

"Thank you, Ian." A wary grin crosses her face. "I bet you say that to all the women."

"Nope, I don't say it to any women."

My fingers slide from her hair with a gentle tug. On the handful of times we've been together, before and now, she's rarely worn it down.

The silkiness of it makes me want to run my fingers through it while we're doing other things that now harbor a spot in the back of my mind. I finger the strands out so that they fan across her back, but I worry the intimate act might cause her anxiety.

The last thing I want is to push her into something she's not ready for. Two years of keeping herself away from the real world must have taken a toll on her social life and self-confidence.

I've spent long periods of my life alone by choice.

This job prevents relationships from flourishing even in the best of conditions. It demands a lot of time.

Yes, we have a schedule to follow, but many days, I can't break away from a situation at the end of the day. Finishing paperwork, following suspects, and lending a hand when needed prevents shifts from ending on set times.

I follow Allison's eyes to the shoreline, where she watches a young family play with their small child in the shallow water. Her glass is empty, so I refill it.

"What are you thinking about?" My voice intrudes her gaze as I hand her the glass back.

"Just watching them have fun. Making memories with their son." Her voice grows quieter with each word.

I stand and offer her my hand. "Let's make some of our own."

She sets down her wine, takes my offered palm, and stands, which almost surprises me, but doesn't say a word.

The water at the edge is warmed by the sun. We kick off our sandals and walk in the shallows. We must look like such a cliché walking hand in hand on a sandy beach in the early evening.

"Do you think we look cheesy to the other couples on the hill?"

My comment caught her off guard, and she laughed naturally.

"If you like pina coladas and getting caught in the

rain," she sang out loud.

"And the feel of the ocean and the taste of champagne," I finish.

I can't help but laugh with her until she reaches down and scoops water, splashing it at me.

"If we're making a cheesy scene for the others, we might as well do it right." She smiles.

Our laughter continues as I reciprocate with a light splash. It's too late in the day to take her deeper into the blue water, so it ends quickly.

Of course, if she'd like to wait until dark and strip down, I'd be completely okay with it, except for the risk of being arrested for public nudity. That's a big *no*.

14

Ian

We make our way back to the blanket. Many families and couples have now left the area, which makes me smile inside. I want to have alone time with Allison— if it happens naturally.

She plops down on the blanket and wipes the water from her shapely legs with the edge. This mother of two has managed to keep herself in great shape. Never wasting away with her husband's death, she has curves and a softness that I love. Feeling bones when I pull a female into my arms causes me to back away for fear I might hurt them.

"Well, that was fun." I grin. "I can't tell you when the last time I've been somewhere to be around water. Not because I don't like it. I just haven't had a chance to go."

She turns and looks at me as I lounge beside her.

"Your tan says you must get a lot of sun somewhere." Her finger traces the line from below my sleeve.

"Product of the job mostly. I keep a farmer's tan year-round from it. On my days off, I prefer to do something outdoors, even just washing my car. I was never one who liked being stuck in the house."

"I love to be outside, but I haven't had much chance for a while." She lets out a long breath before turning back toward the water. Honestly, I haven't tried to find things outdoors to do. Bothering other people to go places like this." She gestures around her. "I don't know. I hate to intrude on their free time."

"You can bother me anytime you want to go somewhere. I'm down for almost anything that involves being close to nature."

God, Ian, that rates up there with the cheesiest. "Close to nature." Ignore that, please.

She turns and stares for a moment, and I wait for her to laugh at me.

Instead, she points to the ice chest. "What else do you have in there?"

Thank God. I sit up, pull the chest close, open it, and gesture for her to take a look.

"I packed a variety because I didn't know what you might like. Fruit, cheeses, crackers, olives, cookies, chocolate. Pretty much anything you'd have with wine."

"Wow, way to be prepared."

"Please help yourself to whatever sounds good to you... some or all. Maybe you like a variety pack. There are plates and silverware too."

We dig through the items and fill the small plates with our favorites. She then goes back and adds a piece of chocolate to each one.

As Allison lays the candy on my plate, she eyes me. "It's for just in case."

"Just in case?"

"Yes, just in case I need two pieces but don't want to appear greedy." She snickers and pops an olive in her mouth.

We devour most of what I brought, and she eats both pieces of candy before I pull the entire bag of Snickers out of the chest and lay it between us.

"You know that's tempting me to be bad, right?"

If she only knew how bad my thoughts are each time she opens those perfect lips or when her pink tongue licks her fingers before she sucks the finger into her mouth, claiming every bit of chocolate. With that one move, I feel my dick stir behind the zipper like a damn teenager.

My voice lowers, "Temptation isn't always bad, Allison."

I want nothing more than to show her how bad we can be together.

Her forehead wrinkles slightly before she straightens it. She has to know exactly what I'm saying but doesn't respond.

I stand and offer her my hand again without giving her a second to overthink. "Come on... I want to show you something."

We walk in the opposite direction toward an outcropping of huge boulders. As children, my parents brought us here to jump and swim.

My family stayed until it was too dark to see us in the water, then let us sleep all the way home. Those were great memories. Now, I want to create new ones.

Stepping up on the top boulder, I pull her up with me. You can see for ten miles across the lake and valley.

"Have you been here before?" I ask.

"No, we never came down this direction. We always went to the river above the dam to swim and play."

"That's too bad. It's a great place to spend the day." I sit, dangling my legs over the side.

Allison hesitates, so I offer her my hand, and she moves in beside me so close our hips touch. It never occurred to me she might be afraid.

"Do you have a fear of heights?"

"Uh, no. I don't usually, but that's a long drop to the water."

"I've jumped here a thousand times. The water is deep enough not to touch the bottom and clear enough to see the surface."

She scans the horizon. "It's so beautiful up here. I'm surprised people don't flock here all the time."

"They do, but most have gone home for the day. Several places around the lake have boulders like this, so none get too crowded, even in the middle of summer."

"Your parents take you to a lot of fun places like this?" she asks.

"Yeah, we never went to places far away. They couldn't get the time off needed, but we saw all the fun places to play around here and in the Texas Hill Country."

"That sounds fun."

The beauty of this spot becomes apparent as we watch the setting sun.

"Wow, talk about getting back to nature." She reminds me of my earlier dumb comment. "I don't think I've been anywhere to compare this sunset to."

The simple times create the moments I wanted to show her. We can always go into the city and do typical things like dinner, shows, and movies. I want to be with her in the easy moments that only require two people to enjoy themselves.

My arm surrounds her back, and I pull her closer to me just as the sun drops. When she looks at me, I know the time is finally right. My lips find hers.

The kiss is brief to start. Our lips touch easily for a few seconds, but I move in again and pull her close for a more intimate kiss. She surprises me when I slide my tongue across her lower lip by opening it for me to explore her sweet mouth.

The chocolate and wine taste lingers on her tongue as we duel for more connection. I tilt her head to open her to me, and she responds by allowing me better access.

Her hand finds my shoulder, and she pulls me to her as she leans back to the flat rock behind us. Not wanting to crush her to the hard surface, I prop on my elbow and wrap my hand around her hip, pulling her sweet body flush with mine.

Her response to me sends a jolt through me. I need to have more of her. I feel my dick hardening when she rubs herself against it.

I never expected her to be as into this as I am, but I am thrilled she is. Breaking the kiss, I move my lips down her cheek and jaw and jump to her neck. Open-mouth kisses and nibbles leave a line across the skin of her neck until I reach the spot where it meets her collarbone. I add my teeth and softly bite the spot.

This drives her into a frenzy, and she wraps her leg around my hip, pulling me to her. My mind says I need to stop because this is not the place. Anyone could come up on us mauling each other like teenagers who've parked in the bushes.

Her need keeps me going, and I take her hip in my hand and move her closer before sliding it around to cup her perfect ass. My squeezing and kneading feel so right. The peach plumpness makes me ache to rid her of the clothing barrier between us so I can caress her warm, soft skin.

When I squeeze and allow myself to rub my dick against her core, she jumps, removes her leg, and backs away.

"So... sorry... sorry. I got carried away," she says as she rubs her swollen lips.

Her eyes dart around, looking to see who might have seen, but I know no one is here but us. I might have gotten carried away, too, but I still had one ear listening for footsteps and voices.

I let her go and move us both to a sitting position. "It's okay. We're alone."

Still looking around, she finally rests her eyes on me. It's not fear I see but a look of panic.

"Are you okay?" I want to know if I've scared her.

"Ye...yes. I'm fine."

I fucking hate fine. It has so many interpretations. Is she fine with what we were doing? Is she fine in that I didn't hurt her? Is she fine but needs to run? I want to know what fine she's thinking of.

"What do you mean, Allison?"

She gives me a strange look.

"What do you mean?" she repeats my question.

"I mean, tell me what's going on up here." I tap her head.

"Oh. Well, uh..." Her eyes scan the area and across the lake before returning to me.

"Are you upset with what we were doing?"

"No. Uh… maybe. I just didn't think about getting so easily carried away there."

"Neither did I. It wasn't planned. You seemed okay with my attention, so I kept going. All you have to do is say 'stop,' and I stop. No questions asked. I don't want you ever to be afraid of me."

"No, I'm not afraid of you, Ian. I don't think you'd ever hurt me."

"Good." I pull her forward and kiss her forehead. "Maybe we should head back."

"It's dark. We should have left earlier."

"I've walked through here so many times I can do it blindfolded. I'll always keep you safe, Allison. Always."

She stares at my face. I feel like she's trying to decide whether I'm telling her the truth. Finally, she nods. "I understand. I do feel safe with you."

"Even better." I stand and take her hand. "Follow me down, and we'll be fine."

"Right. I can do that."

Once we arrive at the blanket, the beach area is completely deserted. I knew it would be, and I feel safe being alone here with her. I'm not sure how she feels, though.

"I suppose we better be on our way," I say as I look around, noticing she does the same.

"It feels strange with it empty after the large crowd from earlier." Her words make her sound worried, so I quickly throw the used items in the ice chest and wrap my arm around her waist to pull her closer to me.

We walk back to a deserted parking lot, where I open her door to get her inside the car before depositing the day's picnic in the back seat. The motor fires up, and we head back toward her home.

I reach for her hand and pull it onto my thigh. Needing her close, I rest our hands there. "I hope you had a fun time today."

"It was the perfect afternoon." She looks over at our hands. "I loved everything about it."

"Great, we'll do something similar again sometime if that's okay with you."

I feel her eyes studying me before she speaks. "Honestly, I'd love to do it again. Like I said, it was the perfect date."

Bringing our hands to my mouth, I kiss the back of her hand. "Good. I want that, too, and I hope it's the first of many."

I want to do so much with Allison—take her places, show her off to friends, and enjoy our time together— if she'll only continue giving me the go-ahead.

15

Allison

After an easy goodnight kiss at my door, I watch Ian drive away from the front window. His insistence that I lock the door before he left makes me laugh. This man takes my safety seriously.

Since Kellen, no one has gone to the trouble to make sure of it. The kids come and go at all hours when they visit for the weekend, but they are careful to lock the doors the same as when they lived here.

With Beth living down the road now, she doesn't spend the night with me anymore. Even when we've knocked out a couple of bottles of wine, she manages to walk home, mostly in a straight line.

I lean against the door once he's out of sight and ponder our day together. I never doubted it would be fun. Ian's a great guy. Always attentive and thinks of everything.

What was I thinking, allowing myself to get so carried away with him on a rock in the middle of nowhere? I don't do things like that. He probably thinks I'm a desperate widow looking for sex now.

Hell, I am a desperate widow looking for sex. It's been too long. Kellen and I had an active sex life. He was always the best lover. God, I miss him, and I miss sex.

I move to my bedroom and immediately remove my shorts and shirt. The day's temperatures were perfect, but I feel dirty after rolling on the sandy blanket, walking in the water, and lounging on a rock while holding Ian.

Not from holding Ian. Nothing we did made me feel dirty. I wouldn't change a damn thing about the day. Everything he did made me feel special, even the way he held me on that boulder.

He waited for me to seek more, and I did. When he rubbed his hard cock against my pussy, I almost orgasmed right then. That's how I know it's been too long.

I don't want to rush into a relationship with Ian, but damn, I can only wait so long. The last thing I intend is for him to think I'm so horny I'll jump into bed under any conditions.

With the shower blasting hot water, I drop my clothes at the door and climb in. Resting under the flow, I turn on the other head and remove the wand.

My mind immediately drifts to the moment he squeezed my ass, and I felt his hardened length move up and down over my clit. Using the wand, I create the scene again in my mind.

If I continue to see Ian, this wand and my vibrator may see a lot of action until we take things further. The way he moved against me caused a fire to start below and work through me.

My breasts felt heavy, and my core trembled with a need that grew with each thrust he made. My clit engorged more with every brush from my lacy underwear.

With his hand holding my ass cheek, he prevented me from moving away from him. Not that I even considered it once he created that ache inside me.

Standing alone in my shower with my leg propped on the seat, I aim the pulsing water back and forth over my clit. My eyes close as my hand pushes against the shower wall in anticipation of what's to come.

Ian's image comes to mind with every swipe of warmth. I feel his lips close over mine and him squeezing my ass, the sensation causing my walls to clamp down on the vacant passage.

An explosive orgasm hits me, and I cry out, bucking with every movement of the wand. With each spasm, my upper body bucks forward, chasing the exquisite feeling of bliss that only comes from an orgasm.

"Holy shit!" My cries echo off the marble walls. "If it

only felt like that every time I made myself come."

Having Ian's image in my mind and remembering his hands on me from earlier made my touch seem more real. For the first time in forever, I felt like a man had led me to reach a pinnacle that amazing.

With Ian on my mind, I wonder how incredible sex will be with him. He is such an attentive man toward me, but what about in the bedroom?

I feel a shiver start at the top of my back and run down my spine. Is he the man I need to show me how to enjoy sex again?

I wash and step out, wrapping a towel around me, and finish my nighttime routine. The exhaustion from the shower and the day leads me to my bed. Dropping the towel, I climb in naked, something I haven't done since Kellen has been gone.

I'll take a little nap and then get up and eat something.

That's the last thing I remember until I hear the crazy grackles who like to wake me at the crack of dawn. Damn birds. If I ever shoot a creature, they'll be the first on my list.

Throwing the covers back, I realize I'm naked.

"That must have been some orgasm," I say, pulling on leggings and an oversized tee with my fluffy slippers, and head to the kitchen where coffee calls my name.

Once I get that first cup dripping into my mug, I look around for my phone. Normally, I take it to bed with me, but last night was not a 'normal' night. A slight quake inside me takes me back to the shower.

Damn woman, you need to jump Ian's bones, and soon.

With my phone in hand, I sit at the island, looking out over the pool in my backyard. We had so much fun when the kids were in it. There were always other children over with constant laughter drifting across the yard.

There may have been some sexy times when the kids were spending the night elsewhere. Kellen and I broke it in on the third day it was up and running because the kids, who were still young and already asleep for the night, would not catch us. We snuck out and skinny-dipped under darkness.

"You are one sick bitch, Allison," I say to my mug as it hangs loosely between my palms. How can I think about having sex with someone else when Kellen still lingers in my mind? A knock at my back door startles me.

"Hey, girl, you here?" Beth's voice relieves my fear. I should have known it was her since she's the only one who comes around back.

"Yeah, come on in." She enters the kitchen, looking around like someone else might be with me.

"Shew, I thought maybe that hot hunk of a policeman might be here. You know, like he got lucky. Or would that be you getting lucky?"

I drill her with my best mean look. "That will

probably never happen."

"But you had a date. At our ages, we don't have to adhere to that shit about three dates before sex." She wiggles her eyebrows, trying to make me laugh. "Shit fire, woman. If I waited for the third date, I'd be wearing out my favorite rabbit in no time, and the good ones are expensive."

"Shut it. I don't even want to know about you and your 'friends.' " I air quote her. "That's not an image I want to have in my head before I finish my first cup of coffee."

She drops a new cup in the machine, starts her cup, and then turns around to me. "I want all the juicy details. Is he hung? Does he know what he's doing? How many orgasms did he give you?"

"I said shut up when you walked in, and now, I'm saying shut the fuck up. I'm not now or ever discussing my sex life or lack of one with you."

"Just what I thought. He left you hanging with your panties wet. Whose fault is that? Yours or his?"

"Again, not talking with you about it."

"If you don't talk about it, then it never happened. I'd ask for pictures, but I know you're too much of a prude to share anything that good with me."

"Beth!" I screech. "You're right. Besides, there will be no pictures, also a never-happening event."

"You can at least give me something. My finger vault is dried up these days."

I stare at her. What the hell is she talking about?

"Oh my God, sister. My spank bank, my fiddle folder?"

I'm still staring.

"For God's sake, Ali, my bang bank as in masturbation."

"Oh my God is right. Where do you get this stuff? Do girls really use those terms like guys do? That's disgusting, Beth. And immature. Very immature."

"Immature or not, I'm still waiting for you to give me something here."

Beth has never hounded me about my sex life before, so why was she so interested in it now? Kellen and I loved each other, but we'd also been married for over twenty years.

Sometimes, he tried new things to keep it exciting and new. We both did, but with kids always keeping us busy, it became more like part of the schedule. Isn't that how most married couples look at sex?

"Earth to Allison?" Beth snaps her fingers in front of my face. "Was it so good that you had to drift off and relive the moment?"

"No, uh, no. I was thinking about Kellen." My head automatically bows with embarrassment. Or is it sorrow?

"You can't do that, Allison." Her arms circle me and hold me tightly. "Kellen's been gone for over two years now. You have the right to move on. To find a new lover and not feel bad about it. Kellen would never want you to live life being sad all the time."

"I know you're right, but the whole idea of having sex with another man is hard to think about."

"So, you plan to never have sex again at your age? That's just damn stupid. You're too young to give it up."

"You're right. I know it in my head. We did some things when we were at the lake yesterday, and it felt so good to feel alive again, but—"

"Yeah, the good stuff. That's what I want to hear about," she jokes to lighten the mood with two sentences, but I'm trying to be serious.

"This is why I don't talk to you about stuff. You make a joke about it. This is hard, Beth. I've only had sex with one man, and now people..." I look directly at her, "... you specifically, expect me to open my arms to the first man who comes along."

"No, Allison. I expect you to want to open your arms, or legs actually, to a man who is kind and gentle and... and... looks like he would make a great lover. I'm not saying you have to fall in love with him. Just see where it goes."

"Don't I first have to know where I want it to go?"

"Yes, that helps, but don't overthink it. You'll know. Just let things happen naturally. Why hold back? You're not some teenager who worries about getting knocked up again. You're a grown-ass woman who has needs. Let someone in to show you how to be that woman."

I can only nod while my head mulls over the words.

Deep down, I know all she's said is right, but why does it have to be so damn hard to let go and just feel again?

This problem never came up before Kellen. I spent every minute of my teen years planning something with friends or for school. College started that way, too, until Kellen came along. I truly need to get my head straight about seeing men.

Beth leaves for an online meeting after we finish our coffee. My brain hurts from our conversation. Then my phone chimes with a text. Looking at the screen, I suppose I might as well start now.

> **Ian:** *How are things this morning?*
> **Me:** *Great, Beth just left.*
> **Ian:** *That's good. I have to you to myself.*
> **Me:***???*
> **Ian:** *Nothing salacious, just like your undivided attention.*
> **Me:** *Salacious, huh?*
> **Ian:** *I'm sitting out here on Highway 222 watching for a certain car to pass. Gotta do something fun to stay awake.*
> **Me:** *Working and texting me?*
> **Ian:** *Multitasking. I'm good at it.*
> **Me:** *Good to know.*

Now, what do I say? I'm not good at flirting, especially over texts. Besides that, I'm a little old to flirt. But isn't that part of the dating thing? Taking a breath, I think about what the right thing to say.

> **Me:** *I had fun yesterday.*
> **Ian:** *Perfect. I want you to always have fun when we're together. The most fun was toward the end;)*

My fingers linger over the phone's keypad. I don't know what to say again. After dealing with Beth's interrogation and her idea of a stern talking to, I'm at a loss for words.

> **Me:** *Yes, that was nice.*

Wow. Lame, Allison.

> **Ian:** *Nice? I thought more like smoking hot.*
> **Me:** *Yes, it was that too.*
> **Ian:** *Glad we're on the same page.*
> **Me:** *I'm just not used to talking about more intimate moments, I guess.*
> **Ian:** *Not a fan of dirty talk?*

"What the hell? How do I answer that?" I can't help but say it out loud.

> **Me:** *Uh... uh... I'm not opposed to it.*
> **Ian:** *Good to know. Next time, I'll see what I*

can do to make you enjoy it. That's got to be better than 'not opposed to it.'

Me: *Maybe. If there's going to be a next time?*

Ian: *I sure as hell hope so. I can't stop thinking about seeing you again.*

Me: *Beth tells me I should just let things happen. This is me doing that.*

Ian: *Glad to know Beth's on my side. I'm off tomorrow. Can we 'just let things happen' tonight?*

Oh shit. Is he saying let us have sex tonight? Already? How do I respond? If I say yes, do I seem anxious for it? But what if I say no, not yet? Will he think I'm the prude my sister believes me to be?

Me: *I'd love to see you tonight if you don't think you'll be too tired after guarding the streets all day.*

Ian: *Haha. For you I'll never be too tired, especially from sitting.*

Me: *Great. What is it the kids say? Netflix and chill?*

Ian: *If that's what you want?*

Me: *Sure. I also have Hulu and Prime and Apple TV.*

Ian: *Okay. I'll come prepared.;) Say about seven?*

Me: *Sure, I'll be waiting.*

Allison

With all my chores done, I decide to go shopping for something nice but casual to wear. My wardrobe needs updating terribly since I've not bought anything nice in a couple of years.

My phone rings, and Siri tells me it's Junie.

"Hey, girl."

"Hi, Mom. Whatcha doin'?" After all her education, she still practices the worst grammar.

"Well, you'll be happy to know, at least I hope you are, I have a date. So I'm going shopping for something to wear."

A scream comes through the phone, followed by a laugh. "Oh, Mom, that's great to hear. Jacks and I want you to be happy, Mom."

"What makes you think I'm unhappy?"

"It's not that you're unhappy, but maybe lonely? It's been two years. You're entitled to move on with your life."

"I know, honey, but moving on is hard." I sigh. "I love your dad very much, and... and I just want to do the right thing."

"We know that, but it's time. So, is it someone we know? We'd both be okay with you dating someone from church. There's a lot of older men who you could date."

"Older as in eighty. I'm not looking for a grandparent."

"No, I mean, like Mr. Border. He's a nice man."

"Yes, he is, and he's at least seventy."

"Oh, yeah. Maybe you're right. What about Mr. Danny, the song leader? He's a nice guy and has never been married."

"Yes, he's nice too, but I think he has a boyfriend."

"What? Mr. Danny is gay? No way."

"Yes, way. His friend is nice, too, and they seem very happy together."

"He brings him to church? In our town?" Her tone says she doesn't believe me.

"Yes, honey, he does. The church knows all about it, and no one seems to think twice. He does an excellent job as choir director, and that's all that matters to the church."

"I know that, and you know that, but I never

thought the conservative people who go there would ever believe it."

"Twenty years ago, it might have caused people to stand up and be angry, but the church has come a long way with the new pastor."

"That's awesome, Mom. Glad to hear it but let's get back to your date," she says, emphasis on 'date.' "Is it someone we know?"

I had hoped she wouldn't ask me this. Both kids met him after the car accident and the funeral. The timing leaves a lot to be desired.

"Yes, you've met him."

"Great, who is it? Do Jacks and me like him?"

"Not that it matters since I'm the one dating him, but it's Ian Windsor, the policeman who came to the hospital and funeral."

Long, dead silence.

"Junie? Are you still there?" I feared this would happen when I told them I was seeing Ian.

"Yeah, I'm here. I just never thought. I mean, uh... well."

"Stop Junie. Ian is a nice guy. He's been nothing but kind to our family since we've met him."

"I know, Mom. It's just that I wasn't prepared for you to see someone connected to the accident. It was a shitty time for us all."

"You're right it was, but Ian knows all about it, and I don't have to do any explaining to him."

"Has he been bothering you to go out with him?"

Her defensive tone tells me exactly where she's going.

"No, your Aunt Beth ran into him, and he asked about me. She told him to call me, so he did. See, nothing like what you were thinking." Junie didn't need to know I reached out first, especially since I'm detecting a note of displeasure about this situation.

"Good because we won't put up with someone who's pushy."

"Like you or your brother have any say so in this matter. I am a grown woman, Junie Len Waller, and I'll date who I see fit to date."

Taking a deep breath, I calm myself down. First, they want me to date, and then they want to choose my dates for me. Hell no. That is not going to happen.

"I know, Mom. Sorry. We want someone who will make you happy and treat you kindly. Someone who'll be proud of who you are and happy they are dating an awesome woman."

"Wow, Junie, that's a lot to ask for, don't you think?"

"No, I don't think it is. You're a great person, Mom. Anyone we know would say so. The men you date also need to know that."

Her praises make me proud to be her mother. Even in the hard teenage times, we always tried to make her understand we loved her. After Kellen died, the three of us banded together and made it through.

"I promise you I will never date someone who makes me feel any less than what you and your brother expect. How about that?"

"Sounds good. So, tell me, where is he taking you?"

"This isn't our first date, and he had to work today, so he's coming here. I told him we could be like the kids and do Netflix and chill."

"*What*! You told him those words?"

"Well, yes, and I also told him we have the other channels. Hulu, Prime, and the others."

"Oh my God. Mother. What have you done?"

"I just invited him over. We're having pizza and watching movies. What's so wrong with that? He works hard at his job." I think back to what he was really doing today and want to laugh, but she is so upset that I decide not to.

"Mom, you invited him over for sex." Her words cause me to choke. Like can't breathe choke. Like have a stroke choke.

"What? I did not."

"Mother, that's what Netflix and chill means. You invited him over to eat, turn on Netflix, and have sex. Then you added all the other channels you have. He probably thinks you're a sex maniac. Or just a desperate widow." I hear her laughing now—falling on the floor laughing.

"Wait till I tell Jackson. I don't know if I should. He might drive home tonight and beat the policeman up."

"Don't you dare tell your brother. Oh, Lord. Junie, what am I going to do? Do you think he'll know what that means too?"

"Yeah, Mom, he will. The man deals with all kinds on the street. Surely, he keeps up current terms people use."

I rub my hand across my forehead. What have I done? Ian will think I'm a nymphomaniac, telling him all the channels we can watch. Leaning over, I place my forehead on the cool quartz and try to control my breathing. This is bad. Really bad.

Junie pipes up again, "You could always message him and tell him y'all need to go somewhere, and that's off the table."

"I can't do that. I told him we'd stay in tonight. I'll just have to inform him we're not having... uh, Netflix and chill."

"You can say sex, Mom. It's okay, I'm an adult, remember?"

"Either way, we aren't doing that." Not tonight anyway, I tell myself. A lot more thought has to go into me getting naked in front of a strange man.

I mean, he saw me at my worst as he removed me from the car and in the hospital when I was in and out of consciousness. Just imagining what I looked like both of those times, he should have run the other way but didn't.

"On that note, I'm going to let you go. I only wanted to check in since it's been a few days. Hey, you said this wasn't your first date. Where did he take you the first time?"

For someone who doesn't want me asking

questions about their life, my daughter seems terribly interested in mine. I will remember that when she is vague about what she's up to.

"We went out to the lake for the afternoon. It was beautiful, and lots of people were around us."

"That's a good first date," she comments.

"Actually, that's the second date. We went for coffee the first time."

"So... this is the third date. And you invite him to Netflix and chill. I'm hanging up now, Mom." She laughs again. "Glad I'm not around to witness this date. Talk to you later."

She hangs up before I have a chance to defend myself. Dammit, what did I do? What does he think about what I said?

I can't even talk to Beth about this. She'll be all over it. I bet she understands what I've told him.

Why didn't I know this? I heard the kids say it all the time. Was that what they were doing? I need to call Jackson. The number of times he told us so casually that he was going to a girl's house to Netflix and chill is astronomical. That boy. Ugh.

What about Junie? I need to think about this. Or maybe I should worry about my own problems? They're adults now like she reminded me. Why does it matter?

Enough of this.

The chime on the antique hall clock tells me I need to get ready. Since I never made it out to buy something new, I search through my closet for something appropriate—comfortable but not too slouchy.

A shirt I haven't worn in a while calls to me from the back of the rack. The vibrant red, silky shirt slides off the hanger. People always compliment me when I'm wearing this color. It's long enough to wear with leggings, and my black ones fit well without showing every bump and bulge.

Turning on the shower, I cover my body in my favorite shower gel. The Blu Atlas smells luscious. I save it for special occasions, so I guess a date is special enough. My skin always feels smooth and soft when I use it.

I decide to shave my legs, too, even though I'm wearing pants. As I pull the razor up my leg, I think about what Junie said about my offer of chilling. What if it does lead to sex?

Lots of women get waxed these days. Maybe I should have gotten waxed. It's been so long since I've needed to, and it hurts like hell. My skin isn't as tight as it used to be, making it hurt worse.

I could shave everywhere that's necessary. Kellen didn't care either way. He just liked sex however we had it, but Ian might have a different opinion.

My eyes look down, and I realize I should clean things up some. I quickly add shaving cream and start the task, careful not to nick or cut myself. Wouldn't that look cute—a huge cut that won't stop bleeding?

With that thought, I realize I've removed a lot of hair on one side. Ugh. I have to make it even, so I start on the other side.

Before I'm finished, I look down carefully and decide my twat resembles an Egyptian hairless cat.

"Very fitting, Allison. A hairless cat."

My God, what will Ian think if we get carried away? A prepubescent girl? A bald spot, like alopecia? No, no, no. What did I do? I should have just left it alone.

The shower door pops open under my force to see how I look in the mirror. A towel barely rakes over me to catch the dripping water before I stand in front of the full-length mirror on the door.

"Holy shit. There will be no sex until it grows back. What will he think when he sees it?" The area is red and splotchy now.

The thought of it growing back reminds me of the last time I waxed and all the prickle and itching it caused.

"What the hell, you dumbass," I mutter. "Why do I have to date? I can stay home and visit my nightstand friend again."

Taking some of my favorite lotion, I smooth it over the freshly shaved area, berating myself for what I did. To be normal, according to today's standards, I created a bigger mess.

I've never been opposed to keeping my pubic area tidy—at least until the accident. I let myself go for two miserable years. Maybe that's where I went wrong.

Keeping myself up should have been a priority after the shock wore off, but I didn't, and now I'm paying for it.

Wouldn't Beth get a laugh out of this? Her voice rings in my head with crude comments, like allowing myself to look like a chia pet. She'd probably sing 'Ch-Ch-Ch Chia' all over my house.

After I smooth the lotion all over my now hairless body, it feels better. I slide on a cute pair of black lace high-cut panties, thanking God it doesn't feel too strange. Of all the things I'll have to get used to again, being smooth down there was never on my list.

The matching bra goes on, and I return to study myself in the mirror. I turn this way and that and then around to study my butt.

Smoothing down the leg lines across the expanded version of my cheeks, I decide it looks okay. Not Cindy Crawford or Christie Brinkley great, but I look pretty decent for a forty-something mom of two.

I refuse to beat myself up over liking to eat. Eating is normal. Starving myself to be thin is not, and I'm okay with that. Could I stand to lose a few pounds? Hell yeah, but what woman doesn't always think that?

But I'm okay with a few extra pounds, and if Ian doesn't like it, he can go suck an egg. The clock chimes again, causing me to rush around to finish getting ready.

I order pizza and salad from my favorite local mom-and-pop pizzeria and move around my den to pick up last-minute clutter. The last thing I want Ian to think is I'm a total slob. With no one living here but me, how do I create little messes everywhere?

Shew, finally done. Now, where's my wine?

Ian

My truck rests at the beginning of her long driveway. When her kids lived here, it probably came in handy. The shine from the decorative house lights illuminates the entire yard. No one can accuse her of lacking visibility around the house.

A small car pulls in behind me and comes to a screeching halt, narrowly missing the back of my truck. The barely-old-enough-to-drive teenager hops out and drags a hot bag from the back along with a plastic grocery sack.

"Hey, got your pizza order right here, sir." He hands me the sack and starts unzipping the other.

Watching him, I ask, "You always come into driveways on two wheels and slide to a stop?"

"Uh, no, sir. Just in a hurry. People only like hot pizza, and I've got two more orders in my car." He hands me the extra-large box and a receipt.

"Thank you for ordering from Pop's Pizza," he calls over his shoulder as he starts running back to his car.

"Wait," I yell. "Did you get a tip?"

"Sure did, thanks."

His car backs out as quickly as it came in, tearing off down the road. Shaking my head, I watch until he's out of sight.

"Slow down, kid, or I'll be dragging you out of that death trap," I mumble, walking to the front door.

The door opens before I can ring the bell.

"Oh, hey. I thought it was Ethan," Allison turns to let me inside.

I hold up the order. "He was in a hurry to get out of here."

"Yes, I tell him every time I order that he's going to have an accident trying to get the pizzas delivered. Scares me sometimes."

"I wish we had guys on the force as anxious to do their jobs as he is." I step into the entryway.

The only other times I've been inside were after the funeral and when I held her while she cried. Tonight needs to be a happy occasion, so I don't dwell on the kid's bad driving.

"Smells delicious," she says, opening the box and taking a big whiff of the cheesy gooeyness. "I always order from Pop's for that reason. Well, that and

Ethan's fast deliveries." She snickers.

"Sure does. Never had it before."

She looks at me like I've grown an extra head from my shoulder.

"You are in a for the greatest treat. They make the best."

I slip behind her as she retrieves plates from the upper cabinet.

"I have a better idea. Let's have this treat first." I spin her and take the plates to deposit on the counter. My arms wrap around her waist as I pull her in for a kiss. I try to keep it tame, but I want her to keep me in mind like she's been jamming into my brain for the last few days.

Tentative arms slide around my shoulders before landing on my neck. When I deepen the kiss, a gentle squeeze causes a quickening pulse to shoot through me. As her hands knead the tight muscle with more force, I realize she also feels the vibrating electricity happening between us.

Even while squeezing her small hands on my traps, she does no harm. Instead, her kneading helps loosen my anxiety over my desire for her. With her pliable in my arms, I back her into the counter. It takes all my strength not to shove her back against the hard surface so I can grind against her willing body.

A low moan escapes her lips with my movements, and as much as I would love to open her before me on the countertop, I know I have to back away. Dammit, I don't want to. Allison's enticing perfume permeates the space, making it even harder to let her go.

Ending the kiss, I continue biting and kissing the warm skin down her neck. My tongue makes circles where I bite, but I don't know if I'm trying to take the pain away or make it more noticeable.

She feels too good in my arms. I reach her collarbone and nip across it until I reach the edge of her shirt.

Dammit, this might be a good time to stop. At least, that's what my head says. I want to rip the offending material off her, or at least pull it aside and continue, but I know how easily I can get carried away with this small tease.

I step back, breathing like I've been held underwater. Watching her chest rise and fall, I believe she feels the same.

The combustion that will happen between us is going to be epic. I can feel it. Not yet, but soon, very soon.

While we sit on the floor behind her coffee table to watch the comedy we agreed on, I enjoy the pizza.

She was right about it being the best in town, but looking at Allison as often as I want makes it all the better. Glancing to the side, brushing her arms and legs, curling her hair around my fingers—a perfect night for me.

I don't need a fancy restaurant to enjoy myself. Not that I don't like to dress up and take a beautiful lady, like this one, to a nice place. I do enjoy it sometimes. But many women think they need wining and dining to be happy, and those are not the women for me. A woman who's happy going anywhere and doing lots of different things is the one I need.

This gorgeous creature warming the spot next to me, laughing at the silly jokes, doesn't strike me as one who always needs fancy. She seems adaptable to any situation.

I plan to take her out soon because I want to show her off to the world. Others can see what I see in her. She rarely meets a stranger and speaks kindly of most people. All I'm waiting for is for her to be ready to face others as a couple out together.

Rolling the chestnut softness around my fingers, I tug lightly on the strands to capture her attention. She turns to me. I believe words rest on the tip of her tongue, but when her eyes meet mine, the words seem to disappear.

My hand goes to the back of her neck, and I meet her halfway. Our lips barely touch and slide across each other's in a soft, tentative kiss. My tongue seeks entry by running the length of the crease, and she opens to me. I love how responsive she is.

I pull her body to mine before I sink inside her mouth to taste and explore its depths. She gives as good as she gets, dueling for space with mine. Her small pink tongue dives in when I retreat some to give her access.

With her head now in my palm, I shift for better access, and as a low growl starts in the back of my throat, she wraps her arm around my neck and climbs across my lap. Getting her where I want her requires no coaxing. This woman reads my mind.

This tells me she's as into this as I am, and it turns me on even more to know she's willing to act on what she wants. No holding back. I fucking love it.

Her hips are lined perfectly with mine, my dick growing to an almost painful point underneath her. My hands slide down Allison's sides to her hips, and I waste no time moving her heat up and down its length. The action makes me want to explode. It's been so long.

I stop and retrace my movements back up her sides to her breasts, palming the globes on top of the material preventing me access.

They feel natural and perfect. Fake tits do nothing for me. I can spot them from a mile away, and these soft, natural breasts only heat my desire.

Squeezing and plumping them, I know I need to taste next, so I reach around with one hand to undo her bra, only to find no clasp. Okay, how does this work?

As I kiss down her neck, I raise my knees, moving her body close to mine. At the neckline, I run my tongue along the edge from side to side, dipping under the edge. I realize there's nothing else under the shirt—perfect easy access.

Allison throws her head back to give me more access. Thank God she's into my movements. She takes a second to slide her shirt straps down, which allows her breasts to partially spill out.

With little effort, I push the offending material out of my way, kissing the pliable skin. They look exquisite, and the fact that they show signs of having children, with large beige rings around the nipples and a few stretch marks, makes me appreciate her being a mother even more. She did what she thought best when having her two.

After licking my way around one and then the other, I twist both nipples between my thumb and index finger and take one in my mouth. Allison moans and arches her back, pushing them closer to me. I want to devour them with my tongue, lips, and teeth.

"God, that feels so good, Ian." She sighs. She rocks her hips across my straining dick that already threatens to bust through my zipper. Her hands move through my hair, lightly scratching as she goes.

I circle each bud with my tongue before I stop and lower my legs, shifting her back. Her eyes pop open instantly at the loss of sensation.

"What's wrong?" she quickly asks.

"Absolutely nothing is wrong, but if we keep doing this, things might end faster than I want." I glance down at the small amount of pre-cum dotting the material under my button.

Her eyes follow mine. "Oh, uh, ohhh… right."

"We can do one of two things. Move this party to a better location with more room, or end the party with a goodnight kiss."

She eyes me carefully for a full minute, which makes me think I'm about to have the case of blue balls from hell. I refuse to push her for sex. I'm ready when she is because I know she's not had a lover since her husband.

Her head drops to her hands in her lap. I lift her chin to look at me. "Allison, I'm ready when you are and not a minute before. You're a beautiful woman, and I want to see where this goes between us, but I will not move forward with the physical side until you're ready."

I can see the gold streaks in her deep brown eyes as they widen. She doesn't speak. After what seems like forever, she opens her mouth and hesitates.

Finally, she says, "I've thought about this a long time, Ian. You know all the reasons why. I want to make the right decision with us because I do want to see where this goes."

"If you want to take sex off the table for now, I get it."

"No, I don't want to take it off the table." She pulls in a deep breath and lets it out. "God knows, I don't ever want it off the table. You're a hot guy, and I'd be a fool."

A bubble of laughter escapes me. I can't help it.

"Don't laugh at me." She swats my chest.

"I'm not laughing at you. I'm laughing at the way you said it."

"What, I didn't say it right?" Her eyebrows raise.

"You mean, your horny, like the rest of the world, and can't bring yourself to say those words, or I'm just such a 'hot guy' you can't resist me." I can't help wagging my eyebrows.

"Yes, that."

"That what, Allison?" I know I'm teasing her, but she's too cute to stop. A grown woman trying to express need and desire to a man she barely knows makes me want to fall over laughing.

"Okay, that I am... horny, and you get me going in all the best ways." The gold flecks become more intense as she speaks.

"Oh, fuck. You're going to kill me."

The words coming out of her mouth send me into overdrive. I stand, pulling her up with me. With ease, I take her over my shoulder in a fireman's hold and almost sprint down the hallway.

18

Ian

I have no clue where I'm going. I open door after door until I find one with a big bed. Allison's laughter when I drop her onto the mattress is sweeter than I know what to do with, but damn, am I ready to figure it out.

My body aims for the one spread before me, but I force myself to take a little of the weight off her with my elbows beside her sides. Allison, small compared to me, wraps her legs around my waist and pulls me down onto her so our bodies line up the best they can.

She shifts her center closer to me, leveraging the position to press herself tighter to me. If it is even possible, my erection swells to a painful point that needs to be alleviated soon.

She pushes herself up to meet my every thrust—

ones I can't seem to resist. The erotic motion we both fight for seems natural between two lovers.

"Stop, Allison, please." My voice sounds like I'm begging for my last meal.

Immediately, she flattens below me. "I'm sorry. Did I do something wrong again?"

"No way. It's just that I want to take my time with you to savor every minute and every inch of your beautiful body."

Her worried face melts in relief, realizing I want to pay attention to the tiniest parts of her.

"Why rush to the end when we've got all night?" I ask, walking my lips down her neck to her exposed breasts once more.

"This needs to go," I trace the fabric. "Mind helping me get it off you?"

"Only if you join me." She playfully wiggles her eyebrows.

I waste no time in grabbing my collar and yanking my shirt off.

"Now there's something to look at... touch... lick," she says, running her tongue over her lower lip.

"Later." With nothing hindering my grip, my hands itch for the exposed softness. "Your tits make my mouth hungry for a better taste than before."

Eyes never leaving my body, Allison raises herself and allows me to pull her shirt over her head. My tongue didn't get enough in the den, so I devote my time now to running my tongue around the wide surface before drawing the hard peak into my mouth.

She whimpers and gasps as I lick, bite, and torture, but nothing matches the moan from her when I first sucked on her nipple.

"You like that, huh?" I tease.

Allison's back arches off the bed. Her response to just my attention on the pebbled peaks tells me we need to try some nipple play another time. Could she come from my manipulating them to the point of torturing us both?

Sliding down, I continue stimulating the stiffened nipples with my fingers while nipping a little harder on the underside. I don't plan to leave a mark, but I can see one has already formed. I cup her breasts and push them together.

"Ugh," Allison blushes. "They used to be there years ago."

"They're one of the best parts of you, sugar. I love them. Tits are at the top of my list of a woman's body, especially real ones." She snickers at my comment. "But I also like other parts. I want to lick every special spot," I emphasize each word with a kiss, traveling down her chest and stomach. By this time, her navel is eye to eye with me. I glance back up to see how she's doing.

"Well, yeah. I'm okay with that." Her words, breathy and sexy, follow a smile, and her hands find their way into my hair again. She hesitates to push or pull me, so I continue kissing my way lower.

When my hand reaches to the band on her tight pants, I glance back up, silently asking for permission. She lifts her hips, and I sit up to help her remove them. She leaves her panties, but I don't push it.

As I leave an open-mouthed kiss on the roundness below her navel, I feel her body tense.

"What's wrong, Allison?"

"Noth... nothing. You know I've had kids, but showing those parts of myself that never returned to the way they were before... makes me nervous." Her skin breaks out in tiny goose bumps.

I stare at her for a second as I weigh my words carefully. Her beautiful body looks like a model for the Greek sculptors, but getting her to see that seems impossible.

"Your breasts represent a body that bore children, and you seem okay with that. They are perfect, by the way." I reach and squeeze the left one again before I roll the nipple between my fingers and give it a slight tug. This earns me a fiery groan from her. She loves it, which makes me love it, so I move to the right one and give it the same attention.

Allison watches my face like she's trying to decide whether I'm talking shit or being honest. Finally, she relaxes.

"The plump layer you're looking at right now is not the same as my breasts. It's just that, well, I was never thin. I've had a pouch there for as long as I can remember." One of her hands leaves my hair to cover her eyes, which makes me understand this truly bothers her.

Before I can reply, she adds, "Guys in school referred to me as chubby forever. It never mattered how thin I got or how hard I worked to get rid of that roll."

"Male stupidity runs wild at that age, Allison. You should know that from raising Jackson. Your body is exactly how it should be for you. No two people are alike. You must know this."

"These stretch marks say it all." I run an easy finger across the supple area. "You grew up, bore children, and became a gorgeous woman. These are simply part of the plan."

I notice the white skin, streaked with fine lines she complains about, appears untouched by the sun, telling me no one outside her husband has seen it in years or possibly ever.

"That's easy for you to say. At fifteen, the last thing I wanted to hear was how I was still a little too thick for them."

"Most adolescent boys need to be herded into a holding pen until they show signs of intelligence." I drop light kisses and nips, not dwelling in one spot too long. Hopefully, I can make her forget about this, even just for now.

If I had my way, this would never come up again. Her body is a true beauty, and any man who thinks differently needs to reconsider his definition of beauty.

The other places I want to spend time enjoying scream my name. Said places hold a much higher spot on my list of importance. And if I do my job right, her mind will be on what I'm doing instead of a pound of flesh.

Reaching her black, silky underwear, I smirk up at her. "You wear these for me?"

"A girl can dream."

"You were dreaming of me?" Teasing her at this point isn't my intention, but if it calms her down, I'm okay with it.

She doesn't respond the way I expect.

"Are you going to spend the night talking or get to the good stuff?"

"Oooh," I draw out my word. "Anxious much? You don't have to ask me twice."

My fingers hook into the silky material by her hips, and I tug her panties down, revealing a nice surprise.

"Well, damn sugar, a gift I didn't expect." I smile, knowing she has been thinking of our night together as much as me.

She rises on her elbows, and her lips open and close, trying to decide what to say.

"I didn't know how you'd prefer. I mean, I wasn't planning on anything specific happening tonight, but just in case..." her words dwindle.

"For you, I prefer any way you allow me to be right

here." I kiss the bare skin before me, just above the hood that's hiding my destination.

"Ohhh," her low moan pushes me to continue. As I slide the panties further down, she squirms, helping me rid her of them. In the process, I treat myself to a good look at this gorgeous, real woman. How can she not see her own perfection?

"Allison, you are a beautiful woman in every way. Your body speaks to me, begging to be set on fire exactly like it makes me feel when I look at you." I rise over her and slam my lips to hers, where she opens instantly, inviting me inside to lap up every inch.

I pull her bottom lip between my teeth, gently sucking the plump flesh inside my mouth. My hand finds its way to her bare pussy where the nub of her desire waits for me to torture it with sweet pleasure.

"I wanted to take it slow, but I'm not sure I can wait too long. I need you, Allison."

"Then, please, don't," she murmurs on a breathy exhale. "I want you, too, Ian."

That is all I need to hear. I've been ready for this moment for a while. My dreams have been locked around this scene since the night she'd fallen apart in my arms. I knew it was the wrong time and chose to bide my time. Waiting. Dreaming. Lusting.

Now, it's here, and I'm nervous. She's only been with her husband, and I have no clue what her expectations might be.

I want to forge a path that is only ours—one that

will not resemble what they had. One we can claim for us.

I've never had a problem pleasing a woman, but none of them were Allison. None had twenty-plus years of knowing what to expect. I can only hope I measure up.

My tongue runs the seam of her from top to bottom and back to the engorged pebble waiting for attention. The squirming and moaning tell me I'm doing something right.

"You like me teasing your pink clit?" I murmur. "There're so many things I want to treat your body to."

I circle the spot before taking it between my lips and applying a light suction. She rewards me with a long, low moan.

"Oh my God." She gasps. "That feels... that feels... I don't even have words, Ian."

"Your sounds say it all, beautiful. Lay back and enjoy while I eat this pretty pussy out until you can't stand another minute."

I continue my delicious assault before moving lower to rim around her opening. Her body rises off the bed to get me closer.

I can tell she wants me to push in, but I want to control this contact. My touch balances her desire and need, and her passion urges me on.

My tongue brushes her distended pebble while my finger slowly rims around her entrance. She grabs my head, trying to help me along, which makes me smile.

"Nuh-uh. I get to decide when, sugar. I'm only inflicting the torturing pleasure to make it better for us both. Your sweetness is flowing already, and I love lapping it up."

"Do you always talk dirty in bed?" Her reply is soft and breathy.

Her fingers run through my hair, pulling, but not to create pain. I'm okay with some pain if it means pleasure is the result.

"Does it bother you? I would love to hear some dirty talk from that adorable mouth of yours."

All she rewards me with is a low moan.

Her craving makes my dick ache with the best pain. I lick from her opening to her clit as I undo my shorts. The tightness causes my dick to suffer. I kick them off before returning my attention to the woman before me.

Without missing a beat, my finger sinks into her opening. The movement causes my whole body to ache. Adding a second elicits a loud cry from her, not from pain but from the best torture.

"Fuck, Ian. Fuck, fuck, fuck. That feels so good." Her words cause my lips to turn up at the ends. She does have some words in there, after all.

Moving my fingers in and out of her lights a fire in my own body, and I rub my dick on the comforter, seeking friction. I desperately want more.

But I also want her ready. It has been a long time

for her, and this is a monumental moment too. I want us both to remember this—the first time, I hope, of many.

"Allison, I don't think I can go much longer. I need you."

"Oh, please, Ian. I need more. Fuck me now. Please," she begs.

I push a third finger in and scissor them before turning them to bend toward the spot that should set her off.

Wow, does it ever. She bucks against my hand, crying out in pleasure.

"Ian, what..." she screams. "What are you doing to me?"

Her muscles clamp down on my fingers as I continue rubbing the textured surface inside her.

I wring the orgasm out, taking pleasure in her raspy moans and screams. Listening to her sexy sounds, I feel more pre-cum leaking from my swollen head.

I kiss the engorged bundle of nerves, making her body tremble.

"Stop, stop, stop. I can't take it anymore." She watches me with hooded eyes.

Removing my fingers and licking them clean, I kiss my way up her body, stopping by the hard peaks for a quick nip.

"No. You can't. Too sensitive," she murmurs, trying to control her breathing. Her eyes never leave mine.

I lightly kiss her lips before lying beside her to look at her bright red face. "You okay?"

Her head shakes no. "How can I be after that? What the fuck did you do to me?"

"Found that spot you needed to have the perfect orgasm. Did you like it?"

She looks at me. "Did I like it?"

I nod.

"Hell yeah, I did. When I've revived, can we try that spot again?"

A snicker escapes me. "Sure. Don't know if I'll be able to set you off like that when I'm inside you, but you never know till you try."

It occurs to me she hasn't had an orgasm from applying pressure and rubbing her G-spot. I'm surprised since hers was easy to find. Allison's was begging me to stroke it.

I smiled to myself. *At least there's one first we can share.*

Allison

Damn. What in the ever-loving hell happened? I'd had years of orgasms, but they never gave me that feeling. Every ounce of my body felt that, from head to toe, and he wasn't even inside me.

I guess it's never too late to learn new tricks. Kellen and I had been adventuresome until the kids got old enough to realize something was happening behind the closed door.

Having teens in the house made doing the deed difficult. The idea they might hear us made me paranoid, which didn't make for a great sex life. Once we had to plan around their schedules, I didn't look as forward to making love as I once had.

"Hey, you okay in there?" Ian taps my temple.

"Thought I'd lost you for a minute."

"No, I'm good." I gave him my sexiest look. "More than good, actually."

I turn and pull him to me for a lingering kiss. The glisten coating his lips tastes of me as I run my tongue along his, seeking entrance.

He opens and rolls over me, covering most of my body and allowing his hand to roam freely over my breast. He is as ready for the main event if his hard length pressing into my hip is any indicator. And so am I.

Somewhere in the middle of coaxing the mind-blowing orgasm out of me, his underwear had disappeared. Open access to his hard cock entices me to wrap my hand around him.

The long length gives me pause, but I refuse to compare him to Kellen. He had no place in this bed with Ian.

As I run my hand up and down his length, Ian shudders. I see his abs contract with each pull. The power I carry in this moment—his every reaction to my touch—makes me realize what this means between us.

Our relationship is moving to a new level of intimacy—the highest level we can go. But I'm not afraid. Even though I have not known him long, I still feel a connection to Ian. The moment he pulled me from the car ties us together in a way that nothing can separate.

"Sugar, fuck, I need you. I won't last long if you keep doing that. We've waited a long time for each other."

His deep ocean eyes stare into mine, and I think I see into his soul.

His truths. His need. His desire. All for me to hold and understand.

I release my hand and wrap my legs around him, pulling him closer.

"We need a condom," he whispers in my ear.

"Not for me. I don't want something between us. Do you need one?"

His eyes stare hard at me because he knows I haven't been with a man other than my husband.

"I have an IUD, so no problems on that front," I add.

Ian's eyes focus on mine as he notches the thick head at my entrance. He pushes in—slowly, which I'm thankful for. Being celibate for over two years now, my worries about the pain linger. I mean, I had two children and years of sex, but lack of use has a way of changing the feel.

Once he reaches about halfway, he stops. "You okay, sugar?"

My words elude me as I try to relax and let the feel of him invading my slick channel be pleasurable. Not that it isn't because, God knows, it's exquisite torture. At my age, I'm not sure I'll be wet enough to stand the intrusion. Damn getting older. But with all the foreplay and that orgasm, I feel like my body is ready.

I nod.

Ian plunges ahead, bottoming out inside me. The full feeling causes me to suck in a breath.

"Still good?" he asks, kissing me lightly.

"Good? No, it's great."

"That's what I wanted to hear because this pace is hell. I wanted to go slow and enjoy every inch sinking in you but fuck that."

He picks up the pace a little, groaning. I feel him needing more, so I circle my legs around his waist once more.

This position gives him the go-ahead to fuck me like he means it. He pulls out and slams in over and over, driving me wild.

A tightness takes over in my abdomen, evidence that another orgasm is not far away. He must realize it, too, because he rises, sits back, and, lifting my hips, he pulls me onto his swelling cock.

This angle allows me to see his huge cock sinking into me over and over.

"Ian, this looks filthy from my view. I think I love it."

My hands go to my breast, pulling and pinching, the sight making him moan louder than me.

"Yes, sugar, torture your tits for me. Makes me want to bite them, but I love this position because seeing my cock sink into you..." he speeds up his movements, "... sends a shock down my spine."

His fingers find my clit and begin circling it with a

heavy touch. "I've held out about as long as I can, sugar."

He pinches my clit, making my body slightly rear as the orgasm takes over. My inner muscles clench and release involuntarily, causing him to follow me into the blissfulness I love.

I feel the warmth of his release buried deep inside me. He pushes in a few more times, extending the orgasm until it's too sensitive for me.

"Stop, stop. It's too much." Not that I want to stop, but I can't take it.

"Yes, but isn't it the best? That moment when it's not quite over, but you know the feeling's almost lost. Makes it hard not to chase it a few more times."

He rolls off me, pulling me into his side so that I never feel a loss of his warm skin.

"Wow," he says. "That was just... fucking wow. Sorry, my brain has taken a break from reality."

"Right there with you. Don't ask me questions right now because I'm incapable of answering."

He snickers and kisses the top of my head. "I gotcha."

We lay suspended in the afterglow, and my mind starts into overdrive.

Did I do the right thing? What will Beth think when I tell her? Will the kids realize we're sleeping together when they see us?

"Ali, you okay, sugar?" He pulls me in tighter.

"Yeah, I'm good."

"Just good?"

I hear some concern in his question.

"No, not 'just good,' " I reassure. "I'm great after that mind-altering round of orgasms. Now my mind won't stop thinking about other stuff."

"I didn't do my job good enough then."

"My body begs to differ." I look up at him. "It feels delicious in all the right places."

"Then you should be either asleep from me wearing you out or thinking hard about round two like I am."

"Yeah, I could sleep, but I worry about dumb stuff, like whether others will think it's too soon."

"Fuck the others. This is just for us. We're adults making adult decisions, Allison. What happens between two consenting adults isn't anyone else's business."

He searches my eyes as I sit up beside him.

"Are you regretting it already?" he asks.

"What, no. Not at all." I reach for his hand, not wanting to be separated from him. "And I know you're right. I shouldn't worry what anyone will think. It's just been such a difficult couple of years. In some ways, I feel like I'm living in a fishbowl with everyone waiting for me to do something stupid or break down."

He brings my hand to his mouth and kisses the palm. "Allison, you've done remarkable from what I see. You are a survivor of the hardest kind. You lived through a dangerous car wreck. I see so many who don't make it."

"Yeah, I know. It was bad, wasn't it."

"Then you buried your husband who grew up with you, raised kids with you, loved you through thick and thin. Many men and women would have fallen apart. Not you, though. You did what you had to do to make it."

His words cause me to think back over all I had endured. The years sucked, but I made it.

"You're right, but I had help. Beth and the kids became my lifeline."

"I'm happy they were here for you."

My eyes lift to his. He's still holding my hand close to his face. I want to see how he reacts to my needing outside help. "I also went to grief counseling."

"That's great. You did what some refuse to do. You tackled your problems head-on. You sought out someone who could help you deal with it all. I'm proud of you for going." He kisses my palm again and moves it to his cheek. I stroke the soft skin as he leans in.

"You are? I worry people will think I need psychological help. Like I was losing it."

"So what? Again, Allison, who cares what others think? You have to do what's best for you. What's going to make you whole again. Everyone's different when it comes to grief or even dealing with any psychological problems."

"I know, but this is me we're talking about."

"Exactly. You, and only you." He sits up beside me. "I see things happen that if people would have sought out any kind of help... a doctor, a counselor, a preacher, anyone, their lives would have been different or spared. Do you know how hard it is to walk into a suicide scene? Or one where it's a double suicide, both spouses dead?"

"Oh, Ian, that must be the worst. I'm so sorry you're forced to go through that."

"It's part of the job, but it doesn't get easier." He pulls me to him, wrapping me up in his strong arms. "Then I see someone like you who does what needs to be done, who seeks help, and I have hope. Hope that others will have the same outcome. That's the only way I can continue to do this job."

We hold each other for a long while. Finally, I lean back.

"Sorry, I didn't mean to take this beautiful moment and ruin it."

"You didn't ruin it. You spoke your truths. I'm happy you shared them. I hope you'll always want to be open this way. I feel closer to you with your honest words."

"Yes, it also makes me feel that way." I lean forward and press my lips to his. Though it starts as a reassuring peck, it quickly morphs into a deep, lust-filled, mind-melting one.

Before I know it, Ian's buried deep inside me with

slow, constant strokes. This time around, it resembles making love instead of having sex.

Am I ready to call this making love?

We share a tenderness that melts my heart. He eases me into another orgasm that hits when I least expect it and causes a tremor to slip down my entire body. My body clenches over his rock-hard erection as though it never intends to release him.

I don't want to let him go. He holds me close and rocks into me, releasing his seed inside me, then follows with a long, luscious kiss that finalizes an exquisite moment we share.

He releases me and goes for a warm washrag to clean me, careful to go easy on my bare skin. The looks he gives me as he softly wipes our liquids away alleviate my earlier thoughts.

This man removes any doubts I might have about trying a relationship. It may be a while before we are ready to have that talk, but I can see it on the horizon.

Once Ian's done, he pulls the covers from under me and spreads them across us. He rolls me over on my side before spooning me closely behind. A strong arm wraps around my middle, and I feel warm kisses spread down my shoulder.

"Sleep, sugar. I'll be right here."

His warmth surrounds me as my eyes close. It's been too long since I have slept like this. So, so long.

20

Ian

"Hey man, how's it going?" Gabriel, my first partner on the force, asks as we prepare for our shift.

I slide my vest over my shirt, not looking forward to another hot Texas day wearing this heavy thing. It's for my own safety, but when it's still almost one hundred degrees in September, I would love to go without.

"Doin' great. How about yourself?"

"Can't complain about work, but these damn temperatures are killing me." Gabe wipes his index finger across his brow.

"That's what happens when you go up north and live a while. Returning must be like moving back to hell." I laugh easily.

"Yeah, but I was ready to get home to Texas. Even with all the shit that goes on, I'd still rather live here than anywhere else."

My locker slams closed as I turn to look at Gabe. He's about my age—we were originally hired in the same small group of officers.

"What's your wife think about living around here?" He had been married for at least fifteen years, with a few kids running around.

"I gotta say, she was thrilled when we moved up by her relatives because she had so much help with our two wild children. It didn't take long for the newness to wear off, though. Her mom and dad popped into our house to see us going at it on the kitchen counter one too many times for her, and she was ready to go back to Texas."

My laughter rang out through the locker room. "Awkward much?"

"Hell yeah, it was awkward with my dick hanging out, looking at her mom. The woman couldn't grasp the concept of knocking. She barged in one time when Anna was sucking my cock like the pro she is. Thought Anna and her mom were both going to die on the spot."

"More than I really wanted to know, dude, but I get it. Her mom should have learned the first time."

"Exactly what I told the old woman. Don't get me wrong, I love Esmerelda. She's great with the kids and helping us out, but a little privacy goes a long way."

"Truth."

"And then the damn woman had the nerve to yell at us that we should save that for the bedroom when it's my fucking house." His volume increases with every word until he gets it under control.

"How old are you kids now?"

"My son, Tony, is fourteen, and his sister, Bella, is ten." He takes a breath and looks at me. "That's another reason we moved too. Tony hated it there, and the guys he went to school with were leading him down a bad path. The big city gave him too many opportunities to find shit to get into."

I nod. Gabe seems like a man who would be heavily involved in his kids' lives. As a policeman, he sees too much that can go sideways quickly. When it comes to his kids, I bet he helicopters over them.

He took the bench next to me, finishing his gear. "Now, Bella, let's just say she *is* going to be the death of me. She's ten but thinks she's twenty. I'm thankful for her involvement with sports and clubs."

"Yes, those usually help keep them tied down with all the coaches' expectations," I say as I stand and get my hat. I'm not a fan of wearing it, but the sergeant insists we keep it with us. It only adds to the heat.

The two of us walk out to our cars. We don't work with partners in our small town, but at least four of us are on every shift for backup.

"I guess with your kids around makes privacy hard to come by. Hope they don't catch y'all in the same positions as your mother-in-law did."

"Oh, hell no. We bought a place with separate bedrooms and put two locks on the door. Esme got her wish since we confine our sex life to the bedroom now. Can't be too careful with kids and their friends always coming and going. Seems like we always have someone extra in our house these days."

This makes me laugh again, and my mind goes to Allison. She lived through that with hers. At least now she knows when they're coming home. We hadn't had kitchen sex yet, but the mood might strike us at some point.

I love that she has an adventurous nature. After that first night, I knew we were going to be having lots of carefree sex. After listening to Gabe, I'm happy her kids are off at college until Christmas break.

"An ice skating rink opens in the town square in a few weeks," Allison announces as I walk into the kitchen. "Do you like to ice skate?"

"Hmm, let's just say I'm not a figure skater. Now, give me some ice hockey skates, and I can go to town. I played on an intermural team in college. We kicked some ass."

Allison turns from her laptop and stares at me. "Guess you liked hitting other people with sticks? It's a very aggressive sport from what I can tell."

Her words and the look on her face cause me to laugh so hard.

"Sure is." I come around behind her, wrap my arms around her, and kiss and nip down her neck to her shoulder. "Kinda like the type of sex I'm thinking of right now."

I spin her around on the barstool to face me. She raises her eyebrows, scrunching up her forehead. "Been thinking about this all day?"

"I didn't get to see you yesterday." My fingers begin undoing her blouse while my lips suck just below her ear. "So yes, I have been thinking about kissing my way up those tasty thighs to get to the promised land."

When the suction gets strong enough to leave a mark, she pulls away, giggling. "You can't do that. I'm too old for a hickey."

She tries to push me away, but I hold onto her with one hand while I finish the buttons with the other.

Sliding the light blue cotton off her shoulder leaves her sitting in a nude bralette. Damn, she looks good enough to eat. The smooth skin she douses nightly with vanilla and lavender still carries the fragrance.

"God, Allison, if only I could mark you everywhere it could be seen. Other men need to know you're off-limits. Keep their fucking hands to themselves."

Her naturally plump lips find mine, and she takes command of a scorching kiss that adds to my desire to take her. Never has a woman held this kind of power over me, but I love every minute I spend with her.

She stays on my mind all the time. Thinking about her is my favorite pastime when I work traffic control or any other downtime I might get.

Her legs open wider, inviting me to move close to her. When I rub my hard length against her soft running shorts, she rewards me with a sexy growl that sets my blood flowing south. This woman keeps me hard all the time with the sounds she makes in response to my touches.

"As much as I love these silky shorts, I like them better off, sugar." My hands slide down her bare sides until I reach the stretchy waistband.

Just as I loop my fingers into it, I hear the back door pop open.

"Yoohoo. Hope everyone's still got their clothes on," Beth yells from the door. No doubt she saw my truck in the driveway.

Damn her timing. I sympathize with Gabe. Beth is as bad as having teenagers in the house.

I step back as Allison quickly buttons her shirt. She finishes the first three before her sister walks through the kitchen door. It's a good thing the back door opens to the laundry room.

"You two up to anything interesting?" she brazenly says with a smirk.

Leaning against the bar to keep my hard-on covered, Allison and I both offer Beth a smile. We know we've been busted, but oh well. My truck should have prompted Beth to keep on going. So much for our privacy.

"Not so much now," Allison says to her annoying sister.

"Well, I'm about to leave anyway. I thought you wanted to go to the sporting goods store for some new running shoes."

"Oh, right," Allison starts. "I forgot you wanted us to go look at the ones on sale. I do need some, but I doubt I need to go now."

"I can come back later?" Beth offers.

"No, I'd rather go alone so I don't have to look at clothes *and* sandals *and* jeans." She looks at me. "This woman gets carried away when it comes to shopping."

Beth eyes me closely. "Yeah, I bet the sporting goods store is one of your favorite places to shop."

Allison jumps in, "Really, I don't have to go. Let's get a glass of wine and sit by the pool. It's not too hot this evening."

I kiss my girl goodbye and head out the door. Beth's cockblocking skills are A+ these days.

Allison

"So, what's up?" I ask, walking out the back door to the pool area. We sit on the lounge chairs in the shade with the sparkles from the sun blinking from the blue water.

"Hadn't talked to you in a while. You seem to always be occupied these days." Beth stares at me over the rim of her glass, expecting a reply.

She's right, though. Ian and I have been almost inseparable since we got together. I should feel ashamed, but I'm not. The hours we spend together keep me going until the next time.

"You know how it is," I start. "I get busy on projects and stuff and zero in on one thing."

"Is that right? Hmm, does *stuff* include the smokin' hot policeman who shows up at dark but is always gone in the morning when I get up?"

Busted. I knew nothing would get by her. There is no use hiding anything from my sister, especially since she lives so close now.

"You're right," I nod. "Ian and I spend a lot of time together, but we haven't taken it public yet."

I turn to look at her, wanting to gauge her reaction. "That's going to change, though. Neither one of us want to hide being together."

"Does this mean you two are *in love?*" Her words sound cartoonish, making me laugh.

"What? No. No one said anything about being in love, Beth. We're having fun and enjoying spending time together. We both like to do the same things. That's all."

"Those same things include knocking boots? You know I prefer juicy details."

My laugh rings out on the verge of hysteria. I pick

up the magazine on the table between us and thumb through it for no reason other than not facing Beth as I lie.

"No juicy details here."

"Riiight. Oh, sister, those of us who've been around the block a few times know the look, and you, my dear, have that recently-fucked look written all over you."

Whipping back to face her, "I most certainly do not. Why would you say such a thing?"

"Because one, you look over-the-top happy, and two, I need to live vicariously through you. So, maybe I'm putting my need onto your reality."

I move around on the recliner, adjusting the back to waste some time before I answer. "When you put it that way, I will confess some hot sex has been going on."

Beth leans over, "How hot are we talking? Say on a scale of one to ten?" Her eyebrows wiggle up and down, making me giggle. "Oh, giggling like a teenager. It must be some Chris Hemsworth-worthy heat."

"Well, I'd have to say a ten each time. He knows things." I end with a smirk.

"Things? Do tell." She leans on my every word. Why does she want me to say these things aloud?

"Nooo. I'm not going into details about what we do in private."

"Oh now, come on, Ali. I'd share with you."

"I am *not* sharing with you. That's just wrong."

"The hell it is. I bet your story would beat watching porn any day if you were willing to get down to the nitty-gritty."

"Nope. Not getting down to any of it. Let's just say Ian knows his way around the female anatomy on a ten basis."

"Yeah, yeah. But does his sex pistol equal his shoe size? Because I noticed they're like LeBron James big. I read LeBron is a size fourteen shoe."

I almost roll out of my chair with laughter. My sister uses some of the most ridiculous comparisons.

"Again, not discussing my sex life. Besides, you shouldn't believe everything you read. They might be bigger than reported."

"*Bigger*?" She practically squeals.

"What? I didn't say it was bigger. I just said..." I end it there. Better to keep her guessing. Beth can get super nosy, so I won't be shocked if she comes out and asks him after enough glasses of Pino.

"Anyway, we've decided to start going out on dates."

"Dating? You know, that's where most people start and then work up to the split-the-sheet action, right? Seems like y'all jumped the gun."

"What's with you and all the police-type euphemisms? Anyway, we've seen each other several times. Just not out in public."

"Why the secrecy? You're both too damn old to be sneaking around."

"We were never sneaking. We wanted to take it slow in case it didn't work out. The people in town will no doubt be wondering what's going on. It's barely been two years now since..." I let my words fade off.

My hand is surrounded by Beth's. "Listen, Ali. You've been through too much shit to let the gossips rule anything you do in life. Fuck them. You need to live the life you want to live."

"I know, but I want to talk to the kids about it first. I want to be the one to tell them we're dating." I look out at the glitters coming off the blue water. "What Jacks and Junie think does matter to me and Ian. He knows they are important to me."

"Yes, they are, Ali, but you can't hold off on your life forever for your kids. They want you to be happy."

"How do you know this?" My eyes turn to her. "What if they aren't ready?"

"They're ready. We've talked about it."

Not sure how I feel about them talking about me behind my back, I put my feet on the ground between us. "What do you mean you've talked about it?"

"They've come over a few times when they've been home for a weekend. Both of them asked me if I thought you were ready to move on or if you were happy as things are."

"And what did you tell them?" With my hackles already raised over this information, I take a deep breath, preparing for her answer.

"The first time Jacks asked, I told him I didn't think you were ready." Her words are spoken in earnest. "Honestly, I didn't think you were back then. It had only been about six months."

"*Six months*? That was way too soon. I had to tread water to keep from drowning at that point." I think back to what six months out looked like. My heart hadn't started to mend at all. My head felt like a balloon skipping along, looking for a place to settle.

"And that's what I told them. Junie asked a little later than Jacks. They both said they hoped that when the time came, you'd go for it. You'd do something to make yourself happy. They realize you're too young to be alone the rest of your life."

"Well... that's good to know." I take her hand back in mine. "Thank you for being there for them. I've tried hard to be strong for them, offering them a safe place to talk."

"Yes, they know that, sis, but they also know you are dealing with the same feelings they are. They don't want to make life harder on you by putting their grief on your shoulders to deal with."

"But I'm their mom. I should have seen their struggles."

"Not if they didn't want you to. Ali, they're adults and need to know you're going to be okay."

Leaning forward, I pull my sister in for a strong hug. "You're the best, Beth. Thank you so much for being here for all of us. I love you."

After the hug and some tears, we let go and take big gulps of our wine, allowing all the emotions to sink in.

"You know, if you really wanted to thank me, you'd give me a play-by-play of hiding the pickle."

"Oh my God, *Beth*." My empty plastic wine glass sails across the chair toward her head. I bust out laughing when she bats it away. Gotta love your sister.

Ian

Two of us in our separate police cars drive to a scene on Highway 71. By the time we arrive to assist, the excitement is over. One actor sits in the back of a cruiser while the other stands bent over the trunk of another as Jennifer, the officer on the scene, snaps the handcuffs shut.

We don't get much action out here, so far from the big city, but it happens. I get out of my car and approach my coworker, who arrives when I do.

"Hey, what's going on?" Sean asks.

"Seems like they got their suspect in the car already. Think it was a road rage situation gone bad."

He looks on as Jennifer puts the suspect in the car.

"Yeah, I've been seeing this too often. People need to chill the fuck out when they're driving, especially this late at night."

"Makes for a helluva week after this happens over and over. Don't know about you, but I'm getting tired of waiting for one to pull a weapon on the other," I add.

"Truth. Last week, I came on a scene with a woman trying to use a two-by-four on the dude's truck. She should be happy I showed when I did. He was twice her size and could have easily taken her."

"You're kidding me? A woman and a two-by-four? Did he hit her car or something?"

"Hell no. Turned out to be a domestic dispute. She caught him with another woman. He took off when she threatened to kill the new chick. He said he wanted to get the wife away from the girlfriend, but the wife had other ideas. Crazy woman wanted to hurt him worse.

"She followed his sorry ass, but when he stopped to talk, she pulled the board and started in on his truck. Managed to get his taillights before I pulled up. I got lucky. My lights and siren got her attention, so she stopped and sat down crying." He grinned at me.

"Oh yeah, I love it when they get all remorseful. Even though they know it's wrong, they let their dumbasses get the best of them."

"Yeah, but he should have thought about it when he cheated. Get a damn divorce if you want to wander is always my advice. Looks like something similar going on here, without the two-by-four." Sean shakes his head as Jennifer walks up to us.

"Hi, guys. Here to join the fun and games?" she asks.

"Don't look too fun if you're the one in the car," I respond.

"Won't last. He's already begging her for forgiveness. She'll take him back. I can't understand why women do that." She shakes her head. "If he hit me, he'd know better than to chase me. It would be a beat down when he caught up to me."

"Just like I said, get a divorce and be done with them before someone goes to jail," Sean reiterates.

I eye him carefully. He's a little older than me, and I wonder what he's been through. "You sound like you know this from experience."

Without missing a beat, Sean says, "Sure do, and you'll never get me to marry again. Once was enough for me."

"Oh yeah? Been divorced long?" Jennifer asks with an eye on him. She's young and has only been on our force for two years. I don't know her very well.

"About five years. I prefer my own company most of the time. Too much effort and too much drama when it comes to relationships."

His bitterness makes me think about how I never want to find myself. Allison and I have something special already. Spending every off day with her gives me something to look forward to. If it were up to me, we would be together every day and night.

I've been single long enough. Even with the few short months together, I know we both want more. We're not two kids jumping into a relationship unaware. We don't need this couple of years shit to see if it's going to work.

Looking at Sean, I shake my head. That could have been me if Allison hadn't come along. I had to wait for her to find her way, but she is worth it.

I get a call from dispatch and leave this scene for one with vandals writing on a wall in the downtown area. The perpetrators have gone before I arrive, so I park and stick around to see if they might return to finish.

The conversation with Sean lingers in my mind. Will Allison feel that way too? Not wanting to remarry? Did her last few years of hell make her bitter toward a permanent relationship? Damn, I hope not.

We need to talk about this to decide whether we're on the same page with relationships. I'm more than willing to put in the time to make it work. What if she's not in it for the long haul? Am I simply someone helping her to find her feet again after her husband's death?

"This is stupid." My words echo around the quiet car. Getting out of my head, I reach for my phone to text her.

Me: *Sleeping?*
Ali: *No. Are you working?*
Me: *For a few more hours.*
Ali: *You've never messaged me while at work. Are you allowed?*
Me: *They frown on phone calls unless it's an emergency. Text, not so much.*
Ali: *Okay. Been busy tonight?*
Me: *In my town? :)*
Me: *Wish I was with you instead.*
Ali: *Of course, me too.*
Me: *Want me to come to you when I get off.*
Ali: *Get off? I like the sound of that.*
Me: *Why Allison are you trying your dirty bedroom words for me?*
Ali: *Maybe...*
Me: *I like it. I'll be there at four and you can use them on me for real.*
Ali: *I'll be waiting.*
Me: *Tease.*
Ali: *Me? Never.*

I put my phone aside and shine my lights on the area below the tagging. A shaggy dog moves out of the alley and turns down the sidewalk like he's on a mission. At least someone knows where they are going tonight.

Dispatch broadcasts suspicious activity, so I take off to the new location.

The garage light shines over Allison's driveway, illuminating the entire side area of her house. Her safety is important to me, so I installed it a month or so ago. The only drawback is the neighbors know when I arrive.

I don't care, but it bothers her that others will think badly of her. I want her to get past the guilt of moving on. The time we spend together makes us both happy. Nosy neighbors need to see this.

Opening her back door with the key she gave me, I slip across the kitchen area and head down to her bedroom. She sits up, waiting for me.

"Sorry, I tried not to wake you, sugar."

"I heard you pull in the driveway." She crooks her finger in my direction. "I've been waiting for you."

The covers drop, and her sweet tits expose themselves—pebbled tips offering an invitation.

"You have? You think you're gonna get lucky or something?" I taunt, wiggling my brow, as I strip off the clothes I changed into after showering at the station.

"I feel like you're the lucky one here." She throws back the covers to reveal the rest of her naked body. *Well, fuck. It's on.*

With no time to waste, I strip off my boxer briefs— no reason to put off the inevitable. Making my way over the top of her, I take her lips with a hard kiss that I've been looking forward to since I left her. Her tongue slides along mine in a series of twists and turns that set me on fire.

This woman knows exactly what to do to make me want her. Warm arms and legs wrap around me, pulling our bodies closer together. The feel of her exposed body against mine, its softness caressing my hardness does things to my mind. I want to get lost in her curves. Touch every inch of skin.

Stopping to pay homage to her luscious breast, I leisurely kiss my way down to the soft skin on the underside of each one. My teeth and tongue can't help themselves, wanting to leave my mark on the supple skin. Every inch calls to me to claim it.

My hands wrap around Allison's hips, flipping her over to allow my lips to kiss the natural curve of her back. Then I return to her slight shoulders, wanting to start at the top. I don't want to miss any part of her.

I run my hands down her arms inch by inch— across the toned muscles and her forearms—until I find her hands to link our fingers, my palms covering the backs of her hands. The contact this move makes causes my dick to harden even more and earns deep moans from her.

My lips dot kisses line a path down her back while I slide our hands over the silky sheets, the friction adding to her pleasure. I let go so I can put my hands to better use on her fine ass. The alabaster skin plumps under my squeezes as she arches, seeking more.

As with her perfect breasts, I can't resist biting and kissing the softness that begs for attention.

"God, what are you doing to me, Ian?" Allison ekes out on an unsure breath.

"Admiring the shape made for squeezing and leaving evidence that this flawless ass has been thoroughly worshiped." I bite down and suck in the soft flesh until I know a sweet spot has been claimed. "This Athena body of yours rivals all those Roman statues, sugar. If we lived in those times, someone would have surely made one of you."

"Why, Ian. Such a romantic," she says, looking over her shoulder at me.

"Only where you're concerned. And besides, it's the truth. Your ass is worth declaring mine."

"The world might think differently."

"Who cares what the world thinks? It's just you and me, sugar. You and me." My lips close over a soft patch of skin, nipping.

Smiling to myself, I know she'll see the mark in the mirror when she takes a bath and be reminded of how hot I am for her body. Not just some tasty locations, but all.

I spread her legs so I can move between them. My fingers slide over her rosebud on their way to feel just how ready for me she is.

"Oh no, not going there," she rises on her elbows,

looking back.

"Not tonight, anyway." The smirk I give her says *maybe later.*

"Not tonight or ever."

"We'll put that on the back burner for now," I say, not wanting to spoil the mood.

"Righ—" Her word cuts off abruptly as I push two fingers inside, just the way she likes it.

It gives me easy access to the front wall of her channel when I flip my fingers over. Now that I've found what pleasure it gives her, I want to send her over the top at least once every time we're together.

This time is no different. I barely push and then swipe across the internal flesh as her entire body seizes up. The sounds I pull from her amaze me, balanced between a cry and a moan.

I glance down to watch her toes curl and know she's coming down from the intensity of the orgasm, making her even more sensitive to my touch.

When I sit back on my calves, I lift her hips and rub my hard cock along her slit. I want to give her a moment to know that the next orgasm happens from a more intimate connection—the pleasure we share.

"Ian," Allison calls out as I enter her. It's not a position we've tried, but my sugar is always game for new things. "What are we doing?"

Her pillow muffles her words before she moves it to lay flat on the bed.

"Don't like it?" I ask as I start moving more.

"Yes, I love it, but it's different. Hits different places."

"Great. I want to fucking hit all the right areas." I sit up some to grind into her further, which earns me moans and words I can't understand.

"Oh my God. Harder. Just like that."

My body pushes faster and deeper, and the movements make me growl each time. "This is going to make me come faster than usual. Are you almost there, sugar? I'm not sure I can hold off."

"Yes, yes, yes!" Her screaming gets louder and more forceful with each word. "Do it!"

My balls draw up after the tingling drops down my spine. I know this time is going to be hard and heavy, so I reach around and circle her swollen clit, setting off clenching in her walls.

"Fuck, sugar. That's it. Fuck." She milks me for all I'm worth as one rope after another spills inside her. Sensations I've never felt before make my body want to continue fucking her with slower thrusts. It feels too damn good to stop, but I know we're both worn down to nothing.

We both fight to capture air in our lungs since we spent what oxygen we had with our cries and moans of pleasure.

We roll together as I pull out of her. She shakes from my withdrawal over her sensitive flesh, so I tighten my hold and wrap her up in my arms.

I'll gladly share my body heat and offer her my

strength when she needs me. The need and desire I've developed for this woman is deep, and something I never thought I'd feel.

The question is, does she feel the same about me?

Chapter 22

Allison

Waking up wrapped in strong arms gives me a sense of safety. After sleeping alone for the past couple of years, I want to bask in the comfort of having Ian beside me before I face the world.

He's scheduled for a three-day weekend this week. I want him to rest. He works weird hours and not always on consecutive days, so I know his body stays in a constant state of upheaval.

"You know I can hear your brain already scheming when we're this close," he whispers, his sleepy voice gravely and sexy. But after last night, I'm not ready for another round yet. Our sexcapades are wearing me out.

"Sorry, I wanted to lay here as long as possible to

simply enjoy being beside you. You're always so warm, and you smell all manly."

"Manly, huh?"

"I love that citric and... something else fragrance. Not sure what it is."

"That other stuff is bergamot. I like the way it smells, and it's in a lot of men's cologne now. The Dior one is my favorite."

"That's what you're wearing now?"

"Yeah, you like it too?" I feel him turn his head to me.

"I love it."

That earns me a squeeze.

"Good. It's a little pricey, but I don't wear it all the time."

I tuck that knowledge away for a gift idea.

"What's on the agenda for today?" I don't expect him to spend all of his free time with me, but I can hope.

"I don't care. No plans on my calendar. What would you like to do? Got things around here that need to be done?"

"That's the last thing I want you to spend your off days doing." I roll over and put my chin on his chest. "Let's do something fun. Maybe go somewhere."

Then I remember he's been working and probably wants to hang out at his home. "Do you want to go to your place? If you have some things you need to take care of, I don't want to stop you."

"No, I want to spend my time with you. What's something you want to do?"

I roll over because I don't want to look at him as I say this. "I was thinking..."

"Uh-oh. Not sure I like the start of this." The humor in his voice tells me he is teasing. His arm comes across my chest, and he pulls me tighter.

"I've been thinking for a while that we might want to go see the kids and let them know we've become more than just friends. How do you feel about that?

"I'm not trying to get ahead of myself here. I mean... if you feel that way too? We haven't talked about us. Not that I'm expecting us to add a label to what we're doing. They need to know that we are... doing something, so they're not blindsided when they come home." My words tumble out. I hope I'm not scaring him.

"I think that's a good idea. When they come home, I want to be here with you. I never want them to think I'm trying to take their dad's place or anything like that. But I want them to know we have feelings for each other."

"Feelings?" My voice sounds shaky to me, so I can imagine what he's thinking.

"Yes, Allison, feelings." He sits up. I think all of our discussions happen this way—in bed and naked. Talk about the raw truth.

"Allison, our time together makes me only want more. I look forward to getting off work because I know you'll be here. My off days are for us. Where I live is temporary, just a place to bathe and sleep.

"Your house is a home. I don't think I've had a home since I left my parents' place years ago. Never really wanted one if I didn't have someone to share it with."

Wow. He laid it all out there. I'm not sure how I feel about this.

"Did I scare you? The look on your face says I did."

My eyes trace his face to stare into his deep blues. "No, not scared of us. More like scared of what my kids are going to say."

"I also care about that. Not like your neighbors. Who gives a shit about them? But your family, Jackson, Junie, and Beth... even your parents. I care what they think of me and us."

"Then we need to tell them. Beth knows, of course, with her living so close."

"What have you told her?"

"I didn't have to tell her anything. She has come in when you're here, remember? I swear my sister has some kind of sex radar or something." We both laugh, but it's the truth.

"Oh yeah? Maybe we should give her some more ammunition." He pulls me to him, kissing me hard.

"No, I need a shower."

"Perfect idea. Shower sex. I like it," he says, dragging me across the bed and throwing me over his shoulder. The nosy neighbors can hear my laughter, but I don't care right now. I have a view of the perfect ass.

Our shower lasts long enough for three, with all the other moves going on under the water from above. Ian makes it even hotter when he turns me and puts my hands against the glass wall, all while thrusting inside me.

We move to the bedroom to dress but hear soft talking from the family room. Looking at me, Ian moves to the door, leaning in to listen.

A loud knock on the door startles him.

"Hey, you two. If you're through in there, we came to visit," Jackson calls. "But if you're too busy, we can go down to Aunt Beth's until you're done."

"Oh my God!" I mouth at Ian. He does all he can to keep from laughing before he returns to the bathroom and snickers lightly.

"Uh, well, Jacks," I stammer. "Be right out. Just, uh, finishing up. I mean, cleaning up a mess... no, uh, taking care of a problem. Shit. Just go sit down. We'll be out."

The cackles echo from the other side of the bedroom door as Jackson returns to the family room, louder than I've heard from him in forever.

"What are we going to do?" I look at Ian, who's still bent over laughing. "This is sooo not funny."

He pulls me into a tight embrace. "Yes, it is Allison. Laugh. You know it's funny. How many kids' brains are completely damaged from hearing their parents having sex?"

My eyes cut to him. "But you're not his parent."

Ian walks to me, taking my hands in his. "I wasn't trying to make it sound like I was his dad, Allison. That's something I'll never do to your kids."

I feel like a total bitch. I know he didn't mean it that way. My feelings rest on my shoulders when it comes to the kids.

"I'm sorry. I know you were trying to make light of their intrusion. It just hit me wrong." I slide my hands up his arms and around his muscular neck, kissing him on the cheek to ease my accusation.

"It's okay, I get it. Now let's dress and go have a laugh at our expense with them."

"Probably a good idea to add clothes. I seriously doubt they'd like seeing either of us naked or in underwear." I grin, and he returns it. How did I get so lucky to find a man who understands my life?

Ian opens the door, waving me through first. I guess he wants me to see Jackson and Junie first to judge for myself how they are taking this news. It's not like I can say we're dating casually because they know better now. I'm not sure exactly what to say about us.

I walk straight to Jackson, who sits closer than his sister, and wrap my arms around him. After kissing his cheek, I back off to look at him. "You look good, honey. School not stressing you out too badly?"

"No, I have a good schedule this year. Seniors get

first choice of classes, so we get the best times to attend and the best profs."

He's so sure of himself now, unlike the first year he went. His junior year wasn't easy on him either. Both kids had to find their way through losing their dad at the beginning. But they pulled it off, better than I made it through the most horrible school year.

Junie stands back, so I have to approach her. She seems reluctant to hug me when I pull her into me. How they found Ian and me must affect her more than Jackson. Knowing this, I hold her close with tears burning the back of my eyes.

I wanted to break it to them differently, but it can't be helped now. They know. We might as well address the situation first thing.

I move to stand by Ian, and his hand brushes the back of mine. He's as unsure how to start this as I am.

"So, do y'all remember Officer Windsor, Ian Windsor? Ian, this is Jackson and Junie, my children. Well, they are definitely not children anymore, but they'll always be mine. They've been away at university. It looks like they decided to come home to surprise me."

"Okay, Mom, you can stop now," Jackson says, offering his hand to Ian.

"Sorry, was I rambling?" My cheeks feel a little warm. Why am I embarrassed?

"More like word vomiting."

We all look at Junie, who stands there looking lost.

"Junie?" I question. She finally steps forward and shakes Ian's hand.

"Hello, Junie," Ian says with a soft smile.

The stare she gives him makes me wonder what's going on in her mind. Is she angry? Surprised? Shocked? All three, maybe? All the emotions are possibilities from the face she's making.

She finally finds her words, but they only shock me.

"So, how long have you two been sleeping together?" she asks.

Wow, just wow. I wasn't ready to jump into our love life quite this way.

"Junie!" Jackson sternly calls to her. "What the hell?"

"What the hell is right. We come home to visit only to catch the two of them romping in the bedroom."

"Yeah, well, last time I checked, Mom is a grown-ass woman and can do whatever the hell she wants in her home. She doesn't snoop around your house waiting to see what kind of douche you drag home."

Ian and I watch them like it's a live soap opera.

"She doesn't have to. She's too busy getting it on with the friendly cop who couldn't stop coming to the hospital. No, he had to show up at the funeral and then at the house afterward."

"Junie, that's enough." I can't watch this for another second.

"Wait a minute. Was this going on before Dad died? When did you really meet *Officer Ian*?" Her condescending tone makes me sick, even though we've done nothing wrong. If she's trying to make me feel guilty, she's doing a great job.

"You're acting like a child, sis," Jackson jumps in to defend me or us. "It's been two long years now. I can guarantee you they weren't hooking up when Dad was alive. I can't believe you'd even accuse her of something like that."

"You can't know that for sure. For all we know, they might have been having an affair for years."

"That's bullshit, and you know it. You think Ian was standing on the side of the road waiting for them to have a wreck so he could rescue Mom? That's absurd."

"Maybe not, but it's sure convenient that he shows up now, isn't it?" She turns to Ian. "How long has this been going on, Ian?"

I answer for him. This is not his problem, even if my daughter seems certain it is. "First of all, Junie Len Waller, what I do with my private time is none of your business. I am a grown woman, and if I want to entertain Ian, I can. And *without* your permission."

"You're right, but I don't have to stand by and watch it." She turns to leave, but Jackson stops her.

"Junie, we've talked about this. We both decided we wanted Mom to move on with her life. She's too young to be alone."

Junie throws her arms around her brother's neck and sobs. "I know that, but I never expected her to go looking for another man this soon."

"What difference does it make? If she feels ready, then we need to respect that. It's not our decision," he says, pulling her in tight for another hug.

Junie holds on in her brother's arms for a few minutes while Ian and I wait to see what happens. She lets him go and turns to face us.

"I'm sorry to both of you. When we walked into the... uh... sounds from the bedroom, it took me totally by surprise. I mean, we knew someone was here because of the truck, but I wasn't prepared for hearing that."

Jackson pipes in, "Yeah, the last thing you want to hear are two old people going at it."

Ian and I bust out laughing, and my face blushes a fiery shade of red I couldn't get rid of if I tried.

"Old people? We are not old," I scold, gesturing between Ian and myself. We're not even mid-life, I'll have you know."

"Okay, okay, maybe not *old-old* but definitely still some weird shit to stumble on, Mom," he says.

Ian, who has been silent this entire time, jumps into the conversation. "I guess I can handle 'not old-old.' "

"Good because I don't know what else to label it."

"How about we agree not to talk about *it*..." Junie points to the bedroom, "... ever again."

"Come on." I laugh. "I'll make something to eat. We can talk about lots of other things. Like, who you are dragging back to your apartment..."

I glance at Junie, who thinks I'm joking, and wink.

Chapter 23

Allison

Having the kids home made for the best weekend. It isn't exactly what Ian and I planned, but I was happy to have him be around the kids. They both want to do nothing but float in the pool, drinking frozen fruity drinks, and Ian seems happy enough to play bartender.

With Junie still being underage, I fear he will balk at serving her, but he explains that, technically, when she is with her parent, it isn't illegal in Texas. I never realized that. He adds that most businesses won't allow it, but we are in our backyard.

Junie and I lounge on the funny flamingo float I bought in the spring. It's big enough for two or three people. We both enjoy talking about what I've been doing, other than Ian.

I want to ask her about the guys at school, but I save it for later. The last thing I want to do now that we've all calmed down is bring up a topic that will end in an argument. From Jackson's comment, I'm afraid it will.

"Anything exciting I should know about?" I watch as she stares up and to the left. I know it's her thinking spot, having seen it often enough.

"Actually, yes. I meant to tell you the trip to Europe is off. Most of the other parents felt the same as you did." She looks over at me. "Did y'all do a Zoom meeting about the trip?"

"What? No. I don't even know who you were going with."

"It seemed funny to all of us that our parents were against it. Even the guy going got a big no from his."

"I did not talk to other parents because I wanted you to come to the conclusion on your own. You don't know how happy it makes me that everyone isn't going so I don't have to be the bad guy."

"Just know, at some point, I am going to leave the country and explore the world, Mom. I want to see what's out there on my own." She closes her eyes, ending the conversation.

I realize it's coming. She wants to be an adult and have all the freedom. It was bad enough when she moved into her own apartment for this year, which scared me. The dorm seemed much safer—even if it was a coed dorm.

"So, Mom, you really like this guy?"

I look over where Ian and Jackson discuss college baseball. "Yeah, baby, I do."

"Does he treat you like a queen?" She stares at me, trying to see if my reaction tells a different story.

"He sure does. Not just that, but he's kind and considerate of my feelings. He's always trying to be helpful not just to me but to other people. You should see the list your Aunt Beth comes up with for him to do at her house."

We laugh. Since Beth is only a few houses down, she always has something one of us needs to help her with.

"Yeah, Jacks and I talk about hiding the car in the garage when we come home so we don't spend all day Saturday working for her."

I pelt her with the heated water from the pool. The house is far enough south that the pool can be used nine or ten months of the year, but the season is almost over.

"Why'd you do that?" She giggles. "It's the truth."

"I don't care. She's your aunt and has been a godsend for me since the wreck. She took on a huge job of getting me to a new normal."

Junie looks at the guys. "Yeah, I guess."

"You and your brother might have had a new roommate without her, so be damn glad she's here."

"Right, but I'm not through asking about Ian."

"Okay. I will be honest with you. Just ask me."

"Did you really not at least know him before Dad died?"

"No, honey, I did not know him. The first time I saw him was when he pulled me from the car. You know he went back to help your dad after getting me out?"

"Really?"

"Yeah, he told me later. He knew Kellen was gone already from the way his eyes looked. I remember seeing your dad's eyes before I was taken out. He was gone, honey. I think I knew it too."

"But Ian tried to help him?"

"Yes, he went back to the driver's side and broke out the side window to get to him. He felt for a pulse and knew it was too late."

Tears stream down Junie's face, and she quickly wipes them away. "Sorry, I wasn't trying to bring up sad things."

"It's okay." My hand finds hers, and I clutch it hard. "If you need to know all the details to move past it, then I'm here to discuss them."

"What else did Ian tell you about it?" She keeps glancing back at the two sitting on the side.

"Hmmm, let's see. He cares about people more than just being a cop. Like him coming to see me in the hospital. He told me he does that often, especially when families are involved."

"Why? That seems over the top to me."

"He likes to know they are okay. He said it made

him happy to see our family rallying around me. I don't know much about his family, but I get the feeling it wasn't always that way for him."

"Oh. So, he wants more family involvement?"

"Seems that way and look what he got with me. Two nosy little shits who show up unannounced." We both laugh out loud, causing the guys to turn and look at us.

"Should we come out there and monitor you two?" Jackson asks.

"No, we're good. Just talking about your love life or, actually, lack of one," Junie says.

Jackson picks up the football and throws it short to spray water on his sister.

Sputtering, Junie yells, "Sorry, but truth."

My daughter turns back to me with a look that says she has more questions.

"What is it, honey?"

"No, I don't want to ask you."

"I said you can ask me anything. Let's hear it." I want there to be honesty between us.

"I mean, is it weird? You know, after being with Dad for so long? Is it different being with another man?"

My spit sticks at the knot in my throat. I wasn't expecting this kind of question from my daughter. My eyes focus on the beak of our huge pink friend.

"It was very strange at first." I choose my words carefully. "I mean, I'd only ever been with your dad, so

I tried to prepare myself for different. But Ian is such a gentle, sweet man. He knew my history because we talked about it. So, his patience was unending."

"Good."

My eyes cut to her. I struggle to voice every damn word to explain, and all I get is 'good.'

"That's it? Good?" The pitch of my voice goes up an octave.

"Mom, it's not like I'm going to ask for details. The last thing I want to know is how he is in the sack. Keep that to yourself." She grins before pausing, eyes wide. "Wait a minute. I bet Aunt Beth asked for every juice tidbit, didn't she?"

The blush moves from my neck to my face.

"*She did!*" Junie almost yells the words.

"Hush. Now they're going to want to know what we're talking about."

Junie lays back and cackles, so I take the opportunity to roll her into the cool water. She goes under, splashing, not expecting me to retaliate. Before she can take revenge, Beth walks out the back door.

Notorious for not thinking before she speaks, my imagination runs wild with what's about to transpire. Junie is almost as bad. Between the two of them, this could be a wild ride for Ian and me.

"What the hell. Everybody is having fun without me.?" she yells across the backyard so that even the neighbors can hear.

Jackson grabs her for a tight hug, swinging her in a

circle before releasing her. "How's it going, Aunt Beth?"

Ian stands next in line to greet her with a cheek kiss. "Where's your swimsuit? You know that pink bird is big enough for three."

"What kind of crazy ass bitches do you mistake us for with all three of us on that bird? It's liable to bust and sink. Too much greatness weighing it down." Her laughter sucks us all in.

Instead of getting her suit, she perches on the barstool under the umbrella to join the guys at the table.

"Who made the girly drinks, and what's in them?"

"I made them," Ian says, picking up another tall glass to pour her one. "It's rum punch with a little of this and that added."

"Ohhh, I like some of this and that." Her eyebrows wiggle suggestively. "Better pour mine full since I've not had any in a long time."

Ian shakes his head, and Jackson turns and looks to see my reaction. What can I say? What am I supposed to do about it? I shrug.

"Hey, Aunt Beth," Junie calls. "Mom and I are telling some 'this and that' stories out here. Go change and join us."

"Junie!" I try to sound like I'm scolding her, but it's useless now.

"Hot damn, put mine back in the cooler. I gotta run home and change." She hops off the stool and takes off through the gate.

"Look what you started." I turn to Junie again. "She'll ask a million more questions."

"I don't want questions. I want descriptions. Oh, wait. That's too weird. No, you're right. No questions."

"Thank God!"

In no time, Beth prances through the gate in her new two-piece, showing a tight midriff. She looks great and doesn't mind wearing it out. This woman needs a male friend, but after the last breakup, she's gun-shy.

A big splash sends water all over Junie and me before Beth surfaces to swim to the shallow end for her cocktail. The reddish punch sloshes over the side of our big bird.

"Hey, you'll get Sandy all sticky from that," I inform my sister.

"Sandy? What kind of name is that for a flamingo?"

"You know, from *Grease*, the Pink Ladies." Junie gives her aunt an indignant look. "Come on, how many times did we watch that movie, Aunt Beth?"

"I'd have voted for Rizzo," Beth says as she takes a big drink.

"Figures," I comment under my breath, joining her with a gulp of my own. Junie laughs.

Climbing up to join us, Beth rolls over on her back, propping her head on the wing. "So, what'd I miss?"

"Nothing." I jump in quickly. "Nothing important anyway."

"Yeah, Mom was just telling me the bare necessities of her and Ian getting it on. Because, you know, Jacks and I had to sit in the family room and listen to them go at it in the shower. By the way, *Mom*, how is shower sex?"

Rum punch covers Sandy when I spit it out of my mouth. "I cannot believe you just ask me that, Junie."

"Hey, you said I could ask you anything, and you'd answer me honestly." She cocks one eyebrow.

"And I told you there would be no details."

"Let me tell you about shower sex, dear girl." Beth grins.

"I'd rather you not," I throw out there, knowing good and well Beth won't let it go.

"When you're young like you and Jackson, shower sex is hot. But when you get our age, the body isn't as limber as it used to be, so it's a little harder to achieve... the best part." She turns and looks at Ian. "But then, from my latest experience, the guy who pushed me against a cold tile wall didn't have the muscles that some men have. Those guys wrap you around them, making it a whole other experience."

I'm dying. Slowly, painfully dying. I can't even speak. My two companions look at Ian again and then at me before they shrug their shoulders.

We are silent before Beth starts a new line of questions.

"I guess since you and Jacks were treated to an audio version of a short story, y'all know the good news about them."

Junie and I look at each other, both taking a minute to think.

"Yeah, I'm not gonna lie, Aunt Beth," Junie finally speaks. "It hit me hard. I mean, Jacks and I had talked about wanting Mom to be happy. She was never meant to be alone, always a people person.

"But walking into that was an in-your-face experience for us. We both stared at each other when it was obvious what was going on behind the closed door."

"Yeah, I can see that was a fucked-up way to find out," Beth tells her.

"We didn't know they were coming home. A text would have been nice." I can't help but grumble.

"Maybe telling us you were already together before we walked in the door would have been nice too." Junie glares at me.

I know she hasn't come to terms with it yet. They both need to spend time with Ian to see what kind of man he is before they understand how he makes me happy.

"Ian is a hard worker in a job that can be difficult and dangerous," Beth tries to smooth it over some. "We should be grateful for guys like him."

"I am grateful for that, but to find the man who was there during the worst part, knowing he saw things and did things. It just makes it hard for me."

"I'm sure Ian would be glad to talk to you about any

of it, Junie." I look down at my drink. "He answered all my questions because I still can't remember every detail about the wreck. My mind blocked out much of it, probably for my own sanity."

"All I can tell you, dear niece, is that the man I've gotten to know so far is a good person." Beth places a hand on Junie's shoulder for a moment. "He cares about your mom. He only wants the best for her.

"He backed off after the wreck and let her have more than two years to come to terms with her grief. Even then, he didn't force his way into her life. He tested the waters to see if she was ready."

I feel Junie's eyes on me while my sister defends Ian. Beth's words explain everything perfectly, bringing tears to my eyes. If someone else sees the Ian I see, then I know I can't be dreaming up his qualities. They must be real.

"Mom, don't cry." Junie wraps her arm around my shoulders. "He sounds like the kind of guy we wanted you to find."

My fingers quickly swipe under my eyes. "Sorry, it's just... listening to Beth tell you all the great parts of Ian that I worried I had imagined..."

"No, doll, you didn't imagine anything." Beth squeezes my hand. "He's all that and a lot more."

Letting my hand go, Beth pushes Junie off Sandy. "Who's ready for another punch and maybe some volleyball? All this mushy stuff gets me excited, and cold water and exercise are the closest things I do these days to cool my libido."

"Eww, Aunt Beth, TMI," Junie yells and swims away.

"Speaking of libido," Beth starts in. "How are things going with the hunky man in uniform? Does he wear it to boss you around?"

My head whips around as I raise my sunglasses. "Beth, you're impossible."

"I've told you I'm living my sex life vicariously through you these days."

"Well, stop. Find your own hunky man in uniform. Mine's off limits."

"As if I could take him away. That guy is so hot for you. Yeah, not going to happen, sis, but maybe he knows a hot firefighter. I can see myself being carried away to my bedroom in a fireman's hold."

We both laugh and clink almost empty glasses.

24

Allison

Looking over at Ian with my two kids, I catch his stare in my direction. Even with sunglasses hiding those deep sapphire eyes, I feel them gliding over my skin as if they were itching to steal me away.

Why does this man want me? I rest my head against the pink wing to consider the answer. I'm not a hot, young twenty-something. My body is not close to perfect in any way. Two adult children vie for my time, and most of the time, they will come first. So why me?

"Something in space calling to you?" Beth disrupts my thoughts.

"Just thinking about Ian and me."

"Oh? Something titillating to share?" She ends with

a look that makes me smile.

"No, nothing like that. I just wonder what he wants with me." I roll over so I can look at her. "Why would this man... this kind, gorgeous man want me when the world is full of women who wait for someone like him to come along?"

"My darling sister, you sell yourself too damn short. Whether you realize it or not, you offer so much more than other women."

"Yeah, right," I say as my eyes roll. She's my sister, and she is required to stroke my ego.

"Girl, really? Your self-realization is shit. First, you're beautiful. I know you don't see yourself that way, but the truth is, you look ten years younger than you are. Second, the maturity you possess puts the young ones to shame.

"In truth, I bet he's dated his fair share of them once or twice only to find their life knowledge is sorely lacking. He doesn't strike me as the kind of man simply looking for a whore in the bed."

"And what do you think he's looking for?" My mind immediately goes to some of the hot sex we've shared. Ian knows his way around the female anatomy and exactly how to set me on fire.

"I feel like he's looking for a lady on the street and a freak in the sheets."

"Please, how dad-like of you to point that out."

"If the shoe fits, sister." Beth lowers her glasses and continues. "Third, you aren't a cheater. My God, you were happily married forever to Kellen after you walked down the aisle. Look how many marriages usually crumble under those circumstances. The fact you made it through those hard times tells him that you are in a relationship for the long haul. Believe me, I know someone like that is almost impossible to find."

Beth's past surfaces when she has time to think about what had started well but ended poorly. Moving on seems like it's on hold for her.

"When are you going to get back out there and look around?" I'm ready to stop talking about my life for a moment.

"Who says I'm not?"

"What, when?"

"Since you've been tied up with your boy toy, I've had plenty of time to go out. I don't sit in my house twenty-four seven."

"How come I didn't know this?" She's always been good at sharing, sometimes even oversharing.

"For one thing, I've not found anyone to write home about. There are men out there, but they're either married, rebounding from divorce, or only looking for a hookup. Don't get me wrong, I'm good with hooking up, but that's not all I want."

"I understand. I doubt I'd be ready to put myself out there if Ian hadn't come along."

"You scored the lottery. Not only did he do the pursuing, but he also waited around for the right one.

That's the kind I need to find."

Watching Ian dive in the pool close to us, I know our discussion is ending. "Someone will find you, Elizabeth. When you least expect it."

Ian's head pops over the side of Sandy, planting a kiss on my lips.

"If he's come for some pool sex, I'm outta here." Beth rolls off her side, taking her empty glass with her.

"Don't leave on my account." Ian wipes the water from his eyes.

"Yeah, yeah. My sister is shit at sharing, and I'm not into watching, at least not in the open with those two around." She throws a thumb over her shoulder at the kids.

Beth gets to the steps before Ian slides his hand over my middle. "If the others weren't here, this flamingo would offer great coverage from the neighbors."

His lips kiss from my neck up to my ear.

"Public nudity is an offense, officer. You might have to arrest me." I roll over and give him a subtle, sexy smile.

"My handcuffs are always available, and there's a spare pair in my trunk."

"Oh yeah? And what would you do with those in the pool?"

He looks around as Sandy glides in a circle from the breeze. "The ladder is a perfect size for hooking them to. I can see your wrist bound to them as I remove these bottoms in my way."

My eyes widen. "Ian, don't say things like that with my family right there."

"They can't hear me, and Jacks put on the portable speaker in the umbrella. It drowns out everything."

I glance in their direction to see for myself, but I'm distracted as his tongue slips around the shell of my ear from top to bottom. Warm lips kiss the spot below my ear before his teeth nip over the skin.

"You're getting me all excited, knowing there will be no finish."

"Oh, there'll be a finish. I may have to wait a while, but anticipation makes it even better, sugar."

"I'm kinda a fan of instant gratification, especially where sex is concerned."

"Then we better find an excuse for going in the house."

Ian's hand pulls mine over the edge of Sandy. He purposely slides it down the front of his abs because he knows the feel of the ridges and valleys makes me tingle. I've traced them with my tongue a few times, and damn, if I wasn't always ready to jump his bones before I was done.

Sill lowering my hand, he ducks it inside his swim trunks to wrap around a very hard, long dick. My palm wraps around the thickness, causing a shiver to overtake my entire body.

"Ian? What the hell?" I check for onlookers

over my shoulder.

"You caused it, not me."

"What? How do you even think that?

"You've been laying out here teasing me with the way your silky legs slide up and down the float like you do to my legs when I'm buried deep inside your sweet pussy. Then your hand cups water, pouring a little over those legs to cool off. I've been forced to watch droplets caress your skin as they make their way down to your ankles."

All I can do is stare at him. My brain goes on sabbatical while I lose myself in his eyes.

"That sexy little giggle you have when you think no one is listening calls me like a siren trying to tease a ship to her. But instead of wrecking me, my beautiful temptress pours oil on these beauties."

His hand starts at my thigh by the bottom of my swimsuit and slowly slips to my ankle. Touching, embracing, almost as if it's his tongue gliding from top to bottom.

I am so turned on with his words and actions that I can't speak. As I tighten the hold on his erection, the torture is all mine now. The water allows me to slide up and down the length, but I keep the motion slow enough not to create ripples.

He leans in and whispers, "You better think about stopping, or the pool will have more than chlorine water in it."

Reluctantly, I release him and move my hand back

to my side. His quiet groan warms my ear. "Torture, sugar. Pure torture."

"What do y'all want to do for dinner?" Jackson interrupts our fun and games. "You want to cook some burgers, Ian?"

"Sure," he calls back, his voice strained. I send him an apologetic look.

"You're going to have to get out, you know."

"Don't remind me, but then again, my woman's son yelling at me is kinda a quick deflator."

"Oh yeah?" I feel my eyebrows raise.

"Nothing like being cockblocked by your kid."

Ian

Jackson and I man the grill, prepping it and sharing a beer. With nothing to cook, the girls leave us alone to buy the supplies. We've not had much time to sit back and get to know each other, so I'm happy they left.

I need the two of us to form a good relationship. Nothing would make his mom happier than me getting along with them both. I want to bond with her kids, too, but never having been in this situation, I hesitate about where to start.

"So, Jackson, what are you going to do when you graduate?" I ask. Talking about college and his future seems a safe choice. "It's coming up soon, right?"

"Yeah, one more semester, and I'm done," Jackson

nods. "At least for a while."

"What are you majoring in?"

"My major is digital marketing with a minor in data analysis."

He says this like it's an everyday degree people go off to college for. Maybe it is these days, but I'm out of the loop for this shit.

"Wow, sounds impressive. Not sure exactly what that means, though," I tell him honestly. I'm sure he can educate me on the nuances of the digital world.

Jackson turns and looks at me, "I'd probably make more with a data analysis job, but I enjoy the media side more."

"Oh yeah?" I bet he's laughing his ass off on the inside, knowing he's talking over my head.

"You're not familiar with any of this, right?" A big smile appears on his face.

"Don't know shit about what you're saying." We both laugh, and he jumps into a dummy version of the two majors.

Before he finishes, the girls return with everything we need and then some.

"Did y'all buy them out?" I ask.

"No, but we got snacks, too, so stop bitching," Beth answers first. "You're going to love this weird cheese we found from samples."

I turn to Jackson, one eyebrow cocked, and he acknowledges my question with a brief nod. Bro language is already forming. Maybe I had made headway with him today.

Earning Junie's trust will prove more difficult. She protested when she first found out, and even though she finally came around to understanding, it wasn't easy. Her view of me still isn't what I want it to be.

From the moment I pulled her mom out of that car, I felt something, like an instant connection. But I knew our time would be in the future. With all the tasks Allison had to deal with, my interference stood way down the line.

I was willing to wait, especially after I went to talk to her about the autopsy. She fell apart in my arms and holding her made me realize we truly did connect on another level.

Junie will force me to be patient, like I was with her mom, but I'm okay with that. My reward will wait for me in the end.

My phone ringing cut into my lunch. The department must want something important to call me on my off days.

"What's up?" My answer isn't typical, but since he's bothering me, I figure he deserves it.

"Yeah, yeah, I get it. I'm calling on your off day, but we need you to come in for an important meeting," my sergeant says.

"Today?" This must be something else if he wants me in on it.

"Yes, today. Why else would I be calling? Get your ass in gear and get to the station."

"Right, see you shortly."

Four people stare at me, waiting to hear what's happening. I hate to leave them because this feels like I'm losing out on quality time with Alli's family.

"It looks like something important is going down, and they want me in on it. This never happens, so it has to be a top priority. I'm sorry to have to leave."

They all offer me words of encouragement, but it doesn't make leaving this impromptu family time any easier. I don't want to cut it short. Who knows how long it will be before we can make it happen again?

Allison follows me in, plops across the bed, and waits for me to change. I can tell she wants to ask questions but doesn't want to pry. Not that I have anything to tell her without finding out more at the station.

"I hate leaving, sugar," I say. "We were having such a great time."

"Yes, but your job is more important than eating burgers with my family."

"Don't say that. Being with your family is essential if we want to make a go of being a couple. The kids and even Beth mean more to you than anyone else. I want them to accept me being around, like an extension of you."

I mean what I'm saying to her. Our relationship is moving to the next level, and her family could accept me or cause problems for her. I'll never come between her and them. I'd walk away first, so I have to make sure it doesn't come down to that.

"I feel like you're safe on that front, Ian. Both the kids appear to be happy having you join us."

"Yeah, but what about on a long-term basis? Will they still be happy with me when I'm around ten years from now?"

She jumps from the bed and stands in front of me. "We don't know what tomorrow is going to look like, Ian, so let's just worry about today, please."

Grabbing her hips, I pull her to me and kiss her hard. I want her to know I'm in this for the long haul, even if she's scared of what's next. Losing Kellen changed her, I realize. I want to give her back the security she felt with him.

When I break away, I look down at her as she fights for the air I stole. "Keep that kiss in mind. I'll be back soon."

I drop one more kiss on her forehead and leave the house.

25

Ian

The station buzzes with excitement as I walk to the conference room. Some workers step aside to let me pass as if I'm someone more important than I was the last time I was here. This strikes me as odd. I am still the same officer.

As I knock and walk into the office, my sergeant sits behind his desk, going through some files. After looking up at me, he motions for some of my coworkers to also come in. *This must be something big.*

"Let me give y'all a brief summary of the situation." He stands and spreads the contents of the top folder over his desktop.

"I've been informed that a major drug deal is in the works here on one of the farms out north of town. The

DEA out of Harris County sent over what they felt we needed to know."

Everyone in the room trades glances. We've dealt with drugs before, but apparently, this situation carries a lot more weight than anything that's happened before. The sergeant makes it sound like it's cartel-level.

We don't live that far from a major drug pipeline, which is an interstate traveling coast to coast. But they rarely call us to assist when they know something is happening. The fact that they call on us to help in any way speaks to the severity.

"DEA is sending in a team and wants us to act as backup or in any other capacity they might need to get these guys. There's a small landing strip out on the property that some of you might be familiar with. They are asking for assistance because we know the people and the area better than they do."

"Makes sense," I offer. "I know we'll be happy to help them."

Everyone around me nods.

"Which brings me down to you, Ian. They looked into your background and know you spent some time working undercover before you joined our force."

I left undercover work in Houston to get away from this type of thing. After a short time, I realized it was not for me. I hated living a double life.

Yeah, it was exciting in the beginning, but after a few years of being assigned to all kinds of bad shit, I moved to the burbs to escape the danger. The thrill of working that way left as quickly as it came.

I nod at my boss. "I'm down to help them if they need me but not permanently. I won't go back to the city."

Sergeant returns my nod, knowing why I left there. "You'll be on special assignment until they wrap this up. Said less than a month if it all went down the way they think it will."

"A month?" That's a long damn time. So many variables go wrong in these cases. You can't outguess these people. I know that from experience.

"Yeah, a month. I'll be kept in the loop on the progress, but I expect you to keep me informed too. That's probably not the way they want it to happen, but you and I understand each other, right?"

"We sure do. So, what's next?"

Sergeant looks over my shoulder and motions for a man and woman to enter.

"This is DEA agents Cora Helms and Paul Kelly."

I turn to shake their hands, memorizing their faces and appearance. If they are undercover with me, I need to know them well.

We spend the next three hours in the conference room getting familiar with all the actors in this situation. Having done this before, I know what's needed to make this have a positive outcome. I quickly realize they do as well, so I can breathe a little easier.

As we walk out the door, Paul turns to me. "This should be wrapped up quickly."

"Good. I'm not in this for the long term. Been there, done that, and figured out it wasn't a permanent position for me."

Paul looks me over briefly before adding, "Yeah, it's not for everyone, but I live for it."

"Good because we need people like you to keep the bad guys at bay." I offer him a small smile and shake their hands before walking to the front with them.

My sergeant stands behind me when I turn around. He watches the two DEA agents walk out before he says, "Let's go to my office."

I know he feels the need to hear me out before this starts. My thoughts ping pong all over the place, starting with the danger I know I'll face.

My budding relationship with Allison crosses my mind first. I don't want to spend time away from her like I'll be forced to.

How will she feel about what I'm going to be doing? I can't tell her much because I'll be bound by secrecy. I know how this goes.

Leaving the station, I head back to Allison's where I find Jackson's car still in the driveway. I could tell them all at once to get their reactions, but do I want to?

My preference is to talk it over with Allison first. She needs to hear everything I can tell her, but there might be only certain parts she prefers to share with her kids.

I approach the side gate, heading for the music still blaring from the backyard. When this family parties, they make a night of it. Easy laughter floats on the night as light, lazy puffs of steam drift from the warm water of their family-size hot tub.

I'm jealous of Allison's daily relationship with her kids. I want this for us, for myself.

A great night like this calls for good news, not bad like mine. I think it's best if that information waits until later.

"Hey, he's back," Jackson calls out. "Miss us?"

"You know it. I busted a gut getting back here. What did I miss?"

"Let's see, these two..." Beth indicates the kids, "... may or may not have found significant others. They're slippery like bare feet on wet pavement when giving up the good stuff."

"Aunt Beth!" Junie scolds her. "I am not discussing my sex life with you and my mother. What I do in my private time isn't any of your business."

Three old people, me included, turn to Jackson with question marks in our eyes.

"Don't put this shit off on me. I'm the gentleman my mother raised me to be. Never kiss and tell." He shuts us down with his well-phrased comment that I feel sure made his mom proud.

"And no one said anything about your sex life, Junie." Beth quickly jumps on her niece's choice of words. "But if you require anything in that department, just ask. I'm a wealth of knowledge—"

"Hell no," Junie spits out before Beth finishes the sentence. "Let's talk about something else, please."

After grabbing a beer, I slide into the seat next to my sugar. Since pulling her into my lap might be frowned on, I wrap my arm around her and pull her closer to me.

"So, what was so important you had to disappear for this long?" Allison asks.

"Just police business." I glance toward her, hoping she will let it go.

She does, but the kids don't.

"Police business? Out with it, big guy. We want all the juicy details. Anyone we know get arrested?" Junie wants to know.

Even if it were, I wouldn't tell her. The local newspaper prints that information in the Tuesday edition.

"Yes, any of our friends around here for the weekend getting into some stupid shit?" Jackson follows up.

"Would you want me spilling my guts to them about you?" I shoot back. What can I possibly change this conversation to without being so obvious?

"Leave Ian alone, you two," my sugar defends me. "If he wanted to share what he's been doing, he would."

I don't need her to run to my aid, but knowing she

has my back is nice.

"The truth is..." I purposely pause, getting them excited. "I can't tell you anything. I'm sworn to secrecy about the aliens we found landing in the fields. You see, we've been finding some crop circles out in Mr. Wilson's hay fields, and it pisses him off when the little green men do that because the horses won't eat it. We don't know what they do with all that hay they cut, but we suspect they are vegetarians on their planet."

Junie sloshes handfuls of water my way, getting Allison and me in the face. "That was just mean, Ian. Mean, mean, mean."

Jackson adds, "Yeah, you had me going there for a hot second."

We all laugh, and Beth shifts to another subject, which I want to hug her for. I'm not going to lie to this family, but I can't share anything.

An hour or so passes before Junie starts nodding off in the warm water. Who knows what she's had to drink today. Despite what she tries to tell us, this girl is still a lightweight. Her partying days at college haven't led her too far astray, which I'm happy to see.

"I think we should call it a night." Beth stands. "Glad I only have to stumble down the block to get home."

We all join her and climb out, helping Junie.

"Little sis, you need to learn to balance your drinking... wine, water, wine, water. You'll last a lot longer if you do," Jackson informs her as he helps her to the back door.

"Let me take her in," Allison says. "You make sure your aunt gets home. Finding her in the neighbor's yard passed out would not be a good look in the morning."

A smile crosses Beth's face, reflecting Allison's, and I wonder if it's happened once or twice before.

"Sure thing, Mom." Jackson wraps his arm around his aunt's shoulder. "Come on, Aunt Beth. I'll walk you home."

"Boy, I've been walking home mildly intoxicated longer than you've been alive." Beth raises an eyebrow.

"Not something I really want to know. Humor me, and let me do this."

Beth puts her arm around his waist, and off they go. His phone rings before they arrive, so we head inside with Junie.

Jackson quickly returns to tell us a high school friend is on their way to pick him up. Allison and I both know he's still got a buzz from the beer, so his choice makes me happy. I hope he's always this careful and not doing it just to please us.

Allison takes Junie to her room, and I head to the shower. It's been a long-ass day, but there's still so much left to talk about. I left that life behind, and now I've been put in the position of explaining it to the woman I care about.

Before it was just me because I never told my parents about what I did. As far as they knew, I patrolled the streets and sometimes arrested a bad guy. I wish Allison only needed to know that.

I step from the shower when she opens the bathroom door, looking me over. Walking right up to me, she pulls the towel from my hands and drops it on the floor.

Her eyes drop to my semi that I've been sporting off and on since the flamingo foreplay. As long as I didn't think about it, I could keep it under control. My mind had drifted back to the teasing in the pool when I climbed into the hot tub and pulled her to me. Her skin held in the warmth of the tub.

With her family there, I forced the images away. It's not cool to sit there sporting a hard-on with them in the same place.

"You look too good, standing there with water running down your body, not to see it all," Allison says before dropping to her knees in front of me. "I've been waiting for this all afternoon. Seeing you joking around with Jackson as you sat there without a shirt made me want you even more."

"Junie's still here," I remind her. "And what about Jackson? He could come back home anytime."

"I messaged him before I walked in, saying we were going to bed. He got the idea." She wiggles her eyebrows at me before wrapping her small hand around my length.

When her mouth joins the party, I wrap my hands in her hair and help her to the finish line.

Allison

Sex with Ian takes on a whole new meaning when I blow him first. He mellows out and takes his time.

Not that I don't like it when he takes me hard and fast. Some of our best times happen when we both get carried away. Who wouldn't like a hot guy like him fucking you against a wall—forceful enough to hit extra deep?

I don't need to share those times with my family in the house, so tonight's lovemaking perfectly fits the bill.

Still kneeling there, I remember he left for the afternoon. He didn't say what the meeting was about. That makes me think he didn't want to share, which scares me.

We often discuss what he does while he's on the streets. It's a thankless job that can be dangerous, and I try not to think about that part.

Lifting me from the floor, he kisses me as he walks me to the bed. I fall back, taking him with me.

He drops kisses down me in a straight line, heading to where I need him the most. But, of course, he stops to pay close attention to my breasts along the way. He loves them.

As he moves lower, he hits ticklish spots on my ribs. I laugh and feel his smile against my skin.

"Hey, mister," I say it forcefully, but in truth, I'm nervous. "I have a question for you."

"Okay." He lightly continues the torture.

"What took so long today? I caught that look you gave me, saying you didn't want to talk about it in front of the others. Is there something you want to tell me?"

He stops, lowering his head to rest on me. "I don't want to talk to you about it, but I know you're going to want to know."

"Then just tell me. Better to get it over with because now I'll worry. My imagination works ten times harder than the actual event."

He draws circles on my skin with a light touch that keeps me on edge. Is he doing it to keep me wanting him or to buy time to come up with an answer?

"You know I did other kinds of police work when I was younger. We've talked about it."

"Sure, as much as you dared to tell me. I know you kept a lot back because you didn't want me to hear the real horror stories."

"Right. I did. No reason to make you panic over something that's already happened. Anyway, DEA has reason to believe some bad actors are creating a situation close to our town."

"And what does that have to do with you?" My heartbeat picks up. This doesn't sound good. With Ian in my inner circle now, thinking about him doing dangerous work puts me on edge.

"I worked undercover with some of their teams before I quit to come to work out here." He stops and looks at me. His voice strains, "They want me to work this assignment with them."

"No way. You don't do that kind of job anymore. You said so yourself." My pulse races from his announcement. DEA means drugs, and illegal drugs equal danger. This could be bad—really bad.

"Sugar, they want me, and Sarg wants me to work with them on it so we can stay in the loop on what might be coming to our town."

"Just tell him no." It seems simple enough to me. Did he sign a contract saying he would be willing to do undercover work? No way.

He snickers at my comment, which causes indignant feelings to rise to my throat. This is not a laughing matter and is not something to take lightly.

"When your boss tells you to do a job, you do it.

There's no physical reason I can't. DEA wants someone a little older to be part of the team, and with my experience in this area, I'm the prime candidate." Strong hands circle my waist and squeeze.

"But... but... Ian. This job is going to be dangerous. And... and... you could be on assignment for a long time. We won't see each other or be able to talk." With my voice raised an octave higher, I know he can hear my worry.

"No, they believe I'll only be with it for about a month. If that. The information gathered shows the key players making a move soon.

"DEA has been watching and waiting to bring me on the team until they need me. I shouldn't be doing anything more than gaining intel, not interacting with the actors."

He kisses above my navel before running his tongue around it. The mood died the minute he told me what I asked about.

Why didn't I wait until we'd had some slow, hot sex? In the mellow aftermath, all words lazily drift around in my head. I enjoy being blissed out.

But no. I asked, he answered, and now I'm too wound up to think about sex.

"Allison," he uses a demanding voice. "Look at me."

I stare into his deep blue smolder. "We will not let my job come between us, especially when I'm between your sweet thighs."

"But this is important." My words eke out.

He slides down and kisses just about my clit. "Not more important than this. Or us."

Before I know it, he pushes my legs apart and, using calloused thumbs, softly spreads me open. I'm lost as he takes me to another place. One where I know love is involved.

Shoving his words to the back of my mind, I enjoy all he gives me.

The rest of the weekend hides behind a shadow of worry. I try hard not to let his upcoming assignment eclipse my time with Ian and the kids. He tells me it will all be fine and assures me the month or less will pass without incident.

My mind goes to all the worst possibilities. Those people carry guns. Of course, so does he, but still. They won't hesitate to shoot at him. It could all end badly for him.

"Mom," Jackson calls, bringing me to the present. "What do you want to do for dinner?"

"Oh, uh, I don't care. Y'all choose."

"No, you also get a vote. I want to go out to that new bar and grill. They have live music," Junie tells us.

"Yes, that's a good idea." I try my best to be invested in the conversation, but with Ian standing close, my mind stays on him.

"What do you want to do, Jacks?" Ian asks him.

"That's fine with me. Let's just go early. I have plans for later."

My son's words capture my attention. "Oh, really? Is she cute?"

"No, Mother. It's not a date. Some friends are meeting at that new club that opened in Austin. One of our favorite bands headline tonight."

"Austin? But that's over an hour away. Why are you leaving so late."

Jackson gives me a look I haven't seen in a while.

"Mom, I'm a big boy. I can go places and do things with friends. We'll be okay. We have a DD that I trust." He pulls his sister into a neck lock. "She's never let me down before."

My eyebrows raise to my hairline. "You're taking your sister?"

"Yes, she's agreed to go, and since she's underage, she can't drink in a club, so we're good."

Ian slips around the bar to stand beside me. "And who's going to keep an eye on your sister while you're otherwise occupied?"

Junie stares at Ian with an evil eye. "Last time I checked, I didn't need a babysitter, Officer Ian. We go clubbing all the damn time when I'm at school."

Her tone says she's pissed at him for suggesting she might be unsafe, but it makes my heart happy. He cares about my kids and only wants them to be safe.

"Are you the only female going?" Ian continues.

"No, Christina is going too." She continues to glare at him.

"And you both trust this girl?" They nod their heads.

"Mom's known her forever, so that should be enough."

Her reply makes him breathe a sigh of relief. "That's good. You won't be alone while the guys are off doing... other stuff."

"Other stuff?" I ask. "Chasing women?"

All three turn and give me a look, causing me to laugh at my own stupidity. Has it been that long since I've been to a club? God, I'm old.

"Promise me you won't drive after drinking, honey. If you decide you're going to drink, call me. We'll come to Austin and get y'all."

"She won't drink, Mom. We both promise you. If she forgets and does some stupid shit, we'll Uber to a hotel for the night. I'll even call so you'll know we're not coming home. See, safe. We'll keep an eye on her and Christina."

With nothing left to say, the kids go dress for the night, leaving Ian and me standing silently in the kitchen. He turns to me and wraps me up in a tight hug.

"They'll be okay. They probably go out to clubs all the time at school, like Junie said. You're not privy to their every move, sugar."

"I know, but it makes me nervous to think she's

driving three or four drunk people back here at God knows what time. Maybe they'd be better off staying in a hotel for the night."

He pins me with a look. "Yeah, then you'd be worried about who's sleeping where."

My shoulders slump. "You're right, I would. Damn, they aren't living under my roof, but I still worry about their every move."

Now that they are adults, I feel so old. I wonder if my comments make Ian think I'm old. I don't feel that way most days, but when those two force me into a position to parent, that old mode kicks in.

Both kids made it through their teen years without causing too many anxious moments, but Kellen and I stood behind each other. Having Ian back me up helps more than he'll ever know. Even if he's never been a parent, he knows what's going on with young adults. Better than me, if I had to guess.

With my head on his chest, I bite the bullet and ask, "Ian, do you think I'm old?"

"What?" He leans back and drops those deep blues on me. "No fucking way. My God, look at you. Nothing about you says old, sugar. You have the body of a young woman, your face attracts guys when we walk in somewhere, and your energy level is that of someone half your age. You think because you have grown kids, that makes you old?"

"Yes and no. I mean, I don't feel old, but when I see them going out to adult places that I used to go to, it's hard not to think of myself that way."

"If you only could see yourself the way I do. You are smart, and beautiful, and sexy in every way, Allison. Anyone who tells you otherwise is crazy." Ian pulls me into his chest again. "I love you just the way you are."

Fine hairs on my arms stand up. Is he saying he loves me? Isn't it too soon for that? I don't know how to respond to it.

"Okay, I can feel your brain spinning. Yes, I love you, Allison. This is not how I saw this happening the first time I said it, but it's an honest moment."

"But it's so soon. Are you sure about this?"

His lips turn up into an easy smile. "Never been more sure about it. I've waited a long time to say those words. Deep down, I think I've known it since the night I came over and first held you in my arms."

"You mean when you told me the results of the autopsy? Oh my God, Ian, that seems like another lifetime ago."

"For you, maybe, but for me, it was only yesterday. I knew there was something there that night, but you were in no place to think such thoughts. So, I sat back and waited."

"You waited for me?" Could I believe this? Someone wanted me enough to hold off over two years to be with me? "What if I found someone else or was not ready?"

"Then we weren't meant to be. But I feel like I did the right thing waiting. You are worth it, sugar." He leans down and softly kisses my lips. "Every single day."

A soft kiss won't work for me, so I join our lips, pouring all my passion for Ian into it. His fingers slide through my hair, and he takes over the kiss, his tongue making love to mine.

"Uh-hmm."

We pull apart, looking toward the interruption.

"Guess y'all can have the house to yourself now," Jackson says, with Junie standing behind him, grinning. "We'll head out and let you know about the drive home."

My arms linger around Ian's neck as I look over my shoulder. "Okay, you two have fun. Be safe."

"Y'all too," my son calls as they walk out the door.

"Y'all too," I mimic him. "What do we have to be safe about?"

I glance at Ian. "We're staying in because I have big plans for you, mister."

Pulling out of his arms, I drag him to the bedroom and kick the door closed before turning the lock.

I turn and smile at his puzzled look. "One can never be too careful with children around. Now, take off your clothes."

Ian

I walk into the station on a normal Monday morning, and my sergeant stops me before I get to the locker room door. The look on his face says information on the shit that's about to go down waits in his office.

The door stands open, and I see a man wearing plain clothes.

"Come in, Ian. You remember Paul Kelly?" the sergeant asks.

I nod and shake his hand, then sit beside my newest friend.

This guy looks too official to be going undercover today. It's more like he's about to join Will Smith and Tommy Lee Jones in his black suit.

"Is there some progress happening sooner than

you thought?" I want to know exactly what's going on before I plunge into a clusterfuck I don't want to be part of.

"We have reason to believe that several of the main players in the scenario we discussed are already here, with a few more heading this way. This says our timeline moves up."

I take in his words, trying to read between the lines. These guys are notorious for only telling us underlings what they feel like we need to know. I'm not used to working on a need-to-know basis any longer.

"When do you see this shit playing out then?" I realize he can't control the players' actions, but a general idea helps me plan my real life.

"We feel like it will be within a week now." He turns, directly facing me. "What we need from you is surveillance done on a local level. A lot of their subordinates work here now. We don't give a fuck about them, but their comings and goings in your city might present some helpful information."

"You want me to watch these guys from the ranch? See where they go, who they talk to, what they do?"

"It would be nice if you could frequent their local hangouts. Chat them up for any info worth knowing. One drunken night in the local bar might turn up something interesting."

The location of the ranch in question is out away from our city, so I doubt anyone would recognize me.

The next city over sits closer to the ranch, and I know for a fact it houses the types of bars those men will want. There are more barflies to choose from.

But my appearance still needs to change. When this is all said and done, I don't want to be easily recognized by anyone who might be connected to this fucking situation. Especially any actors who manage to escape the final roundup.

"Okay, I'm going to need a few days before I start hanging out in these places, but watching around town and maybe shooting some photos for you guys can work now."

"Anything you obtain works. Photos help identify new players." Paul says without much excitement.

"In the meantime, you might want to see what you can do about changing your look. Grow some facial hair. Get rid of the clean-cut, small-town officer." He stands, looks me over, and walks out of the building.

The sergeant and I watch him go.

"You ready for this, Ian?" he asks.

"No." I turn and fall back in the chair. "I came here hoping to escape that life. It's not for me, especially now."

Over his black-framed glasses, my boss looks at me. "What do I need to know?"

His eyes bore into me, searching for the truth.

The truth. Those thoughts constantly linger in my head these days. My heart beats for Allison. She gives purpose to this life I'm living. Before her, I only woke to go to work. I ate to stay alive. I worked out to stay in shape. These were only efforts to kill time.

Killing time is no way to exist. I long to live a real life, have fun, make memories, and enjoy the world around me. With her, I can do all these things. For the first time in forever, I want to do them all.

It's a bonus that her family is part of the package. Even though the kids have left home and started to create their own lives, Allison and I can enjoy making different memories.

Maybe they'll have some kids one day. The idea of playing grandpa later in life appeals to me. Not too soon or anything, but one day.

A harrumph draws my attention to the present. "Oh, sorry. Had some thoughts on the subject."

Leaning forward, I put my forearms on the desk. "The truth is, I've met a woman I'm sure is the one."

"And what did you tell her about this assignment, assuming you've shared your upcoming work with her?"

"Just that I would be doing some undercover work with another department. She needs to be aware I might not be reachable for days at a time if it comes down to that."

He nods, but I can see he's expecting more.

"Her husband passed over a couple of years ago, so she scares easily when it comes to anything possibly dangerous," I add. "For that reason, I don't want her to know anything more than necessary."

"Good call." He leans back in his chair and locks his fingers over his chest. "In her case, the less shit you share, the better off she'll be. You know this situation could go either way. Might be an easy assignment, or things could go fucking sideways in an instant."

It was my turn to nod. I knew how fast a scene flipped. It happened many times while I worked on past assignments. Protecting a partner or others who put their lives in danger for you became the number one goal if an incident went south.

"I will talk to her a little more this evening. I skimmed over a few details when she pressed me, but I can offer a little more to her. Alleviating her fears to allow for less stress is my goal. Nothing more."

"Sounds like a damn good plan. Are you thinking of making changes here in the department if the two of you decide to make things permanent?" He studies me, but I don't make eye contact until I have a good answer.

"Like I said, she's it, the one. It's not a matter of if, but when." I stand with a smile on my face. "I'll let you know about changes after this shit is behind me."

The old man grins at me. I knew he'd been married forever to the same woman.

"When you know, you know," he says with a brief laugh.

I pull his office door behind me and walk out of the station. This meeting leaves me with too much on my mind. Holding off on talking to Allison will not change anything, so I guess now's the time.

She stands knee-deep in laundry when I walk in. Her domestic look makes me hot as hell for her. Visions of taking her on top of the washer bounce around in my head. It's one place we've not had an opportunity to christen.

"They leave you with too much to do?" I say, wrapping my arms around her from behind. The fragrance of her body wash greets me as I kiss below her ear.

"I'm happy to do it if it means they come home to see me. Having them home on the same weekend happens so rarely these days. One or the other always has something going on."

"Living the life of a college student. I remember those days well."

"So do I. I don't think I came home until Thanksgiving that first semester. My mom cried when I walked through the door." She turns the machine on and spins around in my arms.

"Why are you home so early? Not that I'm complaining." Her arms wrap around my neck, and we meet in the middle for a deep, hot kiss. Having the kids home might have been fun, but an empty house meant freedom.

I need her before I approach the bad news. Allison's touch soothes me and makes me feel like I can conquer the world.

Lifting her on the machine behind her, we continue to ravage each other's mouths. Damn, she feels good. I don't know what I did before her, but it was no kind of life for a man my age.

Our need turns into a frenzy for us both—ripping clothes and devouring body parts with lips, tongues, and teeth in a desire that overwhelms us both. Hard and fast sex takes us both over the edge too fast.

"Damn, woman. I needed that more than you'll ever know." My words and breath come out slowly.

"Why are you explaining? I love it hot and heavy sometimes too." Her head rests on my shoulder, with the two of us still wrapped tightly against each other.

I lift her, walk us to the bathroom, and flip on the shower. I step in when the water is perfect, and she drops to her feet. Watching the water slide down her body gets me hard again.

"Wow. Someone's had a morning," she says as she wraps her hand around my length.

"Turn around. Put your hands on the wall." My deep voice commands, and she complies, looking over her shoulder. "You ready for round two?"

She nods more than once while she keeps her eyes on mine. I know she's wondering what the fuck is going on in my head, but right now, I don't care. I crave the closeness only her body gives more than my next breath.

I enter her on one hard thrust before I wrap one hand around her neck and pull her back to devour her swollen lips. The other holds her hip so I can continue to pound into her. Another frantic coupling follows until I slow and wrap my arm around her middle to stroke her hard nub that waits for my attention.

When she screams my name over and over, I join her and fall into oblivion. My arms circle her as I kiss across the back of her neck.

"The things you do to me, Allison," I whisper. "I can't seem to get enough of you."

"If it's going to be like that, I can't get enough of you either," she says as she reaches for her body wash. She turns and looks at me, wanting to know what the hell is happening. I feel her words without her speaking a single one.

"We'll talk when we get out," I offer with a shrug.

Her smile is her only reply. This woman gets me like no one has ever before. She can read my moods and react in a way that puts me at ease. Why am I just now acting on having her as mine?

We shower and dress, then head back downstairs and sit at the kitchen island facing each other. She purposely sits across from me because she knows what I have to say will be important.

I take her small hand in mine. "I'm going undercover for a few weeks. There's some shit going down in the area involving drugs and foreign players."

Looking at her, I know her heart is racing.

"I can't tell you everything," I add. "Except this is the last time I'm going to put us in this situation. I'll quit before I take another assignment involving undercover work."

"Why didn't you say no this time?"

"It wasn't as if they gave me a choice. This is all happening a lot quicker than anyone expected. They'd been keeping an eye on things for a while before dragging me into it."

"So, after this, you promise no more?" Her voice quivers.

With determination in my voice, I say, "No more. Like I said, I'll quit first."

She moves around the island and stands between my legs. I hold her like my life depends on this moment.

28

Allison

"When will you leave?" My mind wants to plan every minute we have together. "Will I see you again before the assignment starts?"

I have no idea how these things work. Other than what I see on police shows on television, how else would I know?

"I'm going to start in a couple of days. I need to grow some thicker facial hair and spend some time with the agents to get up to speed on all the work they've done so far."

"Am I going to see you again before all of this?" He seems pretty nonchalant about everything, while every word from his mouth unnerves me. I consider freaking out on his behalf. Someone needs to.

"Yes, sugar. We have tonight and tomorrow night, but I probably won't contact you for a few days or more when I leave on Wednesday morning. It might even be a week."

"A week? I can't talk to you for weeks at a time?" With my voice jumping octaves, he realizes I'm about to go into full-blown panic mode.

Ian wraps me tightly in his strong arms. The same arms I'm getting used to having around me at night as I fall asleep. Being surrounded by his warmth makes me feel safer than I've felt since the wreck.

I try not to think about all the danger this job entails. I need to find something to keep my mind and body busy so that I'll be exhausted when I fall into bed while Ian's gone. Trying to go to sleep with him on my mind will be a challenge. If I'm too tired to stay awake, I won't have time to worry about what he's doing or if he's okay.

"This is hard for you, Ali, but you're the strongest woman I know. You've come out on the other side of tragedy like a champ."

"But I don't want to be a champ alone anymore. I want you home with me."

"Good, because that's where I want to be too. When this is behind us, I want more between us than we have now. Playing house some days of the week isn't going to be enough. You need to be by my side. Permanently."

"Permanently? That's a long time, Ian."

"Bottom line is, I'm in love with you, Allison. I think I knew it from the beginning. The night I held you while you grieved the loss of your husband, my head and heart agreed about you. I understood I would wait until you found yourself again, but I never forgot what holding you felt like."

I know he'd said it before, but it felt like it was a dream then. Ian saying it again makes me realize I never want to stop hearing it from him.

"Yes, Allison, I love you. Hell, I love everything about you. Your sense of humor, your kids, your crazy sister. I love it all. The way you understand me says you're the one.

"And when I walk away from this assignment, we'll talk more about how we move forward." He holds me close, and warmth spreads like a cozy blanket fresh from a warming rack.

I consider what he professes, and my heart knows he's right. Being on my own for over two years left me with a loneliness I never knew existed. All I want now is to be happy. Ian fits that bill perfectly. Everything about him makes my heart feel new again. Happy again.

What I feel for him is a new sensation running rampant through my soul. It's not simply a need to fill my hours with another human. The desire bouncing around inside has facets I hadn't considered before now.

I care about this man. My desire for him is

insatiable. I only want the best for him in all areas of his life.

Oh my God. I've fallen for this man. I'm in love with him. I love Ian.

"I think you might be right because I love you too," I confess. "I'm not as sure as you about when or how it happened. All I do know is that my feelings for you run deep, and my heart tells me it's love." I squeeze him tightly, feeling our hearts beating rapidly.

"Thank God. I'd hate to know we weren't in this together." He laughs before he kisses me. "If we hadn't just had some hot, needy sex, I'd have you again."

I move away, taunting him with a look that I hope he sees as sexy and desirable. "What's the matter, old man? Can't hang with the young guys?"

"I'll show you how it's hanging," he yells as he chases me into the bedroom.

Our days and nights fly by, and before we blink, I'm watching him take a few things and drive away. I try to hold back the tears, a lump lodging in my throat. I can't allow myself to think this could be the last time I see him alive.

"He'll be home soon," I tell myself. With plenty of time to think, I open the notes app on my phone to list things I could do while he's away.

Beth knows nothing about Ian's assignment. Ian and I talked about what to tell her and the kids. He understood they would ask questions about him suddenly disappearing from my life.

I might as well get it over with, so I text all three.

Me: *I have some news.*
Beth: *Do tell.*
Junie: *Good or bad?*
Jacks: *Listening*
Me: *Ian is going to do some undercover work and could be gone for a few weeks. I'm going to be looking for things to do while he's away.*
Beth: *Hell yeah. Vacation time.*
Junie: *Do I need to come home?*
Jackson: *Lot coming up at school, but I'll come home if you need me.*
Me: *I'll let y'all know what's going on. Maybe he won't be out of reach for very long.*
Beth: *I'll come down later*
Junie: *K*
Jackson: *K, let me know*

That went better than I thought. I figured they'd bombard me with questions about Ian's assignment. Glad they didn't ask because my limited knowledge makes me feel foolish.

Projects wait around the house, so I know I can occupy my time. Opening my notes again, I think about places Beth and I might go. Maybe Fredericksburg for a wine country tour? Or we could head to the San Antonio River Walk or the Galveston boardwalk.

A knock and then the opening of the back door tells me Beth is already here.

"Hey, girl," she says and hugs me. It's unusual. Not that I don't love a hug from my sister, but she rarely ever does that since we see each other all the time.

"Thank you. I can always use a hug."

"You're quite welcome. I figured you could use it with your mind on overtime worrying over that hot hunk of a man who keeps you sexed up over here. I mean, if I had constant dick, I'd never get out of the bedroom."

Leave it to Beth to pinpoint my anxiety and then make me laugh.

I wiggle my eyebrows. "He is a hot hunk of a man, isn't he?"

She nods, but concern clouds her face. "On a scale of one to ten of angst, how are you?"

"Right now, about an eight." A deep breath rushes out of me. "I'm trying hard not to think about it. Besides, he left this morning, so I'm not close to a panic attack. Yet."

"Good. I mean, undercover doesn't mean it has to be all guns and fighting shit, right?"

My eyes cut to her. "You had to go there, didn't you? I refuse to think that."

Beth's arm wraps around my shoulder, pulling me into a side hug as we stand in front of the sink. "You've been through a lot worse. I'm sorry I said anything."

"Don't be sorry. Deep down, I know it's possible."

"Did he give you any deets?" she says as she lets go and sits on the barstool.

Pulling out the other stool, I join her. "Not much. He isn't allowed to share information with anyone for his safety."

"Right. The less you know, the better."

"I started a list of places to go and things to do."

"Do we need a spreadsheet?" Her question captures my attention, causing us both to laugh hard. I love my sister. She may be quirky, but her ability to make me laugh is wonderful, especially when I need it—like now.

Ian video calls with me a few days later, and I hardly recognize him. The bearded face catches me off guard. He told me he needed to change appearances, but he grew so much facial hair quickly.

"Wow. Who is this hot, bearded guy on my phone?"

"Yeah, it's a good thing it's cooler out." He runs his hands over the facial hair. I think I like it. "This damn mess is too hot for Texas."

"But men wear them all the time."

"I don't give a fuck. It's hot, and it itches."

My laughter catches his attention.

"Tell me how you really feel," he grumbles.

I continue laughing. "Sorry. You look good enough to eat."

"Hmm. That sounds fun."

I bat my eyelashes.

"Don't be teasing me with that come-over-and-fuck-me look." He groans.

"What? I was trying to make you laugh."

"For three days and nights, I've lain in bed thinking about your hot body, and now you want me to laugh. Not happening, sugar."

The frustration is clear. "Man, someone's in a mood. I'd tell you to stop by, but I don't think you want to do that now."

"I would love to, but no damn way. I've made some progress with the actors. These people are dangerous. I probably shouldn't even be calling you, but I miss you."

"Oh, Ian. I'm sorry. I miss you too, but this will be over soon."

"Not soon enough." He lets go of a deep breath. The frustration in his words tells me how much he hates the assignment. "Look, sugar. I gotta go, but I wanted to tell you how much I love you. I might not call for a while, so try not to worry."

A light laugh escapes me. How can I not worry?

"I love you too. You be extra safe and come home to me."

"You know it. Love you." He hangs up abruptly, telling me he's busy.

I glance around the den. Maybe I'll do some remodeling while he's gone. Beth and I like to paint. With so many great colors that designers use now, we could transform this room. Maybe returning to a house with a new look will say we have a new start.

I need to do some shopping.

Ian

It takes no time at all to see this assignment is going to be a bitch. These guys are take-no-prisoner types.

I went to the bar the first night looking for a job.

When I told people I'd be willing to do anything to make a quick buck, I got a few looks from the suspects I know work with our target. I expect to have an in with the group bringing in the product soon.

I fake drinking a little too much and let my mouth run about being a great shot from my days in the army. Now that I am 'out,' I want to use my skills to get a job.

No one approaches me that night or the next. I keep my words closer to the vest the second night and my drinking to a minimum. The last thing they need to believe is I'm a drunk.

The pretty redhead behind the bar sidles up to me. "How come you're not slugging them back tonight?"

I'd left her a great tip for my drinks that were wasted the night before.

"Hell, I don't drink like that often. Only wanted to get it out of my system. Now I need a fucking job, so being sober seems important."

"There's not too much to do around here. Most of the ranchers and farmers don't hire off the street. You gotta know someone."

"Yeah, I can see that." I glance around behind me. The huge mirror running the length of the bar allows me to keep an eye on the entire place. "Any other types hang out here?"

She wipes the bar down before quietly answering, "Sometimes."

Her head nods toward the three men sitting at a table close enough to hear me. I glance at the group's reflection.

"I hear ya," I tell the pretty woman. "Think I'll see about playing some darts."

Making my way to the unoccupied dart board, I pull a few out and purposely aim at the outer rings and the wall beside the board. The pock-marked wall tells me I'm not the only one who aims poorly. Mine is intentional, though.

The men sit close enough to see what I'm doing. After a few hits, I catch one looking right at me. "You guys want to play?"

They ignore me, so I continue to throw, purposely missing the bull's eye. When I was in the Marines, we played this game so often that I swear I could hit the eye in my sleep.

One of the men stands and walks over, picking up three darts. "Let me practice. Been a while."

"Sure thing." He throws and hits the outer rings like I do. I figure he knows what he's doing by the way he holds the dart, but he doesn't want to show his hand.

We play a round, and he wins, just as planned. I want him to believe I suck at this game. It's not that I intend to beat him, but he needs to see that I can come close.

In the second round, my score is better. His smirk says he knows he's got me beat.

"Let's play one more," I say with confidence. "I think I can beat you. After all, three's a charm, right?"

"Whatever you say, man."

"How about we make it more interesting? A hundred says I can whoop your ass at this game."

"Oh yeah. You're on. One fucking crisp Benjamin." We both take one from our billfolds before my new friend turns to his group.

"Amigos, this dumbass thinks he can beat me. I've kicked his ass on every game."

The table breaks into laughter.

"Does he know you're a champ at the ranch in darts?" one asks.

"And how would I know that? Where the fuck is

this ranch anyway? They hiring out there? I got ranching skills."

"No," my opponent says as he cuts his eyes to his friends. "We don't have anything to do with the hiring. The boss is picky as fuck about that."

"That's cool, but if he asks, you'll put in a good word for me, right?" I keep my eyes on the board we're about to use, not wanting to seem too desperate.

"Sure, but look at other damn ranches because I can tell you it ain't gonna happen."

The guys sitting at the table order more drinks and continue talking. They heard me ask because their talking stopped, but none looked in my direction as my challenger spoke to me.

I've accomplished my first goal of getting on their radar.

"Let's get this party started," I say, taking a swig of my beer.

The hands run neck and neck until the very end. He wins again, and I fork over the green.

"Dammit. You win again. I thought I could fucking take you on this one." I stick my hand out.

He shakes it with a big smile. "Anytime you feel like giving up your next paycheck, come on out and play. It was pure pleasure on my part to watch you go down."

It's all said in jest, but he never knew I would have the last laugh if I found my way into their circle.

I return his smirk from earlier. "Yeah, I'll be sure to

put in some time to practice before I do that. You gotta give me a chance to win some of my money back."

"Yeah, don't hold your breath on that shit. I'll take you every fucking time, dude." He laughs again as he returns to his table of friends.

"Right. See ya later." Walking back to the barstool I sat on earlier, my redheaded friend wipes down the bartop in my direction.

"Thought I told you to stay the fuck away from them. You got a death wish or some shit like that?"

"No, no. Just wanted to make a contact on a different ranch. You know, for a job and all."

"That's not the place you want to work. Another?" She nods to my empty bottle.

"No, I'm about to head on home. Got things to do."

Her green eyes catch me as I step back from the stool. "Coming back again?"

I recognize her look of desire. It's not something I want to see when I could have my sugar if I dared to go there. Not tonight, though. Not until this shit is over and done.

"Yeah, I gotta win my money back. Can't have some wrinkled old bastard showing me up." I laugh and wink.

"Right. Keep telling yourself that. Maybe your fucked-up brain will start believing it. I watched that game, by the way. You met your match. Just admit it."

I grin and push open the wooden door, staring at

the swarm of insects hovering around the lit-up sign. Little bastards bite anything with a pulse this time of year. Jumping in my car, I shut the blood-sucking threat outside. If only all threats were that easy to leave behind.

Ian

I message Paul and await his reply as I head to my house. Part of me thought about moving to a temporary place while I worked on this assignment. The people I need to gain access to still hang in the wind, but I'm holding off as long as I can.

> **Paul:** *Anything?*
> **Me:** *Nada. Gained ground tonight*
> **Paul:** *Keep me informed. Big actors making moves down south*
> **Me:** *K thanks*
> **Paul:** *Delete*
> **Me:** *Done*

I delete the messages. When I get home, I'll wipe the phone. People like them retain the best IT people. They can retrieve anything, but why make it easy? A new burner will be delivered in a day or so.

With my refrigerator full of cold beer, I take one out, pop off the cap, and take a long pull. The stress of the night makes me want a drink to take the edge off.

I slide into my favorite chair and pull up Allison's number. This might be my last chance to contact her for a while. With this job, I never know the time frame. Her soft voice soothes me, and I want to hear it right now.

Pressing the green button, the phone rings. She answers quickly, telling me she's still awake. I never know with her. She sleeps at odd hours. Maybe she was hoping I would call tonight, and perhaps I was hoping she would answer.

"Hey, you," a sultry voice comes over the speaker. "Missing me?"

"Hell yeah, I am. Damn, woman, I really need to see you."

"I'm awake. Come over."

"As good as that sounds, I can't put you in danger. God only knows who's watching me. You can't second-guess them."

"I'm glad you're sharing this, but it only makes me more worried about your safety."

"Sorry. I didn't call to scare you." Even though we

talked a little about this assignment, she is smart enough to know it's dangerous. Television is probably to blame for that, and it's her only frame of reference for what I'm getting into.

"I know. Guess watching *True Detective* right now gives me too many ideas."

"Exactly. Since that's TV and so far from the real thing, it's funny."

"Okay, tell me something good then."

"I'm missing the hell out of you."

"That's not good, Ian." She snickers. "I want to hear something like... you saw something today that I need to see too. Or someplace we need to go."

"Sorry. I did some online searches on the actors, read some reports, and went to a dive bar. That about sums up my entire day."

"Boring." She laughs.

I love hearing that sweet sound. I've noticed her laughing more and more since we started seeing each other. The beginning, when she was still grieving, had little laughter.

"You're right, boring shit to do all day. That's a lot closer to the truth about this job."

"Until it's not." Her words come with force behind them.

"Right, until it's not. Then it becomes crucial to make snap decisions that possibly could cost lives. I hate the exciting times."

"Okay, enough of that. I don't want to go to sleep

thinking about you being in danger."

"So, what was your day like?" Hers should be far more exciting and a hell of a long way from anything I can get into on the job.

"Not much. I've been thinking about updating the house some, so I spent time online looking at color trends, furniture, light fixtures. I can get by for cheap by making those few changes."

"Uh-huh." That's all I got.

"You make it sound like that's your idea of a nightmare." Her teasing tone makes me smile.

"Yeah, yeah. I mean, who doesn't love painting and shopping for new furniture?"

"Okay, smart-ass. You asked what I was doing. And, by the way, I love shopping for new furniture or painting the walls. It makes the whole house smell new."

"Give me a comfortable recliner, blue walls, and an eighty-inch TV, and I'm all good."

"Spoken like a true man."

We both laugh, taking away from the reality of what's going on with my life right now.

"Okay, really, I don't mind painting. The sense of accomplishment when you get a whole wall done and stand back to look at it makes me feel a satisfaction like no other."

"Wow. This coming from my alpha, hunky strong man. You trying to impress me or something?"

"No, it's the truth. The smell doesn't do it for me,

but stepping back when I'm done—I feel as though I've achieved a goal."

"Maybe you should look into opening a house painting business."

"Oh, hell no. Then it would be work like any other job. I don't want another job unless it involves spending time with you."

"So, spending time with me is like work?"

"Don't twist my words, sugar. That's not what I said."

I hear her laughter coming through the phone. It's an easy sound, the kind I love to hear. This is why I wanted to talk to her tonight.

The connection we share only grows when we laugh together over something as mundane as painting. This life borders on normal, and that's what I want with Allison. I might not deserve it, but I've waited a long time to find a woman I can enjoy simple things with.

Since we've been together, I've found pleasure in effortless times, where we enjoy being ourselves without pretense. I think she also feels it. The relaxed moments make memories I carry with me when we're apart.

"Are you still there?" She pulls me back to our conversation.

"Yes, just thinking about how much I love spending time with you. I miss you every time we're apart, Allison. I want to come home to you when my work is done."

"That's exactly how I feel, Ian. I hate you doing work that keeps us apart."

A dead silence between us makes me wonder if she realizes what we are both saying. I want this woman. This lost person who has finally found herself again needs to be mine. Mine.

If I say this soon, will it drive her away? From what she's said, I don't think so. The strides she's made surprise me because she's come so far from when we first met.

Her effort to find a new normal took work, but she did it. Now, she can see a life in the future and is not stuck in the past.

"What's going on, Ian?"

"I'm thinking about how much I love you, sugar, and whether I'm jumping the gun by saying I want us to live together. I don't want a drawer or a few things hanging in your closet. I want us to come home looking forward to the other being there. I love you so much, and I don't want to be apart anymore after this assignment."

Dead silence.

It stretches on forever.

"Now who's quiet? You asked, remember? Is it too soon?"

"Uh, no. I thought of this before you started this job, but I didn't know if you also felt that way. I miss you when we're apart. Damn, I miss you so bad right now.

I want to feel your arms around me, holding me close."

"And I'd like nothing better than to be there beside you in the bed with you wrapped around me. I'd like to roll you over and sink into you, connecting to make us one."

"Oh, Ian. It's like I can feel you through the words. The warmth of your body wrapped around me while you make love to me."

"You're making me so fucking hard, sugar."

"Did you really call me for phone sex?" she barely whispers.

"No, but right now, it can be arranged because going to bed with blue balls isn't on my list of good times. Dammit, I want to feel you right fucking now."

"Tell me, what would you do to me?"

"I'd strip that hot body of yours so I can lay my eyes on every single inch of you. Next, I'd lick my way down over your perfect tits and torture your nipples until you begged me to take you."

"Is it possible to come with just words? Because I feel like it's about to happen."

"Fuck, Ali." I pull my hard length out from the confines of my jeans, not able to stand the tightness any longer. The pre-cum adds some lube to my strokes.

"Are you touching yourself?" she asks.

"Hell yeah, and I want you to do the same. Lick those long fingers and grab your nipples. Roll them around, pulling and squeezing until it's painful. Pretend it's my mouth, ravishing them with my tongue and teeth."

Long, hard moans come through the speaker, making me squeeze my dick harder, mimicking being inside her tight pussy. More pre-cum leaks, and I gather it with my thumb to help my movement.

"Move one hand down to the sweet spot and run those fingers around the swollen nub waiting for my attention, sugar. Think of how my tongue feels circling it before I take it between my teeth and give it a soft nip."

We both eke out guttural moans for the other to hear while we continue our personal torture. God, what I wouldn't give to have her straddling me on this chair.

"I'm gonna come, Ian."

"Pinch that nipple and tease that clit like I would. Come, baby. Do it now. Fuckkk." My load shoots into my hand as I continue to pump until nothing more is left.

I hear her panting and know she's close before I can hear her orgasm through the phone. I picture the face she makes and the way her body seizes and her toes curl under.

The entire experience of her orgasm makes me want to start all over again. Not being able to touch or hold her while she's coming makes me jealous of her fingers. I want to be the one eating her or filling her full of hard thrusts while she comes.

"Oh wow," I hear the soft words. "That was amazing. I needed to hear your voice, Ian."

Taking my T-shirt from the floor, I wipe the load from my hand and stomach. What a damn mess I made when I could be wiping it from between her thighs. I fucking hate this job.

"I needed it, too, sugar, but next time, I'll be the one making you come with everything I have."

"Good, because phone sex is only a substitute for what you do to me. And now I miss you holding me."

"Well, fuck. Did I say I hate this job?"

She snickers across the line. "Yes, I think you mentioned it."

"Next time, sugar. I promise."

"I love you, Ian."

"I love you, Allison. Sleep well."

With sleepy words, she says, "You too."

I hear the rustling of covers before the line goes dead. Standing, I pick up my beer and finish it on my way to the bathroom for a shower. I might have to repeat that performance once more. Picturing her coming makes my dick stir. Another time, and I might be able to sleep too.

I wrap my hand around my dick and rub one out with Allison's hot body the star of my head show.

30

Ian

I listen to Paul's dissertation on the actions of our players, trying to extract what I need to know. The guy is too long-winded. A need-to-know summary works for me.

"Tonight, you gotta work on being hired or gaining access to the ranch."

I've been hanging out at the few bars the workers frequent for over a week. Something needs to happen soon.

"Right. I'll push as hard as I dare without raising suspicion. They've all seemed spooked for some reason."

"A flight plan was filed for the ranch this morning. We don't have true intel on who's aboard, but we suspect it's the big boss."

"Good. Let's get this guy and be done with this shit. I'm ready for the end."

"I realize it's been going on longer than we thought, but there's nothing we can do to force it."

"Right. I know."

"Talk soon."

I've met with some group of the bastards every day this past week. They aren't taking the bait to get me access to the ranch. Trust is taking more time than I thought.

Tonight, I plan to make a bigger push. Walking into their favorite bar, I see a few new players sitting with them. All of the faces aren't visible from the bar, so I can't decide if I need to make my way over there.

I move to the bar and order a beer from the bartender. She knows me by now, even though we've had little interaction.

The last thing I need is to get her mixed up in this shit. The woman is just doing her job, but with these guys, she could end up being collateral damage. There almost always is—another reason I want to move this to the ranch.

After drinking a few sips that I make look like gulps, I watch them in the mirror over the bar. One makes eye contact with me as he stands and makes his way over to me.

"Dude, join us. The guy you need to talk to about a job is here tonight."

I turn with an incredulous look. "You sure? I don't want to interrupt, Luis."

Looking like a pussy is never on my agenda, but I need to play this cool, like I'm honored to be invited.

"Yeah, we told him about you." Louis grins. "He's interested in taking on a few more workers to finish the job we have coming up in the next few days."

"Sure, then. If you think it's a good plan."

He motions with his head to follow him, so I grab my beer and walk toward the table. The only chair left sits next to Louis, so I round the table to take the seat.

Before my ass even hits the chair, I look to see the face of the new man. Well, fuck. This is going to be a shit show. He resembles a mountain lion searching for its next meal, and I'm a newborn fawn. I hold his stare, refusing to be the one to look away.

We're not strangers by any means. In the last job I worked before leaving Houston, Matias Espinosa surfaced as a major player. He managed to escape when we rounded up the crew and the millions in cocaine headed for the United States.

There's no way he forgot me. My beard was long then too. Even with the few pounds of muscle I've gained pumping iron over the last few years, my appearance looks about the same.

"Well, well, if it isn't the pretty boy from Houston, Wilson. Or should I call you Ian?" I see Matias's arms move under the table, and there's no doubt a gun points in my direction. How did he get my real name?

The others at the table look between the two of us. Their faces say they're surprised at the scene.

Luis speaks up quickly. "No, Boss, this guy's name is Cord. He's looking for a job at the ranch."

"Yes, I bet he is. The truth will be your last nightmare, Luis. Cord is an undercover cop. Burned us a few years ago in Houston. Stole millions from us in product."

The others look around, probably for the exits. Like me, they'll be lucky to get out of here alive. If I could look away from this fucker, I'd probably see faces full of terror.

My eyes never leave his as I wonder where this is heading. He could kill me in the next thirty seconds. He could take me outside and kill me in the next five minutes. He could let me walk out without a problem. Hell no, we all know that won't happen.

How do I play this? Pretend I'm someone else? It might buy me an extra minute or two. Just when my life starts taking on meaning, this shit happens. At least the last thing I told Allison was I love her. Her life will be shattered all over again. I can't let that happen.

My phone rests in my hand on my lap. Can I make a call without alerting this fucking group of criminals? I doubt it, but it's worth a try.

Paul was my last contact, so all I need to do is hit send. Paul will have to figure it out from there.

"Put your hands on the table, motherfucker," he says.

"Now, Matias. I thought we parted old friends. You smiled at me the last time I saw you."

"The last time you saw me, I scrambled for my life. You'll never see that again. This smile..." Matias points to his face with the biggest shit-eating grin, "... it's the last fucking thing you'll ever see."

"Boss, is that a wise thing to do with all the witnesses around us?" Another man at the table asks.

Apparently, none of my table mates want to be caught in the crossfire, especially since Matias has already declared Luis a dead man.

Matias finally looks at the others. This might be my only chance. I raise my boot, reaching for the gun strapped within it—enough to get my hand to it. But not before my enemy catches the movement.

"I suggest you put your hands on the table immediately if you don't want to cause a mess in this fine establishment," Matias glares. "From this angle, I'm sure you'd be castrated with my first shot. Hate to see you go out that way."

Slowly, not to raise suspicion, I move my hands to the tabletop. "Now what?"

"Now, we're going to stand up and move until you're standing in front of me. Then we're going to walk out the door with this gun aimed at your kidney."

I stand without pausing, sliding my phone under

the table. I make sure it lands on my booted foot to keep them from hearing the slight thump.

Getting this group outside will be best for all the patrons around us who enjoy their evening without suspecting a gun is aimed at me.

Walking around the table, Matias stands with me, and the others follow. I turn toward the door with him on my heels. I make eye contact with the bartender, sending her a calm look and hoping she will not realize what's actually going on. She seems fearless and might try something stupid, like pulling the shotgun that sits under the bar.

Before I push the door open, two beauties walk in. With big smiles, they eye me.

"Hey, the fun's just arriving. There's no need to leave," the first one says and glances at the group following.

"Not tonight, ladies. Got a ranch to go run," I say calmly but loud enough for the bartender to hear me, which earns me a hard push of the barrel into my back.

"Let's go." Matias growls.

"Y'all come back when the work's done," the black-haired one calls out while we pass through the doorway. The other men say nothing, afraid to set Matias off.

"What's it gonna be, Matias?" I ask when we clear the entrance. This man holds the key to my future. His answer holds the key to his.

The ranch workers mill around, watching Matias's every move. I never understood how anyone sought out jobs that had the potential of another man stepping in one day and killing you. They all know that Matias's gun waving around means they could be next. The deranged man could end us all.

"I'll tell you, Cord," he emphasizes my alias, "I've decided we are taking you to the ranch. You told these stupid fuckers you wanted a job. Well, we have one for you, and I'm going to take great pleasure in watching you work for your life."

A loud, clown-like, demented laugh bellows from him. This nightmare keeps getting better and better.

After binding my hands behind me, they cover my head and shove me into the back seat of a truck. I hoped they would throw me in the back so I could jump out, but who knew these dumbasses had a brain.

Little is said between the workers as we drive. After several turns in both directions and lengthy roads in between, the truck finally comes to a halt. They drag me out, stand me up, and rip off the hood. Since it's dark out, my eyes quickly adjust to my surroundings. Typical looking ranch for this part of Texas, several outbuildings from a large home stand around me.

Matias stands before me, wearing a manic grin.

"Take him to the den," he yells at the men.

"Oh, are we visiting like normal friends in your den?" I can't resist commenting. While I might be shaking in my boots, showing fear will never happen.

He laughs loud enough to wake the dead, but it goes unheard out here in the rolling hills with nothing around for miles. I can't see bright spots in the sky telling me we're far from the city.

Walking into the den, I realize our ideas of this room's title vary greatly. It's underground, for one. My head thinks of a torture chamber as I stare at pain devices lying around with a chair attached to the floor in the center of the cement floor.

"Exactly what kind of fucking work you want me to do here?" I ask, keeping my tone light.

"Your work won't be physical labor, Ian. Your job is to stay alive and provide us with information. Sadly, your pretty face will be the first thing to go."

Again with the laughter. I swear the guy has listened to Pennywise laughing too much.

I keep my mouth shut as the men attach my legs and arms to the chair. Matias's message is loud and clear. The only thing that might save me is my phone call reaching Paul.

The first fist flies into my nose. The second, a right hook, smashes across my face. The blows that follow land equally hard and litter my body, head, and arms. All I can think about is staying alive to see Allison once more so I can say goodbye. She didn't get to do that with Kellen.

I don't want her to see my face rearranged, but at least she can have closure with my impending death.

"Okay, let's have a talk now, shall we?" Matias speaks, stopping the goon working me over.

As best I can, I spit a stream of blood from my mouth. It's been a long damn time since I took a real beating without being able to defend myself.

"What?" That's all he gets from me.

"Who are you working for? Local police? DEA? Any of the other fuckers who think they control Texas?"

"No one. Need a job."

"That's bullshit, and we both know it," my personal abuser says as he takes a shot at my face.

Matias raises his hand, glaring at the attacker. "Did I tell you to continue?"

The man retreats to a stool at the side of the room.

"Now, Ian," Matias says, full of fake kindness and patience. "Let's begin again. Who sent you to infiltrate our operation?"

I stare at Matias. "Me? I work for myself."

He knows he'll never get information from me.

"Wrong answer." He makes his way around my chair, breathing heavily. Stopping directly in front of me, he leans in. "You would do well to help yourself by answering. You see, we've also been watching you. Your work must be getting sloppy here in this country town since you never made our guys. We know there is a certain widow you've also been entertaining."

This captures my attention, but I don't want to show my hand at anything he says.

"She's very beautiful, like her children."

Goddammit. He's been all over my movements, and I missed it. Allison is in danger and has no clue. How could I let this happen? I must be getting sloppy.

"She's just an easy lay I picked up in a bar. Desperate for some attention since her old man ate it in a car wreck. Bitch cried every time we were together. Became too much work."

"So, if we bring her here, you'll be okay for my men to service her since you're tired of her?"

It takes everything in me not to react.

"I mean, if your guys are into a crier." I desperately maintain my neutral face.

There's no fucking way they are going to touch Allison.

"Enough of this. We need intel on what the DEA is planning. I started with the easy questions because we already know who you work for. Surprised the hell out of me when they called you back in for undercover work."

I stare at him. If they knew Matias from the Houston bust was involved, no one informed me. I remember all the players from the last assignment. Paul was brought on after it, but he should have been familiar with the case.

When I give Matias nothing, he walks to the door. "See if you can get his attention, but don't kill him. Understood?"

"I'll try my best, sir, but sometimes accidents happen," the goon says.

I get it. If I die, I die. Not his problem.

"You better. We have plans for him."

The attacker finally gets the message when he nods in Matias's direction. A slam rings in my ears before the brutal beating begins.

Paul

"The situation has escalated. They're taking Ian to the ranch, and we don't even know where it is exactly," Paul tells the room of agents. "Cora, thoughts?"

Cora stands before the group to speak. "Only new intel we've gathered is someone is watching his girlfriend, Allison Waller. We were right to keep her under surveillance."

"True. These men will go after anything and anyone connected to Ian to get what they want this time," Paul continues. "Let's keep a constant tail on her. We don't want to be searching for two missing people."

Cora nods and leaves the room.

"This situation will most likely move fast from here on out. We need to keep all avenues of information open. You see or hear anything in the bar, relay it immediately." Paul looks out over his small audience, observing head nods.

"Any questions?" No one moves or says anything

else. "Okay, relieve your people. Eyes and ears, people."

The room empties to quiet words.

31

Ian

Before blacking out again, I feel rocks pierce my skin as I roll several times. Like a pig on a skewer being coated with dust and rocks, I finally come to a stop. Did they throw me from the back of a moving truck?

"Son of a bitch," I grunt out when someone moves me. Peoples' voices sink in. I must be in hell because the pain they cause hurts like a motherfucker. Just let me be. Let me die in peace.

My eyes are swollen shut, and my head swims, but I wake enough to hear the bells and whistles of a hospital room.

"He's coming to. Get the lady," someone standing close to me says, but that's all I hear with my mind drifting back into the blackness.

I try to open my eyes again sometime later. They refuse to budge, but I can move my fingers some.

"He's awake again. Mr. Windsor, can you hear me?" a strange, soft voice says next to my ear. "I know you can't open your eyes, but can you wiggle your finger if you hear me?"

Trying my best, I wiggle two fingers for her. Damn, it hurts all over just to move them. There is something in my nose that also hurts. If I could reach it, I'd jerk that son of a bitch out.

"You can talk to him, but he can't talk back. He can wiggle his fingers if you ask simple questions," the stranger says to someone else.

A warm hand caresses mine without squeezing.

"Ian? Ian, it's me, Allison." Her soft voice soothes my aching head.

It's Allison, my Allison. They didn't get her. She's here with me.

I try to take her hand in mine. It's too hard to move it that much, so my fingers wrap around hers as much as they can. She's here, and that's all that matters.

A sob breaks through the noisy machines around me.

"You can't leave me, Ian, please. I can't do this again. I can't lose you." Her sobs begin to edge on hysterical crying. "I just can't handle losing you, too, Ian. You're my everything. I need you with me. Please don't leave me this way."

My body aches to hold her to me. Everything in me

says take her in my arms and hold her tightly. I need to reassure her I'm not going anywhere, but it's impossible when I can't talk or move.

The pain continues shooting up my arm as I squeeze her hand and pull until I sense her looking at me. I whisper, "Hug me."

She delicately lays her head on my chest and wraps her arms around my sides. One of my hands surrounds her and holds her to me.

She's supporting her weight with one arm, but I feel her against me. My body relaxes at her touch. I'm going to be okay. I know it from the way my body responds to her closeness.

After a minute or two, Allison pulls the chair closer to the bed. I lay my hand on top of hers and move my fingers around hers.

"I'm afraid to hold your hand, Ian," she whispers. "It might hurt you."

I turn my hand over and open my fingers wide. She responds to my motion by laying her palm against mine without embracing my entire hand, so I do my best to wrap my fingers around it. It costs me some, but not enough to let go. The warmth from her hands gives me something to hold onto inside me—a connection I need right now.

Taking in my first deep breath hurts, but as I exhale, I feel the strength she offers through our hands—the best feeling ever.

I wake with a start, my mind clearer than before. It's quiet in the room. Maybe they removed the machines while I slept or at least turned the noise down.

My hand still feels her palm touching mine, and I know she's here waiting for me. Her touch makes my heartbeat want to perk up. She makes me want to get well sooner.

Damn, I love this woman. Thank God I'm still alive for her. For us.

"Are you awake?" The sound of her sleepy voice drifts around me.

I try to talk, but I can barely manage a whisper. "Yeah."

"Don't try to talk. Your throat was damaged from some hits you took."

Fuck. All I want is to tell her I love her.

"I love you," I rasp.

"Oh, Ian." She sobs. "I love you too. Now, stop talking. The doctor says it will heal, and you'll have full use of your voice in time."

I squeeze her hand as best I can. One of my eyes barely opens. My sugar looks at me, and it's the best sight I've had in forever.

"Ian. Don't open them yet. They're too swollen."

"Don't leave me," I barely eke out.

"I'll never leave you," she replies as I watch tears

stream down her face.

Talk about a sight for sore eyes. I'm the poster child for that old saying.

The nurse swings open the door, looking at the two of us. "Guess this means you're more awake, Mr. Windsor."

I slightly nod. Everything in my body hurts, but I want to stay awake.

She writes down my vitals and checks the tubes running in and out of me. The one in my nose needs to go since it's causing me more pain.

"Nose?" I whisper.

"Don't talk," she and Allison say simultaneously.

Got it. Don't talk. But then, how can I tell them anything?

"Your nose hurts?" the older nurse asks.

I nod again.

"That tube is feeding you. You've been out since your surgery. The doctor felt it would be easier to feed you short term with your throat damage with an NG tube. He'll be in shortly, so you can let your friend here ask about it."

"I'll be sure to talk to the doctor about it for you," Allison offers. "Also, your parents are waiting to come in. They've been so worried about you."

I nod, and she tries to let go of my hand, but I wrap all my fingers as tight as I can around it and shake my head.

"I have to go get them. I'll come right back."

Reluctantly, I slide my hand from hers. Letting her go hurts since it's something I never want to do again. My desire for this amazing woman goes much deeper than sex. I crave her being beside me, laughing, holding, and loving me. I want it all.

My parents slip through the door quietly, and Allison follows. Their faces change from smiles to concern with one look at me. All the tubes—some necessary and others not, in my opinion—scare them.

My mom's face grows paler as she walks to my side, taking my hand in hers. I love my parents, but it's not the same as having Allison's warmth seep through my skin when she touches me.

Once they see that I'm going to be okay, they decide to go home. It's hard to visit with them without being able to hold a conversation. They both promise to see me again when I can talk more. Neither can drive after dark, so I don't want to keep them either.

"Your mom and dad are such nice people, Ian. I wish I'd met them in a less stressful situation."

I nod. I wanted to take her to meet them, but there never was a good time. We will plan a day under better circumstances so they can get to know the woman I plan to marry as soon as I can stand.

The time I've had to think in this damn bed has brought clarity to my situation in life. Having Allison by my side tops my list of goals. Hopefully, she will feel the same way, and I can convince her to marry me.

My nurse pops in to retake my vitals. This seems like such a waste of time to come in so often, but they're just doing their job. This one always has something to say to me, unlike some who do the bare minimum.

"Mr. Windsor, how are you feeling this afternoon?"

"Good, better every hour."

The blood pressure cuff lets go as it finishes. Her face scrunches slightly but immediately returns to a smile. Allison stares at the machine behind my line of vision.

To get her attention, I squeeze her hand. In a light whisper, I ask," What's wrong?"

"No, no, nothing's wrong." Her tone tells me all I need to know. I turn to the nurse and raise my eyebrows in question. "Let me try it on the other arm."

She moves around and wraps the pad around my arm before starting the machine again. The decompression happens quickly.

"It's fine, Mr. Windsor. Your BP is a little low, is all. I'll come back in a few minutes to take it again. The doctor will probably prescribe something to bump it up." She pats my arm. "No need to worry at all. I'll get in contact with him right now."

After the nurse straightens my covers, she smiles and says she'll be back soon before closing my door.

"How bad?" I ask Allison. She saw the numbers when the machine stopped.

She moves in closer and leans over me. Her hair falls forward, sending the softness across my arm and the light fragrance wafting around me. I want nothing more than to grab it and pull her in for a kiss—a hot, deep, tongue-lashing kiss.

"It's not that low," she says. "I'm sure meds will bring it back up quickly."

Her face, tone, and words set my nerves on edge. What the hell is going on?

Before I can muster enough energy to ask more questions, the pain in my stomach doubles. The doctor did what he called a minor surgery to remove my spleen, which had been damaged from the ass whipping I took. He didn't seem concerned when I cringed as he poked at the wound left from the surgery.

This is more than a little pain going on now. It hurts like a motherfucker now, to the point I have to moan.

"What's wrong?" Allison stands over me. "Did I hurt you when we hugged?"

I shake my head no and point to the wound on me where the incision is healing.

"Hurts bad," I eke out.

"Maybe you need more pain meds," she offers.

I shrug my shoulders, not knowing what to think. Allison pushes the call button when I moan again, louder this time. The nurse's voice crackles over the speaker, asking what I need.

"He's in a lot of pain at the incision site. Can you come in here or call the doctor?" Thank God Allison is here to speak for me.

This time, a male nurse, Collin, comes in.

"What's going on, Mr. Windsor?" Collin asks, looking me over. "Looks like your respiration is elevated."

"The nurse was in here a few minutes ago, and Ian's blood pressure was down. She was going to call the doctor," Allison provides while I hold my stomach as best as I can.

When I let out a loud moan, the nurse raises my shirt. He must see something he doesn't like. Allison's face goes pale. What the fuck is going on?

Trying to look makes me feel dizzy, so I lay back, but things start happening fast. The doctor on call runs in with a few other people in tow. Allison makes a terrible noise while looking at my exposed abdomen.

Lights whiz by overhead as they move me somewhere. People talk all around me, but none say anything directly to me. Will someone tell me what's going on?

I lose the warmth when Allison lets go of my hand. *No, don't let go.*

"I love you," she says, but her words are fleeting since I'm still moving forward.

I love you too. I only think the words.

32

Allison

Several police officers march silently through the door while I sit and wait. Brave women and men from around the county and beyond come to offer everything—solace, help, and strength. Small towns support each other that way. Ian knows a countless number of people, so I'm beginning to learn.

"Ma'am," an older man in uniform addresses me. "We were told we could find Ian's fiancé here."

"Yes, that's me. I mean, I'm not really his fiancé, but that's the only way they would allow me to stay." I stand addressing the group of men.

"We wanted to stop by and check in, but they told us he's back in surgery. The nurse said to come here." They stare, expecting me to give them some news. The problem is there is no news.

"He was fine yesterday. Trying to talk. Wanting to get up."

"Sounds like Ian," one of the other men comments.

"Yes, it does, doesn't it?" I smile at him.

"He started hurting." My eyes go from person to person, not really knowing what I'm looking for.

"Then everything happened so fast. They took him back into surgery so quickly, I hardly had time to tell him I love him." My feelings pour out to total strangers, but they understand. How often do they find this situation before them? A time to show support or maybe a shoulder to cry on.

We all turn when we hear footsteps getting louder, obviously running toward us. Jackson, Junie, and Beth round the corner, and I burst into tears. Familiar faces break the tension I've held in since they took Ian away. The flood escaping my eyes draws all three to me. They wrap me tight, holding me up.

"Mom, tell us what's happening?" Jackson asks, his arms keeping me upright as my knees buckle.

"I don't know yet. It's something to do with the first surgery or the injuries he sustained when those horrid people had him."

They back away, confusion in their eyes. I never shared what Ian was doing, only that he was on a special assignment.

"Ian was working undercover. He was dealing with drug dealers. Bad men."

"Wow."

"Holy shit."

"Oh no."

All three exclaim at the same second. This might be comical at any other time, but right now, I can only cry more.

My eyes shift from Junie to Jackson and then to Beth, and I fall apart.

"Why? Why am I doing this again?" I grab my sister and pull her nose to nose. "What did I do, Beth? What if he doesn't make it? How do I live through this again?"

"He'll make it. Have faith, Ali."

I can feel that her words are genuine and sincere.

"I can't live through another death of someone I love. I love him, Elizabeth." Our eyes lock together. "I love him with all my heart, and now he's going to leave me just like Kellen. I told myself not to fall in love again. I screamed it out loud when Kellen died. I swore never to love another man."

"I'm sorry, Ali, but you can't know he won't pull through. They are fixing him right now."

I bawl and bellow, "But what if they can't? What if he dies on the table? I need to go."

I let her go and grab my purse. My actions are frantic and erratic.

"Where are you going?" Beth's face twists in question.

"I'm leaving. I can't do this again. I can't, I can't. I'll

go somewhere. I have money, time, and nowhere to be. If I run far enough, I can escape the pain of losing him. I'll forget it all. I'll live life differently this time. I'll guard my heart." Choppy words pour out of me.

Jackson steps between me and my escape route and grabs my arms. "Mom. Stop. Just stop."

"No, Jacks, you don't understand. You've never been in love. Don't ever fall in love. It only ends in pain. Now let me go. Let me go, please," I beg him.

"Mom. You love him. He's a good man. He's good for you."

I repeatedly shake my head no while my eyes blink back tears.

"Yes, Mom, you do," Jackson keeps his voice low and slow. "You have a second chance at love. A second chance to enjoy life with a man who would walk over burning coals for you. You don't want to leave him while he's hurt. That's not the mom I know."

"But it hurts too much, son. It hurts to live it all over again."

"You don't know he's not going to make it. Think how badly he'll hurt if you're not here when he wakes up. Losing you will be a pain he can't deal with. You don't want to be responsible for that, do you?"

Staring into my son's eyes, I see the truth. I hear words from my child, who's not a child anymore. I see maturity beyond his years. The death we've endured together made him a man before my eyes.

I stop trying to run. My legs buckle, and I fold down

to the floor. Jackson and Junie go with me. The three of us grieve for our loss in a tight pile on the floor.

For the first time, we shed tears together. As we grieve for Kellen, our hope for this new force in our lives grows.

I'm emotionally spent. My adrenaline has depleted. I sit limp in the arms of my children and my sister.

"God, please let Ian get through this." I pray aloud to the others in the room. "I, no we, need him, his strength, his love, him... just him, please God. Please."

Eventually, Jackson stands and pulls Junie and me up. We make our way to the chairs.

I'm empty.

Numb.

Tired.

Part of me realizes I've made a spectacle of myself, but I truly don't give a rat's ass what anyone thinks. I need Ian back. That is the only thing I care about.

As time passes, I wear a rut in the floor. A generic clock hanging askew and too close to the ceiling tells everyone how many hours it has been. Is that good or bad?

With my patience wrecked, I reach the locked doors leading to the operating area. A window in the door only shows a hallway ending in a solid doorway. I can only stare at it because I'm blank just like it—a wall of nothing.

"Mom?" Junie says softly, and I turn to see a scrub-clad man and woman walking toward us from a different direction. I can't bring myself to hope. It's too hard.

"Is this the family of Officer Windsor?" the doctor asks.

"Yes, yes. I'm here," I reply, moving to them. Part of me wants to attack these two, but I realize how crazy that would be.

"We were able to locate the bleed. Actually, there was more than one. The initial surgery didn't locate them behind the liver. This time, I explored further to make sure nothing else was waiting to cause a problem."

"Thank you, doctors." I move forward and shake the hands that held Ian's precious organs only minutes before. They both nod.

Beth has the mind to continue asking important questions while I am simply satisfied he's alive.

"Will this lead to a complete recovery for him?" she inquires further.

The female doctor speaks up. "Yes, he should have a complete recovery. Of course, it's going to be several weeks before he's up and moving, but in time, he'll be back to his usual active self."

"So, the surgery went fine?" Beth continues probing.

"Yes, but he's bruised throughout the abdomen from the blows he took. Those will heal over time just as his face will. Mr. Windsor has solid bones to take hits like he did and not have facial fractures."

"Sounds like his attackers wanted to do more internal damage than hurt his pretty face."

Leave it to Beth to comment on his face—everyone around snickers, including the doctors.

"If you have no more questions, we'll leave you then," the man says.

"Yes," I pipe up. "When can I see him? How long until he wakes up?"

Suddenly, I'm filled with needy questions.

"He's in recovery right now. I'll tell the nurse to alert you when he's awake. You can slip in briefly to see him, and then he'll be moved to his room."

"Yeah, Mom, we need to let them do their job," Junie informs me.

"I can't say thank you enough, doctors. He's very important to our family," I look around at the other officers, who are also nodding. "All of his families."

"You're all welcome," they both address the crowd before returning from the way they came.

Tears of joy pour from me, and my family joins me in a tight hug. What would I do without them? They keep me sane through everything.

Now that three days have passed, Ian is starting to show signs of getting better, even if he's grumpy. I feel a sense of relief when I look up and see two welcome visitors. Another uniformed man comes in after the first. These two were here in the beginning, but I never had a chance to talk to them with all the action taking place.

"Hey, old man," a policeman calls to Ian from the doorway. He's wearing his uniform, so I immediately know who he is.

"Hey, who are you calling old?" Ian grunts. It still hurts him to speak. He looks at me, "This is Gabe and my sergeant. This is Allison, my girlfriend."

"Nice to meet you both," I extend my hand. "I'm happy someone else can listen to him complaining."

While the three of us laugh, Ian grimaces.

"It's nice to finally meet you, too," the sergeant begins. "We've only seen you from afar."

I turn my head and look at the two men. "What?"

"We kept an eye on you while Ian did his job. Never know what those crazy people will do for revenge." I blink several times, trying to wrap my head around this information.

"Why would they want me?"

"These kinds of people will do anything to get what they want. They had Ian, and if they could use you to get him to talk, they would," the sergeant says.

Gabe adds, "Yeah, but we weren't your only protection. We also spotted DEA there. You were double covered."

"I never knew." My voice is barely above a whisper.

"Good, that's the whole idea. We didn't want to be obvious enough to cause you to worry more than you already were." The sergeant pats me on the shoulder. "But it's all good now."

Was it, though? What if they came back later? These are bad guys. Drug people. Cartel types.

Over the next week, the kids come back from school occasionally to check on the two of us. They say it's to see Ian, but I know they worry about me. Ian's assignment still has us all on edge and I know it causes more concern for everyone.

Beth magically appears at odd hours to get progress reports, but she brings good food because she worries I won't eat. I need to keep up my strength so I can care for Ian.

The DEA team stops by to see Ian too. The first question he asks them is whether they have caught Matias. While they haven't caught him, the DEA team lets him know they've shut down the ranch activities and tracked Matias to Mexico. Ian assures me these guys will move the operation elsewhere, so the problem looms for others to worry about.

Six days later, the doctor announces he's sending Ian home, though someone would be checking in on him several times a week. We're all thrilled to take our patient home, but not as much as Ian is to be leaving the hospital.

With the time I've spent here, I've been able to make a list of questions about his care. The first one is, are you sure he's ready?

His doctor smiles and nods.

I'm glad to be leaving. These last two days of his stay have been harder because Ian feels good. He is healing inside and out. His grumpy side shows more often, and I'm not a fan.

Ian is not going to be an easy patient when we get home. I may have to tie him to the bed to keep him from overdoing it.

It doesn't take long after we get home before my patient is becoming more impatient. It's hard not to give into him.

"So, you want to tie me up?" he asks with a smile. "I could be down for play like that."

I lean over to straighten the blankets he had thrown off all night for the past week and a half. "That's not the kind of tying up I'm talking about, and you know it."

He grins at me and does his eyebrow wiggle. I swear sex hovers around in his brain constantly.

"You're injured, Ian," I remind him. "No sex. The doctor told you no strenuous activities for three to four more weeks."

"If I'm tied up, there won't be any strenuous activity on my part. I'm happy to let you do all the work. I'll just lay here."

"Like you could do that. And isn't that supposed to be what you tell me to do?" I move to the other side of the bed and sit down, facing him as he laughs.

I'd love nothing better than to have hot, steamy sex with this fine specimen of a man, but not until he's healed. Talk about a tease, though. Giving him a sponge bath leaves me worked up every single time.

"If you think I'm waiting three more weeks to have you bouncing on my dick, you're sorely mistaken. You bounce in here with no bra or in those tight workout tops and shorts, leaving me with a case of blue balls every time."

I guess he's feeling it too. "I'm guessing you're getting tired of sponge baths then?"

"Oh, hell no. I love it until you walk away without finishing me off."

My head jerks up, and our eyes meet. "What?"

"Don't play dumb with me, sugar. I see you watching my aching dick while you slowly wrap the washcloth around it and cup my balls in the pretense of making sure they're dry. Every fucking time, I think she'll surely see what pain she leaves me in and will wrap those pretty pink lips around it. But nooo... you walk away."

"Ian." I choose my words carefully. "I want to follow the doctor's orders. The last thing I want is for you to have a setback. I want you well as quickly as you can be."

"A blow job isn't going to impede my recuperation. It will only help it along. All that blood flow can finally leave my hard dick and go to areas trying to heal. See, that's exactly why you should want to provide me with a home healing option."

Oh my God. This man. Where does he come up with this shit? He makes giving head sound like homeopathic medicine.

Thia Finn

"Maybe you should spend some time online looking up that type of therapy. It'll give you something to do besides think about sex."

"Come closer and tell me that." His alpha male personality comes out in full force the hornier he gets. He gestures with his hand for me to come to him. If he only knew how badly I want to comply, but I can't risk hurting him.

"Ian, you had internal injuries that are healing. It scares me to think what your muscles will do if we do any kind of sex."

"I'll put the doctor on speed dial. If I see a bruise or have any kind of twitch, you can call him first thing." He sounds like a begging man dying for water.

"And then you'd have to explain to the doctor that we were having sex. No. Not doing it."

He throws back the cover where his hard length stands as it greets me and looks at me through hooded eyes. "You talking about sex, sugar, only makes it worse. Please, Allison."

His begging gets to me. I can't stand it, so I move to crawl up between his spread legs and take over with my own hands and mouth until he's coating my throat.

The look on his face is the sexiest thing I've ever seen as I watch him come. I've given him a blow job before, but never has he looked at me with the dark ink eyes I see before he throws his head back and gutturally moans, calling my name over and over.

Watching this man experience such deep emotions leaves me overwhelmed.

33

Allison

"Dammit, I want out of this fucking bed."

I can hear Ian even as I stand in front of the washer. He's been a bear for the last full week. Keeping him down gets harder with each passing day.

He walks around the house until he can't. We walk down the driveway several times a day, and the movement wears him out to the point that he has to nap. I can see his progress, but it's not fast enough for him.

"Allison, please come in here," he asks so nicely I do as he asks.

As I turn the corner in the bedroom, I see him sitting on the side of the bed. He turns and motions for me to come closer, so I move to him. His hands take mine and pull me to stand between his legs.

My arms automatically wrap around his neck. The bruises that took over every inch of his face are finally gone. His body looks healed on the outside, with only a few marks still on his torso. The doctor comments each time how great he's looking.

Ian's temper gets heated easily all day long. He wants to go to work or help around the house, but I won't let him.

"Sugar, if the doctor doesn't turn me loose pretty soon, I'm going to go crazy. I feel like I'm in a psych ward or something. Only they're torturing me instead of helping me."

"It's not for much longer. He promised you could start doing more after the next X-ray."

"I'm sick of sitting around doing nothing. I feel great. Better than great." He wraps his arms around me so we're body to body. I feel his desire between us.

"What if we went for a ride or maybe out to dinner?" I ask. "I know you went with Gabe to lunch a few days ago like you've been doing a few times a week, but we haven't been out in a while."

"Right. He's been a good friend since I've been on the injured list. How about we go to the lake where I took you the first time we went out? You don't have to cook. We'll buy something on the way. It's a great day outside. Warm enough to enjoy being out."

Ian's not wrong. It's a great day for a fall picnic,

even if we're approaching winter already—typical Texas weather. I go to the kitchen and begin packing so we can leave quickly. He's so impatient now.

He walks out dressed in a long-sleeved Henley and jeans that fit him nicely again. Now that he's gained a little weight back, he seems to be filling out his clothes better. With his arms getting back the muscle from lifting dumbbells, the material stretches over his biceps. He looks like the hot guy I met for coffee.

The drive is short, so I let Ian get behind the wheel. His doctor told him he could try driving locally, but no long trips yet. Positive comments happen each time Ian sees him, which gives us hope that the end of this time at home is near.

"You feel good sitting in the driver's seat?" I smile at him, loving the smirk on his face. It's as though each new accomplishment gives him a sense of freedom and normalcy.

"You know it, sugar. What more could I ask for? Blue skies, gorgeous woman, fast car. Perfect day."

We laugh together. This is a perfect day. Seeing Ian so close to his old self gives me hope that life will return to normal. Maybe not my old normal—Ian and I will create a new normal—our normal.

The park remains empty, just like the last time we were here. The lake sparkles with the sun glinting off the blue water. It's a close second to the beautiful cobalt blue of Ian's eyes.

We spread a blanket under the same tree with the

sun peeking through the branches. Ian hesitates, trying to lower himself to the ground without causing pain. This tells us that he's not completely back to himself but is so close.

After removing our lunch from the ice chest, I spread it out so we can enjoy the afternoon without anyone interfering with our time. The apples with caramel dip are great this time of year, so I feed him bites.

The atmosphere is light and easy between us. We both enjoy these moments together.

Ian rolls over and stands up.

"What are you doing?" I ask, watching him flinch on his way up.

"Stand up," he says in his alpha voice. I think the man is dying to growl at me when we have actual sex for the first time. He sure enjoys practicing it.

I stand only to watch him get down on one knee. "What the hell, Ian? You just got up."

He seems determined to hurt himself on our first real outing.

"Allison," he takes my hand. "From the moment we first looked at each other, I knew there was something between us. You and I were both scared, but we got through it and much more."

Oh no. He's... he's... I can't even think the word.

"I don't want anything else to stand in our way of being together. No one, no accident, no hospitals, nothing." He reaches into his pocket and pulls out a beautiful ring. "I love you, Allison, with all my heart. Will you marry me? Will you be my wife? Will you spend the rest of your life with me?"

As badly as I want to attack him, I drop down to my knees and gently wrap my arms around him. "Yes, yes, yes. I'll marry you and be your wife and spend forever loving you. I love you so much, Ian. So, so much."

We pull apart, and he slides the ring on my finger before he plunders my lips, like he did before he was hurt. His tongue invades my lips as he deepens the kiss. Our bodies align as we fall over on the blanket, and he rolls on top of me. The feeling sends a shiver down my spine.

For the first time in months, his body weight holds me. I love the closeness, the feeling of belonging only he can give me this way. The wait for him to possess my body the way only Ian can is finally over.

My life longs for the feelings he gives me—the love, affection, and security. God, I love this man. I love us being a team.

With all the emotion surrounding the moment, he undresses us both and slams into me. I'm ready to feel him inside me as much as he wants to be there.

Being in public doesn't matter to either of us. Our want and need for each other take over every sane thought we might possess. It's hot and heavy and just what we both need.

"Wow. Just wow," Ian says as he rolls off, pulling me with him. I cuddle into his side and wrap my leg over his after pulling up my leggings and covering myself.

"I promise to last longer next time, Allison. It's just been so long," his apology almost a whisper.

"Yeah, I get it. I think I came when you bottomed out the first time, and you hit the best places inside me." I smile against his side. "That was pretty intense, though."

"So, you're going to be my wife. Let's get married tomorrow."

I look at him. "Don't you think we need to tell a few people first?"

"I talked to Jackson and Junie when they were home the last time. They agreed it was about time." He picks up my left hand and kisses my ring finger.

"And what about this ring? When did you have time to get it? It's gorgeous, by the way."

"Gabe took me to the jewelry store after Junie gave me a ring of yours from your jewelry box."

My eyebrows raise, "You had the kids in on this from the beginning?"

"Yes, I talked to them just after I got home from the hospital."

"The traitors, keeping secrets from their mom. What about Beth?"

He glances down at me. "She was a little harder sell. That woman can be scary. Her threats seriously made me afraid. I'm glad, though. You need someone in your corner to always be looking out for your best interest.

Beth is that person. I want to be that person now."

I lean up and offer him a sweet kiss. "I think that can be arranged."

"Good because I told her to find her own person. That job is taken." He takes my lips in a hard kiss.

Breaking the kiss, he stares at me, "Now about that date?"

Thank you for reading *About That Date*.
Be sure to watch for Beth's story coming soon.

If you enjoyed this book, check out,
Kiss Me Before Flight,
another seasoned romance.

MORE BOOKS FROM THIA FINN

Before the Second Show

Kiss Me Before Flight

Be Understanding

Becks Part One and Two

Fall Boys (Three book series)

Assured Distraction (Four book series)
Hayden's Timbre (An Assured Distraction Novel)

ACKNOWLEDGMENTS

Thank you so much to Roux Cantrell, Ginger Lee, Carson Mackenzie, and Elaine Marie for alpha reading *About That Date.* Your questions and comments were invaluable to me. The CCT has given me so much support in all areas. Julie Lafrance, the head Badger, keeps me sane.

Thank you to Kaylene Osborn, owner of Swish Design & Editing, for helping me in so many ways I cannot list them all. She is the best BFF, an awesome editor, and a wonderful mentor in my small book world. Laughing or crying, we make it work. I am so grateful to Kay and Kim for all the moral support they give me.

Thank you to Stephanie Seay for showing up when I need her the most. She takes care of me at signings, comes to my home to get me organized, and sends me to various Buccees to collect shirts! She's the best helper ever!

Thank you to my sister, Mary LeFebvre, for always being there. Our adventures have been few but perfect for us!

Thank you to my sweet husband, Steve, for giving me the time I need to pour out words when my heart is ready to do so. These past few years have been some of the hardest.

Thank you to my children and their spouses for all their support. I cannot say enough about how much love and kindness I receive from them. And now they've given me three sweet grandchildren to spread the love with. Austin, Logan, and Sabrie, y'all are the best ever!

AMAZON
http://amzn.to/2mgw5oq

WEBSITE
http://www.thiafinn.com

EMAIL
author@thiafinn.com

TWITTER
http://twitter.com/ThiaFinnCGrif

INSTAGRAM
@cegriffin.thiafinn

FACEBOOK
https://www.facebook.com/ThiaFinn/?fref=ts

GOODREADS
https://www.goodreads.com/author/show/
14206242.Thia_Finn

BOOKBUB
https://www.bookbub.com/profile/thia-finn

THE AUTHOR

Growing up in small-town Texas, Thia Finn discovered life outside of it by attending The University of Texas, only to return home and marry her high school sweetheart. They raised two successful and beautiful daughters while she taught middle school Language Arts and eventually became a middle school librarian. After thirty-four years, she retired to do her favorite things, like travel, spending time off-roading with family and friends, hanging out at one of the Texas Hill Country's beautiful rivers, reading, and writing.

She currently lives in a small town similar to where she grew up, with her husband and Chihuahua, Josie, and closer to the kids and grandkids. She can often be found stalking on social media, reading or traveling the world.